THE PARTY

ALSO BY NATASHA PRESTON

THE PARTY

NATASHA PRESTON

DELACORTE PRESS

Text copyright © 2024 by Natasha Preston
Cover photograph © 2024 by Michael Trevillion/Trevillion Images

All rights reserved. Published in the United States by Delacorte Press, an imprint of Random House Children's Books, a division of Penguin Random House LLC, New York.

Delacorte Press is a registered trademark
and the colophon is a trademark of Penguin Random House LLC.

GetUnderlined.com

Educators and librarians, for a variety of teaching tools,
visit us at RHTeachersLibrarians.com

Library of Congress Cataloging-in-Publication Data is available upon request.
ISBN 978-0-593-70408-0 (pbk.) — ISBN 978-0-593-70409-7 (ebook)

The text of this book is set in 11-point Janson MT.
Interior design by Ken Crossland

Printed in the United States of America
10 9 8 7 6 5 4 3 2 1
First Edition

This is for everyone who takes an emergency book with them when forced to socialize.

1

"Have you seen the size of this castle?" I ask my best friend, Kashvi, angling my phone screen toward her.

She rolls over on her bed in our dorm room, the warm light above her head reflecting in her dark eyes. She has tan skin, black hair that reaches her butt, and the brightest smile I have ever seen in my life. Kash has been my best friend since we met on our first day at St. Mary's Grammar School when we were four.

We share the same love for Taylor Swift, rom-com movies, and sneaking out to parties. We've roomed together for the past seven years, both of us absolutely refusing to share with anyone else. I've heard that a lot of the girls snore, and I would definitely end up committing murder if I was stuck in a room with one of them.

"Allegra said her dad renovated the outside and that's why it doesn't look derelict," Kash says. "Don't get too excited, because the inside is a different story. We're camping in a cold, empty castle."

"Fun. That makes me feel so much better about lying to the dean and my parents so we can stay there over spring break," I say dryly.

Kash smiles. "You're *not* bailing on this trip, Bessie. Do you know how difficult it was to get my parents to let me go to 'Allegra's house' instead of New Delhi? They really wanted me to visit relatives I've only met about two or three time in my life." She does air quotes with her fingers because we've all told a little lie to our parents. An abandoned castle isn't somewhere my parents would want me spending a long weekend.

"I vividly remember the crying and begging, Kash."

She sits up on her yellow tie-dye bedding, pointing a pink-tipped finger at me. "I did *not* beg."

"Whatever. Look at this! It has a *moat*. Think the water is safe to swim in?" I ask her. "It looks okay. And didn't Fergus say there's a generator, so we'll have heating and electricity? I'm sure he told me that."

"I asked Allegra the same thing about the moat. She said, and I quote, 'If you want to catch ten different plagues, go ahead,' so I'm thinking no. But yes to the generator."

"Well, what does she know? The weather is uncharacteristically hot for English springtime. I'm packing my bikini just in case," I tell her.

She shrugs, looking at me like she thinks I'm the one who doesn't know what she's talking about. "You know there's a big storm the first two days, right?"

"I can swim on Sunday," I say rather pathetically, since I can already tell it's a bust.

The weather looks awful for this afternoon and Saturday, but after that I see only sunshine on my app. Party for two days, swim for two days. There's a *chance*.

"It's your funeral," she replies.

"Someone will come in with me."

"I can't believe we've managed to keep this a secret. One massive, weekend-long party in a remote castle in the country and no one has said a word. It's a miracle when you think about it. Jia and Odette are both enormous gossips."

Odette, not in our year, has been invited because she's friends with Hugo—a total heartthrob who would never look twice at any of us because we're younger than him. Allegra tried getting with him and then went for Shen, the hottie who moved from China to the UK to board at the same time as Jia.

Hugo is also our friend Raif's brother, but Raif doesn't want anything to do with us anymore.

"We haven't managed to leave campus yet. Let's not get ahead of ourselves," I tell her.

Sure, we've sneaked off campus before, but it was always for just a few hours. We'd be tucked back in bed when Mrs. Evans, our dorm's houseparent, did her morning rounds.

This time we're leaving for spring break alone, not with an adult as mandated by school policy.

She waves my worry away in true Kash style. When it comes to planning, she is the queen. She knows every single aspect of what we're about to do. She's been through it in her head hundreds of times, from the destination to the accommodations, and I'm not sure that's much of an exaggeration.

The planning part of our weekend adventure is the easy part.

Zeke is driving, and he's supposed to be taking me to my parents', since our families live twenty minutes apart. I emailed the school from my mom's account, giving me permission to leave school grounds without being collected by a parent. I've had access to her email for years, since she never changes her password.

Kash, Shen, and Jia are getting a taxi to the station. They're meant to be taking a train to the airport, where Kash will in theory board a plane to New Delhi and Shen and Jia will fly to Beijing.

However, Zeke and I will pick Kash up. Allegra will get the others.

Allegra and her twin brother, Fergus, both drive too, so they're taking their cars.

"We'll be fine. This isn't the first time we've lied to every adult we know," Kash says, studying a printout of the castle's plans. Before we go away anywhere, Kash has to do her research. She doesn't like being surprised. The red folder containing property and location information from Allegra has curled at the edges, she's opened it so many times.

"No, it's just the first time we've lied in order to head to an abandoned castle."

No adults, no one other than us, knowing where we are. It's exciting, the most anticipated party of the year.

"Cool, isn't it?" she says, wiggling her dark brows.

I drop my phone on the bed and smile. "I can't wait."

The castle is gorgeous, and it's in a pretty countryside village, miles from anything or anyone else, in the middle of a huge forest.

"You commit the layout to memory yet?" I ask, only half joking, because she probably has. Maybe she's being extra diligent this time because there will be no adults.

Unless you count Hugo, who's eighteen, but after watching him snort ice cream through his nose I certainly do not.

She holds up the paper. "I think I have it."

Of course you do.

The castle has been in Allegra and Fergus Beaufort's family for generations, and their parents are now trying to develop the area since they own about a hundred acres of land surrounding it. Apparently it's the last chance we have for a weekend there, and we're not passing it up.

The seven of us, a friend group forged during Getting to Know You Week at the start of senior year—though I knew most of them already—will go tomorrow morning to set up. Allegra has a trunk full of party supplies to decorate the ballroom, where we'll spend most of our time.

Allegra is *big* on aesthetics, her life one big Pinterest board. That's the only reason we're going early. We couldn't possibly allow everyone to arrive at anything less than a perfect venue.

The rest come in the evening, and the party will last until we leave on Monday.

"Allegra has given us a very specific route to the castle," Kash says, holding up her phone next to show me a map. "It's been bothering me for a while. Okay, look here—there's a more direct journey, but that goes through the village. Do you think she just doesn't want to be seen?"

"But why would she worry about people in town seeing us? No one there knows who we are."

"I guess she wants to make sure word about the party doesn't get back to our parents and the school."

We'd be in *so* much trouble if we were caught, but could the school really expel nearly the entire class? It wouldn't look good on the tours when there are no students left in the junior year.

Allegra's route is the one I will be taking. We'll be okay if no one knows we're not where we're supposed to be this weekend. We can be discreet when the stakes are this high.

"Should we go over the plan again at breakfast?" I ask, checking the time on my phone. Fifteen minutes to go. I'm starving, my snacks depleted after last night's movie. Kash and I hid under my covers with an iPad, her holding the bowl of our remaining candy, the volume low in case Mrs. Evans came by to do *another* one of her lights-out checks. She takes her job way too seriously.

"We can, but you know how Allegra is. She's already been through it, and we don't want her to think we don't trust her. She's thought of *everything*, apparently. All we need to do is pack a bag and prepare for little to no sleep for the next three nights."

Kash isn't wrong: Allegra can't be questioned. Not ever. But to be fair to her, she does usually think of everything.

"Okay. I mean, if anything changed or if something was wrong, Allegra and Fergus would tell us, right?"

There's an air of secrecy shrouding the weekend that I don't like, and I'm not talking about the fact that we have to keep the party to ourselves. Details have been few and far between, nothing close to the usual bombardment of texts and constant reminders.

Kash laughs, throwing her head back. "No, she wouldn't tell us at all, but you're going in Zeke's car and picking me up at the station. We're the ones in control of that."

"We've got this."

"We'll have a much better time if we sneak into that castle without the constant worrying. No more stressing, Bessie."

I hold my palms up. "No more stressing . . . if you promise to pack your bikini too."

She rolls her eyes. "Nicely played. I'll pack it, but I'm not promising anything. I don't want to spend the whole weekend vomiting."

"Have you heard how much beer Shen wants to bring? You'll definitely vomit."

She laughs and then bites her lip, her playful expression dropping. "Bessie, can I ask you a question?"

"You just did."

She waves my comment away. "Do you feel like we're all drifting? Not you and me. But the others?"

I've been ignoring that feeling since summer break. The seven of us are like a family. We're growing apart but all desperately holding on. I hate it, because I genuinely love my friends.

"That was random."

"Well, I figured while we're overthinking things . . ."

I hold up my hand. "I'm done with the sneaking-away drama.

But I get how you feel about our group. Things are different after . . . ," I say, then snap my lips together because we agreed not to talk about it. It's done and over. "But we're all still here, and Allegra has put a lot of effort into this weekend. Let's have the best break ever."

"Starting with the castle."

"Exactly. Starting with the potentially life-ruining castle."

She laughs. "The danger aspect makes it more fun. Come on, I'm starving."

I swing my legs off the bed, trying to push any negative thoughts out of my mind. How often do you get to take over a castle for one massive party? It's what teen dreams are made of.

A chance to let off steam and be wild with no adults there to ruin our fun. With no one knowing where we are. It'll be like we're the only people on the planet.

We can get away with anything.

2

"They're going to know. Look at Mrs. Sinclair. Just look at her. She's doing that x-ray vision thing again, Bessie." Kash's fingertips dig into the flesh of my arm. We've successfully switched places—Kash is now the nervous wreck.

I was ready for this. Kash is confident, thanks to all her research, until we're walking out the door and the theory turns to practice.

I turn to my paranoid best friend and lightly backhand her wrist, making her let go before she draws blood.

She shakes her hand, scowling at me. "What was that for?"

"One, so I don't lose circulation. And two, because you're the one who said we should stick to the plan. Which is *not* acting suspiciously and leaving the same way we do at any other break. Relax."

Her eyes are wild as she looks around for . . . well, who knows.

"Bessie, if we're caught . . ."

All right, it would be bad. Catastrophic, actually. Boarding school, apparently, isn't an opportunity to "run amok" with our friends. In the words of Mrs. Sinclair, the dean, obviously.

It's not like our parents couldn't just make another donation to the school to get the whole thing expunged. Probably.

"She doesn't know. No one does, so please will you just calm down before you give us away."

"Allegra invited the whole class—do you really believe that none of the teachers are hearing the whispers? Gossip spreads like wildfire here, you know that."

"That's still only twenty-two people, Kash. Let's get you some breakfast—you've stopped being rational."

We take the main staircase and walk along the freshly painted hallway past Mrs. Sinclair, who doesn't appear to know what we're up to. Her head is held high, back straight, shiny choppy bob bouncing as she walks. She's always wearing a no-nonsense bob.

After the break, the Duke of Edinburgh will be opening the new science lab, so the school has undergone an expensive renovation for his ten-minute visit.

The cafeteria is bustling already, the energy level so high it gives me an instant buzz. The atmosphere is always like this on the last day of term—everyone is animated and laughing. Some people left after class yesterday, but most stayed and will travel this morning.

A few classmates give us knowing looks as they pass, and I want to punch them. If they keep that up, a teacher will become suspicious. Kash waves her hands at them, drawing more attention to us.

Nothing to see here, just getting ready to go home.

Mrs. Sinclair walks around the cafeteria, speaking to groups of students as she goes. Our friends have snagged one of the tables with a sofa by the Georgian bar windows that reach from the floor to the ceiling. If you sit there in the afternoon, you'll get a tan and singed corneas.

We grab breakfast and head over to our group, taking a longer route because we don't want to run into the dean. Well, Kash doesn't. You know, in case she accidently blurts out the entire plan upon Mrs. Sinclair's hello.

Allegra looks over her fruit tea and smiles. "Have you packed?"

"We're leaving in twenty minutes," I reply, sitting down next to Zeke with my tea and cinnamon bun, not wanting to admit I haven't actually finished. "Do we have enough food and drinks?"

All Kash and I have packed is sugary treats. At some point I'm going to need something with nutritional value.

"We have some things that are easy to prepare since the electricity is limited. Allegra doesn't think it's enough, so we'll have to stop on the way," Fergus replies, flashing me a smile. He still has the power to make me feel a little bit dizzy. He has gorgeous pale green eyes, light hair, cheekbones that make me want to cry, fair skin, and a warm smile. "Zeke and I loaded the cars late last night so no one would see the extras I'm taking," he adds.

It also helps that they know exactly where the school's CCTV cameras are.

Zeke, Allegra, and Fergus are the only ones who have their driver's licenses. I'm not seventeen until the summer, so I can't even start learning with a proper instructor yet. I've only been driving with Fergus on his private land. But there's a positive to being younger in the class—I get to be a passenger princess and snack distributor.

"Okay, good. Has anyone else noticed Mrs. Sinclair?" Kash asks, her eyes darting around the room. "I think she's getting suspicious."

"Is she serious or just hungry?" Jia asks me, jabbing her thumb in Kash's direction. Her dark hair is tied in a neat ponytail and her near-black eyes shine with amusement.

"Hungry. No one's mentioned anything, and if a teacher got even a hint of what we're doing, we'd be in Sinclair's office by now."

Kash looks between me and Jia with hope.

"See, Kash, we're fine," Shen says, wrapping his arm around Allegra. They've been together for a year now, since almost immediately after Hugo turned Allegra down. He's loyal and good-looking with spiky black hair and a jawline to swoon over. "God, I love the last day of term. No class for three weeks. No study hall."

"Right, because you go to study hall when school's in session," I say sarcastically.

He points at me. "I'll get a break from having to skip it."

"Hey, Fergus, you know there's a quicker route to the castle, right?" Zeke says, staring at his screen.

I quickly exchange a glance with Kash and then turn my attention to Allegra, though Zeke asked Fergus and not her.

Zeke was one of the first friends I made at the school. We had plenty of playdates before boarding because of our proximity growing up. He has dark skin, a hair fade that is nothing less than perfection at *all* times, and a surprising number of abs given he's only seventeen. He drags me to the school's gym three times a week, but it's not working quite as well for me.

Allegra stares at Fergus, but he ignores her, not at all intimidated by his twin. He's probably the only one who isn't, and that's just because of their bond.

When neither of them replies, Zeke, undeterred, adds, "There a reason we're taking the scenic route?"

Translation: Who have you pissed off so thoroughly in town?

"Going through the village takes a couple of miles out of the journey, but the roads through the village are slow," Fergus says, his voice too controlled, as if he's rehearsed. "Okay?"

Allegra quickly pipes up. "Besides, we can't get caught, Zeke. They know who Fergus and I are in town, so it could get back to our parents. It's not worth the risk."

Zeke lifts a dark brow. "The route says it's an extra twenty minutes, and who in the village even knows you?"

Excellent points. Ones Kash and I have already thought about.

They might have researched the family when the plans for the castle were submitted, but it seems like a stretch to assume they know their cars or recognize them from a distance. Not to mention they wouldn't know Zeke's vehicle at all.

Allegra sighs. "Look, we shouldn't be there. Not only because we should all be with our families but because the castle isn't fit for habitation. Not yet. And it's not as if my dad would give us permission even if it was finished."

"Not fit for habitation. What does that mean?" Zeke replies.

Shen leans forward. "Cut it out, mate. Their castle, their rules. You can handle a few days without your TV and therapy lamp."

Zeke and I synchronize an eye roll. I have one of those lamps too, absolute game changers on cold, dark mornings.

No one is surprised that Shen is being a lemming and obediently going along with whatever Allegra tells him to do. She's dominant and sometimes overbearing. And he's totally in love with her. It'd be cute if they didn't make me want to vomit.

I expect Zeke to say something else, but he continues eating his breakfast, bored and probably aware the conversation is going nowhere.

I take a breath, because although I know she's about to make this seem tiny, I can't sit back and not mention anything. Her mild attack on Zeke has irritated me, and I'm fed up with her picking and choosing what information to tell us.

"So, we were looking up the castle online and found some stuff," I tell Allegra. "There's a group on Facebook that seems to *really* dislike your family."

Allegra's pale eyes flash with anger but she tries to conceal it with a Hollywood smile. She runs her hands through her shiny dark blond hair before speaking. "Bessie, every village, town, and city has people like that. Sad individuals who can't stand the fact that change is coming. They'd still be riding around in a horse and carriage if they could."

"You actually can still do that," Kash says, then shrinks back in her seat as Fergus shoots her a dark look.

Allegra knows. Her family owns horses, a few of them successful at Ascot Racecourse.

"Right, so none of this village avoidance has anything to do with
that group, then? They're kind of . . . passionate about the castle not
becoming apartments and the area remaining fields and woodland.
You're not *at all* concerned about them?"

"Why would we be?" Fergus asks. "Honestly, Bess, they walk
around with cardboard posters and clipboards. They're annoying as
hell but harmless. Ignore them."

"One of them said they'd rather the castle burned down than be
developed," Kash adds. "That doesn't sound harmless."

Fergus's eyes slide back to her. "No, that sounds like a keyboard
warrior."

"Can we not ruin the weekend before it's even begun?" Allegra
says, putting her cup down with trembling hands as if she's fighting to keep it together. "This party is a huge deal, the first one I've
organized independently, and I'm *not* going to let anyone ruin it."

"We're on board," Shen says. "Nothing is getting in the way of
the plan. It's going to be the party of the year."

The tension in her shoulders melts away and she smiles. I can
tell she thinks the conversation is permanently over. She claps her
hands together. "Four days in the castle. Let's load up and go. We
have a lot to do. I have jobs for everyone."

Her parties are always off the charts, but it takes a lot of effort
to make them happen, even with the professionals she usually hires.
This time it's just us. I have a feeling I'm going to ache more from
setting up than I ever have from the gym.

"I'm going to brush my teeth," I tell them, picking up my plate. "I'll meet you all in the parking lot in ten, okay?"

Allegra checks her watch. "Yes, it's almost time to go!"

I put my mug and plate on the cart and make my way out of the cafeteria. As I move along the hall, I'm mentally going over the few things I still need to pack when I run straight into someone.

"Whoa," Hugo says, steadying me as I almost bounce off his chest and fall on my ass. "You okay, Bessie?"

I step back and nod, pushing my long hair behind my ears. *What is wrong with you?* "Yes, sorry. I wasn't looking. Are you okay?"

"Uh, yeah, I'm fine." He scratches his jaw and smiles. He has tan skin, dark green eyes, and the physique of someone who plays a lot of soccer, his favorite sport.

He's in his final year of school and usually too cool to hang out with us. But there have been a couple of times. None since Raif.

Forget Raif.

"Are you still coming to the party?" I ask. I feel like I'm under a microscope with that intense gaze of his.

"Abbas, Odette, and I are coming later," he says, standing under the wooden arch, his head so much closer to the top than mine. "I heard Allegra is on one."

"She's just . . . ambitious and . . ."

He smirks, leaning a little closer until I can smell his aftershave. *Don't you dare lean in and sniff him.*

"She's a pain in the ass, Bessie."

"Well, sometimes. She means well. Wants this weekend to be

perfect," I say, annoyed at myself for feeling like I should defend her to anyone outside our group. It's one of those situations where we can say things about her but no one else can.

He nods and goes to turn away.

"Wait, Hugo."

"Yeah?" he asks, lifting a brow as if he's not really interested in what I'm about to say. Always hot and cold.

I wring my hands and force myself to keep eye contact. This isn't something we've spoken about since it happened. Hugo has barely said one word to me. "Is Raif coming?"

Rubbing his forehead, he sighs heavily. "No, he's not."

"I miss him."

"Another time," he says, looking around distracted. "Okay? Not now. I have to go. Things to do before we leave this evening. I'll see you there, yeah?"

"Okay, sure," I mutter as he walks off, taking long strides to get away from me as fast as he can.

Well, that went horribly.

I run up the stairs and to my dorm room. Students are rushing by, almost knocking into me with their bags and boxes, ready to return home for spring break. The scent of artificial lemon drifts along the hallway, the deep clean of the school underway.

Last year I traveled around more of Europe with my parents, visiting Spain, Italy, Denmark, and Sweden. This year I'm spending the first weekend of my break in an abandoned castle.

Which, yes, is *so* much cooler.

I brush my teeth and chuck the final toiletries in my backpack. My suitcase is stuffed, full of both endless outfits and some snacks. I'll grab drinks in the supermarket on the way.

"Bessie, all packed?" Mrs. Evans asks, her tight bun almost on the very top of her head. She's wearing a cream knitted sweater and smart black trousers. There's no uniform for her as houseparent, but she wears a version of a cream top and black trousers or skirt every single day.

Kash's theory is that she's read consistency is the key to making boarders feel safe. We can rely on her wardrobe the same as we can rely on weekly math assessments from evil Mrs. Lane.

"Oh, yeah. I'm ready. Are you doing anything over the break?" I ask, voice high as a kite.

She smiles widely, her lips stretching until they disappear. "Visiting my daughter and grandchildren."

"Nice. Well, I should head out. Zeke is giving me a lift home . . . as you know."

"Yes, you have a lovely break, and I'll see you in a few weeks."

"Thanks. Bye," I say, and dash past her with my things, my suitcase bashing the wall. Good job that bit hasn't been repainted yet.

I hate lying, because then you have to keep it going, and I constantly worry that I'm going to trip myself up. No one wants to face the wrath of Allegra if someone lets this slip.

I carry my suitcase down the stairs, kicking myself for not getting Fergus or Zeke to load up my things last night. The suitcase weighs a ton. Why did I think I'd need so many clothes for a weekend?

Fergus is at the bottom of the stairs, leaning against the chunky banister. He watches me with a smirk and a sparkle in his eyes. It gives me a major flashback to when he took me to the early-summer ball last year, right as we started dating.

"Hey, don't worry about helping, will you?"

He laughs. "I'm sorry. It's just quite funny watching you."

"Thanks," I say, almost dropping the suitcase on the last step. Fergus laughs again when I shake my arms out. More lifting with Zeke at the gym needed. "You can carry it from here."

"Fine," he replies, taking the suitcase without an argument. "Are you feeling okay now? You seemed freaked about the group of crazies. I've read what they're writing too, Bess."

"You have?"

"I actually joined the group."

My jaw drops. "Really?"

"My dad kept getting letters from them, and they're all over the comments section on the planning application."

"Do they know you're in the group?"

He shrugs. "They figured it out and blocked me after we took legal action over the threats, but I'd seen enough by that point."

"You're honestly not worried?"

"My dad has it under control. He has a restraining order for a couple of them. The threats got a little too personal, but they're all talk," he tells me as we walk out of the school. "They come near any of us or the castle and they'll face the consequences."

They must be at least a little worried to have taken that action. That's the reason we're going out of our way, I'm sure of it.

Nothing in the group mentioned any legal action from the Beauforts, and I think that would've come up. When I get a chance, I'm going back to look further into it.

"Kash and I have been looking at pictures of the castle. It's amazing."

He smiles, dragging my suitcase behind him. It's not often that I see a big, genuine smile from Fergus anymore. I've missed it. "It's incredible, and unfortunately I couldn't convince my parents to give it to me."

I do a double take. "You tried?"

He laughs. "Of course I tried! Wouldn't you?"

"Oh, I would beg twenty-four seven."

"All I'm getting is the manor house on the Scottish border."

That makes me laugh out loud. "How selfish of them."

"It's colder up there," he says, smirking. "I'm joking. I'm not ungrateful. See, you shouldn't have broken up with me. You're missing out on a manor house."

"Get the castle and I'm yours again."

We both laugh this time, and I think maybe we're finally past the teeny-tiny relationship we had last year. Never fall for someone in your friend group. *Terrible* idea. Though he's been the one I've relied on since the accident.

Sometimes I wonder if we'd still be together if it had never happened.

"Where's Kash?" I ask as Fergus loads my suitcase into Zeke's car.

"Taxi took her a couple of minutes ago. Let's hit the road—she'll be waiting at the train station soon," Zeke says, slapping Fergus on the back. "Your car ready?"

Fergus nods. "Everyone's in. Allegra's ready too."

I look back at the school as I get into Zeke's car. Teachers are milling around outside, some parents have arrived, and a couple taxis are waiting for students. I love it here . . . though I constantly feel Raif's absence.

Zeke starts the engine and we pull out of the parking lot, following Fergus and Allegra.

My excitement is momentarily dampened when I spot the reflection of Hugo watching us leave from the great hall in the side-view mirror.

3

"Where are we going?" I ask, watching Fergus take a left instead of a right. Zeke's pointless GPS instantly informs us we've gone the wrong way, and not for the first time.

"Supermarket up ahead," Kash says. "This must be where we're getting even more food and drink. We're only minutes away. This car is already rammed."

"That's because Zeke bought a toy car," I retort, smirking at him.

"Hey, no one speaks ill of my baby. Unless you think your legs can get you there faster."

"Sorry," I mutter as he parks between Fergus and Allegra. His Audi is the most important thing in his life. I don't think he's ever been as happy as when his parents bought it for him.

I stretch as I get out; being cooped up in a roller skate of a car for two hours has seized my muscles.

Zeke stares at me over the roof from his side. "That's rather dramatic, Bess."

"You want to stretch out too. I know it."

"Okay," Fergus says, calling for everyone's attention. "Beer. Snacks. Car. Let's do this."

"Is he hyping himself up to go run an errand?" Kash asks, linking her arm with mine.

"I remember when we were dating and we went to a shop. Poor thing was completely lost."

Now, I'm not saying I'm not privileged, but I have bought bread before. Fergus is only at home in Apple and Porsche.

Kash laughs. "He's cute, though."

Well, there is that. He's the definition of cute preppy, with his chinos and polo shirts.

Allegra looks up at the building like it's going to inhale her. The only shopping she does is for clothes and makeup. To be fair, this little store does look rather uninviting—a dated sign and window posters peeling at the edges—but I guess it's enough for a village.

We split up inside, Kash and I going for sodas and extra snacks and the rest of them, the ones who remembered their fake IDs, for beer.

I push a tiny cart that looks as if it was made for small children, one wheel spinning like it's having a breakdown, and narrowly miss an elderly lady with faded purple hair who cuts across the aisle without a glance.

Instead of running into her, I sway sideways, stopping short of scraping the legs of a guy pinning up a flyer on an overcrowded noticeboard.

He looks up, startled. Wide brown eyes meet mine, and his mouth forms an O shape.

"Sorry," I say, ignoring Kash muttering about the woman.

He takes a step back, laughing as he scratches his neck. "It's cool. Who needs ankles anyway?"

I barely hear what he says because the flyer catches my attention. Pinned over thick layers of posters is a picture of the very castle I'm on my way to.

A caption at the top in bright red ink reads STOP THE DEVELOP-MENT.

He looks from the poster to me. He's tall and handsome with tan skin and dark eyes that you can't look away from. I'd say he was a similar age to us, so this development isn't exactly what I'd expect him to be passionate about.

"What's the poster for?" I ask, pointing to the board. Kash nudges my arm, and I can feel her eyes burning into the side of my head.

"Oh, just the castle down the road. Been standing since the sixteenth century and now some rich snob is trying to develop it. Make luxury apartments." The disgusted tone in his voice makes me wish I'd apologized and walked on.

As he explains how detrimental the development is to the area, I steal glances at the poster to read it. It details a meeting location, time, and goal. The name of the Facebook group is at the bottom, proudly stating their cause and asking for people to join.

"An actual castle?" Kash asks, not even a little bit subtle.

"Yep. My folks set up the group to try to stop these people. We don't want our village turning into some bougie paradise. Come along to the meeting if you can make it," he says, pointing to the time on the poster. "Though I've not seen you around . . ."

"We're passing through," I reply. "Spring break road trip. I'm Bessie."

He nods. "Oscar."

"I'm Kash. What are you going to do to stop the rich guy?"

Ironic that they're trying to save the historical home of rich people from present-day rich people.

"We have an ongoing petition. We're trying to get a protection order on the castle. It was never used in a battle or anything of historical relevance, so it's proving difficult. But it's ours, a part of the community, and we'll do whatever it takes to protect it. We have a couple of members with a few other ideas, but I'm not sure burning the place down is going to do much."

"Burn it down?" I ask, laughing somewhat nervously. It's as unsettling to hear that again as it was the first time. "Surely that's counterproductive."

His eyes twitch as if he's trying incredibly hard to control his emotions. His parents might have started a save-the-castle group, but I get the impression he's a solid part of it. "We won't do it, of course. But some of us feel that it would be better flat than as posh apartments."

They could just build on the land, but I'm not about to point that out.

"Oh," I mutter, not really knowing what to say and feeling more than a little uncomfortable at the turn this conversation has taken.

"Well, we should grab what we need and get back on the road," I say. "I hope you save your castle, Oscar."

He smiles wide, baring his teeth. "Yeah, thanks. Hey, drive safe. There's a bad storm coming."

I nod, maneuvering the cart around him. Kash is gripping the handle so hard her knuckles are white.

"Keep cool," I whisper to her.

"They actually want to burn the castle down. They have a whole group, and you want me to stay calm. He was weird, right? The type of person who you wouldn't be surprised has slaughtered his whole family."

She has me beat for most dramatic reaction to the weird stranger.

"I heard, Kash, and they don't want to burn it down. He's probably not a murderer."

"Your use of *probably* is less than encouraging."

I look over my shoulder and nearly trip. Oscar is standing there, watching us walk away. "He's still looking," I mutter. "*Don't* turn back around, just grab snacks and drinks."

We're not in our school uniforms, and I'm pretty sure he wouldn't recognize them even if he knew where Fergus and Allegra go . . . so why do I feel like he's trying to figure out where he knows us from?

"Should we tell the others?" she asks.

"Fergus is aware of the group and what they've said. His family has taken legal action against some threats."

Her eyes widen so big she looks comical. "So they're taking the threats seriously? They believe the group could burn the castle to the ground. We're about to spend the weekend in it!"

"They just want to keep them away. There's no way they can actually do that now without the police knowing exactly who's behind it. That was said in anger. Who's going to risk their freedom for a building?" I ask, grabbing share-size bags of pretzels and cans of barbecue Pringles. Then more.

"We're not mentioning it? For real?"

"What would be the point? We'll be long gone before the group's meeting next week. Ooh, grab some M&M's, I love those."

More sugar. I feel like we need it now. Running into Oscar has rattled me too, even if I need to pretend otherwise for Kash's benefit.

"Bessie, you're far too chill about this."

I shrug. "My dad's had plenty of opposition to some of his developments. It's no surprise that this group exists. Besides, we're only about fifteen minutes from the castle now, so the party starts *soon*."

She grabs packs of instant noodles and chucks them into the cart. "Good thing it's going to rain, I guess."

We load the cart up, having the good sense to add a few pieces of fruit, plus some milk and fresh juice, since Shen has a mini fridge.

Once we have enough snacks to feed an entire army for a week, we pay and head out, both pushing the cart to keep it in a straight line.

I look around for any sign of Oscar as we cross the parking lot.

Avoid going through the village, but shop in one of their local supermarkets. Real smart.

Oscar is nowhere to be seen, thankfully. It's as if he disappeared. I shudder.

The others are waiting by the cars when we get out, Zeke just loading the final of . . . five more crates of beer to Fergus's trunk.

Everyone attending is bringing food and drinks too. We're going to be drunk and stuffed the entire time.

"Let's go," Allegra says, raising her arms and twisting her body. "We have *so* much to do when we arrive."

"Yeah, that'll get us moving," Fergus says sarcastically, taking a bag from me and wedging it into the last inch of space in his car. He flashes me a shy smile.

Kash and I get back in Zeke's car and we follow the others. I quickly glance back and nearly shout when I catch a glimpse of Oscar. But when I do a double take, he's gone. It reminds me of how Hugo was watching us leave.

I turn back in my seat, trying to focus on whatever Zeke and Kash are talking about.

I really wish I had never found that online group or met Oscar.

Soon we turn off the main road and drive along what can only be described as a dirt track.

"You think he'd have the road done with all his billions," Zeke says, wincing as we hit a pothole.

The Beauforts are by far the richest family at our school. They could afford to pay every student's tuition and buy the school, and they'd still have money left over.

"I'm sure they will. You wouldn't spend millions on an apartment if you needed a tractor to get to it," Kash replies.

We turn a sharp corner, the car's suspension bouncing me so high I nearly hit my head on the roof. The holes in the ground make it look like Swiss cheese.

"Slow down, Zeke," I say, placing my hands on the dash. His car handles the uneven road surprisingly well, but it's also likely to be the reason I lose my breakfast.

That could also be the crippling anxiety at lying and sneaking around. Or the fact that Kash and I chickened out of mentioning Oscar to our friends. I can still see him watching us every time I blink.

Zeke chuckles and lifts his foot what must only be a millimeter, just enough so he can say he's technically slowed. It's still too fast.

"I hope you get a puncture," Kash says from the back seat. She has one palm on the roof and the other on the window. "My teeth are vibrating, Zeke."

"That's not possible, Kash."

Zeke's retort is ignored by Kash, who has closed her eyes and is probably praying. I hope she asks for me to be safe too, because Zeke's driving only seems to get worse.

"Look," I say, pointing ahead as the road curves and the huge castle slides into view from behind the trees. It's even more breathtaking than the pictures.

The castle rises high in the middle of the clearing, an actual moat protecting it from the outside world. I don't think I've ever seen a moat that big before—it's easily fifty yards wide.

I count six tall windows along the width, and it looks like there are four floors, the tops of frames peeking above the grass suggesting one level is belowground. There's a freaking *turret* that stands tall and steady at one end of the building—the pictures did not do that justice either. I want to live up there. If Fergus's dad won't give him the castle, maybe he can ask for whichever apartment includes the turret.

It appears remarkably robust for something that was built in the sixteenth century, but it must've had a lot of work done over the years. The windows and balcony look more modern. Allegra and Fergus did say there had been some external renovation recently.

I'm with Fergus here. I wouldn't want to develop this. I'd want to live in it.

"Wow," Kash mutters.

"I hope my bedroom is in the turret," I say.

"Is any of it livable?" Zeke asks. "Didn't Fergus say the inside is a wreck?"

I shrug. "By wreck I think he means it's been abandoned for about fifty years. It's dated, and there's only power to some of it."

"Right. So we're thinking it's more camping than glamping," Kash adds. "Because I can see there are portable toilets over there, but I *really* don't want to use them."

"Agreed," Zeke says. "We'll be fine. I'm having all the beer this weekend anyway."

"It's so pretty," Kash whispers as we get closer.

I fully appreciate why the locals don't want it to be developed. Moving walls and creating apartments will completely alter the feel of the castle.

Zeke whistles. "That group must be able to get a protection order on something like this."

Kash pokes her head between the front seats. "Is anything protected if you have enough money?"

"This must be," I say, taking in the moat around the castle again. Surely it's a lake. I can't get over it.

"Wait . . . is anyone else noticing the issue? How do we get over there?" Zeke asks, following Fergus as he parks between trees and dense vegetation.

Are we hiding the cars off the road?

Why would we be hiding the cars?

I can see why Zeke asked about getting to the front door. The bridge from here to the castle is made of wood and only wide enough for about three people to walk it side by side. Not only will a car not fit, but it would probably collapse the bridge. It's the same width as the long path that sweeps around the castle. A horse and cart sound good about now.

"We have to drag our bags and the equipment up there?" Kash asks.

"Doesn't look like there's another way," I tell her. "I hope you're feeling strong, because my arms still ache after lugging my suitcase down the stairs."

Zeke shakes his head as he parks. "How many more times do I have to explain about lifting?"

"No more times." I'm so ready to take his advice. Straight back. Bend the knees.

"This is incredible. . . . Right?" Kash asks.

"It'll be cool once we've finished dragging all our things over the bridge," I reply.

Zeke sticks the car in park. "This weekend is going to be sick!"

"Do you think there's a boat somewhere?" I ask.

"For the moat?"

"No, for the tennis court."

Kash laughs at my remark. Zeke . . . not so much. "I really hope so. I miss sailing."

I don't have the heart to tell her that it'll likely be a rowboat. But it'll be fun regardless.

"You two realize that water is probably full of disease, right?" Zeke gives us a side-eye.

We all get out and I grab my backpack, throwing it over my shoulder. "We've heard and we'll be fine."

"Okay, everyone take as much as you can carry," Fergus says, watching the lid of his trunk slowly rise. "All of this equipment needs to go to the ballroom. Second door on the right when you get inside."

"I'll lead the way," Allegra says, as if we couldn't possibly find where we're going with only Fergus's directions. She likes to be the one in charge.

"How many rooms have electricity?" I ask, picking up a speaker and handing it to Zeke.

"The generator will power a few."

"Oh my god, is there heating?" Kash asks. "I'm always cold, you know this."

Fergus smirks at her. "There's a fireplace in the ballroom and in what Allegra has claimed as the girls' bedroom above it. I promise I won't let you freeze to death."

Looks like I'm not getting my bedroom in the turret. I want to pout, but that's ridiculous beyond the age of three.

Our arms loaded with equipment, food, drinks, and clothing, we make our way to the bridge.

No one wants to come back for a second trip.

The air is warm but sharp. A floral scent wafts by in a breeze and makes me smile. Flowers have sprung up all over the grounds despite the site being abandoned. Nature is determined to keep the castle looking its best.

"Erm, is anyone else seeing how rickety this thing looks?" I ask, stopping short of the first plank, my arms aching from carrying my backpack, two bags from the supermarket, plus dragging my suitcase.

The murky green water in the moat *does* look like it's harboring a few thousand diseases. I turn my nose up because it smells like it too. My bikini can stay in my suitcase.

Allegra walks first, rolling her eyes as she goes. "It's fine. Stop being so precious."

"Says the girl carrying a pink suitcase and not much else," Kash mutters.

Can't say I'm thrilled to be called precious by her.

I wait for everyone else to go ahead before I put my foot on the first plank. When I don't instantly fall through it, I take another step. It doesn't move as much as I thought, the wood solid and stable. I had images of it swaying and one of us, likely me, falling into the water. With my backpack weighing me down I'd probably drown too.

Fergus, Shen, and Zeke laugh ahead of me. Shen is leaning to the side, pretending to fall in.

Come on, karma.

"Don't do anything risky!" Kash shouts. "I'm not pulling you out of there!"

Allegra laughs and adds, "Yeah, and you're so not coming anywhere near me if you end up in there."

"Does the castle have running water?" I ask, kicking myself for not thinking of that earlier. Now I'm stuck.

"Dad had it turned on for the builders so the bathroom and kitchen sinks can be used," Fergus says. "We've had a lot of people in lately, prepping for the work to start."

He couldn't have had the electricity and heating turned on already too? Though I guess if they've only been working outside, they wouldn't need those yet. At least I'll be able to wash in the bathroom sink—it's better than nothing.

The muscles in my arms begin to burn as the bags seem to double in weight with every second I carry them. I step off the bridge, thankful that the thing held up.

They're going to need a new one of those before it becomes apartments. One that can carry the weight and size of cars.

I crane my neck, looking up at the beautiful castle.

"Unlock the door, Allegra, this shit is heavy and you're absolutely no help as usual," Fergus tells his sister, half teasing.

She rolls those pale eyes again and holds up a key. "Shut up, Fergus."

"This is staying here," I say, lowering the bags as soon as she lets us in.

"I'll come grab them in a bit," Zeke tells me, following Allegra and Fergus through the foyer with the speakers in his arms.

The foyer is freaking *huge*. The walls stretch up high, decorated at the top with ornate stone coving, the same sandy color as the floor. It smells kind of stagnant in here, but it's something we'll get used to.

"This place is amazing," I say.

"Yeah, why aren't you living here?" Shen asks Allegra. "We could inherit this place, babe."

"If you think I'm living in an old castle, you don't know me *at all*."

"Meanwhile I would sell my whole family to live here," Kash says, staring up at the dust-covered five-tiered crystal chandelier that's nearly bigger than me.

I bet this place was off the charts before it was left to degrade.

"Okay, a couple of ground rules," Allegra says, spinning on her toes and grinning at us.

"There's a lot of electrical work going on at the moment and the power is off. As Fergus has mentioned, there is a generator, but it isn't big enough to light the entire place. That means we have power in the ballroom, a bathroom, and two other rooms. We'll use those to sleep in. The girls' bedroom is above the ballroom and the boys will take the room next to it. We'll light fires, but the temperature isn't freezing, so I don't want to hear any whining."

Shen wraps his arm around her. "The beer will keep us warm."

"Yeah!" Zeke says, high-fiving him.

Incorrect. I need heating and my hoodie. Kash needs both of those, plus thermals and gloves. She's petite and always shivering.

"You can have a quick tour of the castle once the ballroom is set up. Then I want you to stick to the rooms I just mentioned. We're not supposed to be here, so let's not leave any evidence behind."

"Everyone is helping with cleanup on Monday," Fergus adds, clearly bored of her lecture.

I'm pretty sure by that he means he will be supervising and the rest of us will be cleaning. Not once has he pulled his weight when it comes to anything post-party. Unless you count messing around and making everyone laugh. He does. I don't.

"We're starting the tour with the cellar, right?" Kash asks me.

"The creepiest room in the place? Absolutely."

Though I can't imagine anything being creepy in this place. It's too beautiful.

4

An hour later and the ballroom looks utterly ridiculous. The grand room swamps our sound system and decorations. But there will be a bunch of people arriving later, and we'll fill the space with more bodies.

The heavy dark red curtains clash with the bright pink pom-poms, and the class banner only reaches halfway up to the tall ceiling. Somehow, we got glitter all over the wood parquet flooring, the planks now littered with welts, dust, and flecks of gold.

Allegra went wild—she didn't realize some of the pom-poms had glitter. Which, in fairness, they don't anymore.

The long windows stretch up high, set into thick pale stone, their peaks pointing to the sky.

Allegra dashes past me and squeals, "Shen! Are you kidding me?"

He looks down from where he's balancing rather precariously on a dark wooden end table that looks like it's about to collapse underneath him. "What?"

"The banner isn't even in the middle of the wall. Everything looks horrendous!" She places her hand over her heart. "This party is going to be a disaster."

The banner could never be in the middle of the wall without a ladder. It looks like a toddler has decorated an ordinary room.

Zeke nudges me. "We've hit the meltdown phase of setup."

"Uh-huh."

This happens every single time she hosts a party. With a reputation to maintain—think Kardashian-level hosting—she's going to *hate* not being able to have much decor in here. We could only bring what would wedge into the cars. It's not as if she could hire the usual planners to help her out.

A banner and balloons and pom-poms are all we can manage. No fresh flower displays or expensive charcuterie boards that look great on her Insta.

I walk away to one of the tall windows, leaving the others to their new argument. The curtains are full of dust, and in the creases I can see that the red is much brighter. Zeke stays to help Shen, trying to grab the other end of the banner so they can center it before Allegra kills them.

The sky has transformed to an angry shade of gray, the bulging clouds ready to burst. I check my phone. The storm is still not supposed to hit until this evening. The others should make it in time.

"I don't think we'll be taking the party outside," I say to whoever is listening.

"There's a storm forecast, Bessie, of course we won't be," Fergus replies, stopping beside me to peer up at the sky. "We'll be fine in here."

"Why wouldn't we be?"

"I'm just trying to be positive, Bess. The moat is only half-full. We'd need a lot more rainfall than forecast to fill it."

I hadn't even considered the possibility of a flood . . . but now I am. He's right, though. There would need to be a lot of rainfall before anything happened here. It's odd that he'd even bring it up.

I wave my hand. "As long as we can keep this room warm and the drinks flowing, I don't care."

He touches my back. "That's my girl."

I stare at him, deadpan, trying to figure out how that makes me feel, and he rolls his eyes.

"Figure of speech, Bessie."

I haven't been his girl for a long time. Not since last year, and it was hardly the most committed relationship. We were never going to ride off into the sunset together. We were a couple for five months before we realized that we're better as friends. Sometimes I wonder if the accident had never happened . . .

Stop. No point in going there.

"Hey, Fergus," I say as he starts to walk away from me. "Are we good?"

He nods, his full lips stretching into a half smile. "The absolute best."

Kash laughs as she approaches me, and judging by the smug look on her face I'm not going to like what she's about to say. "That was so smooth."

"Shut up. Ugh, it's been months since we broke up, and I still feel this lingering awkwardness. Every time I think we're past it, something pops back up. Won't it go away?"

"You're a bit of an overthinker . . . and you're probably regretting breaking up with him now that you've seen this castle."

"Well, there is that. I can definitely picture myself—" I snap my teeth together, spinning around as something hits the window behind me.

"Whoa," Kash says, almost pressing her nose to the glass.

It takes a second to register that what's flying past us is rain. *Hours* early. A few fat drops hit the glass. Then, as if someone has opened a dam, it *pours.* Water hammers down loudly, bouncing off the building and dancing in the moat.

"That's . . . alarming." She looks at me. "Isn't it?"

About five seconds ago there was no rain at all.

"Well, it means our sail and swim is out. Come on, we only have about four hours left before everyone else arrives and I want to check out the castle." We've been stuck in the ballroom for ages now, and I'm dying to see the rest, to imagine how people throughout history made this their home.

Kash looks over her shoulder, seeing the others distracted with the class banner position. She pushes at my arm with hers as if I'm her boxing bag. "Go! Go!"

I spin and tiptoe out of the room with Kash right behind me.

"The cellar first?" I ask as we step around the corner, keeping as quiet as possible on the stone floor.

"Definitely. I don't want to go down there after dark."

"Did you say it's accessible through the kitchen?"

"The servants' kitchen, yeah," she responds.

"I think they just call them working kitchens now."

She shrugs. "Sounds nicer, I guess. If I remember correctly, it's this way."

"I love your organized mind, Kash. And the fact that you remember *everything,* unlike me."

I'm certain she has a photographic memory, but she's too modest to agree.

I follow her along the hallway, past doors that look like they were made for giants and walls that are half-clad in wood and intricately designed red and gold wallpaper. All has faded over time, but you still get a sense of how grand this place once was. The glitter would look much better on the floor out here.

There are huge portraits of people from years ago hanging proudly in chunky frames on the walls. Each one of them is staring at the artist with a bored arrogance, dressed in clothes that look equally heavy and uncomfortable.

"Here," she says, pushing open a door.

We both take out our phones and use the flashlight function to light the way. Since the rain started, it's darkened outside, but I didn't think it'd be this bad yet. I feel for everyone who will have to walk from their cars to the castle in this weather. The bridge is probably slippery as hell.

I shine the light around the large kitchen, though visibility isn't too bad. There are no appliances in here anymore, only old cabinets and a wooden countertop with so many notches scratched into it I'm surprised the whole thing hasn't rotted. There's a layer of grime covering all the surfaces that turns my stomach. I would never prepare food in here.

This room belongs in another house. It's plain and dull, but it was only for the staff.

I wrinkle my nose, trying not to cough as the musty air dives down my throat.

"Door to the cellar is here," Kash says, wiggling the light over the faded gold doorknob.

"Can you get into there from the outside?"

"Yeah. I was looking at the plans and that's where they must've brought the food in back in the day."

"What are you waiting for?"

"For you to go first."

"Are you kidding me?"

"I was the one who did most of the research on this place and—"

"All right, all right," I say, waving my hand and then opening the door. "I'm going."

The staircase leads down rather steeply, and the handrail moves the second I touch it; it's holding on for dear life by what appear to be rusty nails.

This is probably how I die.

"Careful," I say as Kash steps down behind me. "It doesn't feel stable."

"It's very much not."

The stairs are concrete, with far more cracks in them than I care for, and it looks like they're held together with dirt and dust. This room has had absolutely no TLC.

It's a relief to reach the bottom. The room opens up into a large sparse space with two narrow horizontal windows at the top that, thanks to overgrown bushes outside and the storm, allow absolutely no light to reach the cellar. One of the windows has a long crack in it. At first I thought it was a spider's web.

There isn't a lot down here. A few storage cabinets with the doors hanging off, two sets of metal shelving units that hold a couple of boxes I will absolutely not be looking inside of. There's probably old food rotting in there.

The dampness of the room seeps into my clothes, instantly giving me a chill. I know we're underground, but it feels about fifty degrees cooler all of a sudden.

"There's no way there's not mold here," I say.

Kash clears her throat. "It smells like death."

I retch as the stench hits the back of my throat.

I turn around, shining the light on the far wall, and gasp. Covering the external door is a *lot* of awful, hateful graffiti . . . and not much of it seems to be about the development.

5

"Kash . . . are you seeing this?"

"Uh-huh," she mutters, and shines her light from left to right as she reads some of the red sprawl. " 'You won't get away with this.' And look here. 'I'm not going anywhere.' 'You're getting what's coming to you.' Wow. I knew the locals were angry, but this is a bit much, right? I mean, we didn't know they'd broken in."

Oh, I'm reading it.

"You think this is about the development?" I ask, frowning at the words.

They're not even on a little part of the wall either, it's the whole thing. Scrawls and scrawls of hateful sentences, some overlapping, as if the writers couldn't contain their hate and had to keep going.

"Of course it is, Bess. What else would it be about? They're majorly angry. You've read the posts in that group."

"Yes, but . . . read it again. '*I'm* not going anywhere,' not *we're*.

And then there's the 'You won't get away with this' and 'You're getting what's coming to you.'"

"Okay, you're just rereading what I said."

Oh my god. "It reads like *one* person who has a major grudge."

She's silent for a few seconds and then says, "Right . . . that makes
sense. Someone in the village hates one of the Beauforts?"

"I think so. They're sure not Beaufort fans. It's probably aimed
at their dad," I tell her. "What do you think this all means?"

"That one of the save-the-castle crew is massively pissed off.
Wants to let Mr. Beaufort know."

"Do you think he's seen this?"

"If he hasn't, it would've been reported to him. We probably
shouldn't tell anyone. It won't be nice for Allegra or Fergus to see
this about their dad."

I turn to her. "Have you met Allegra and Fergus?"

They're used to stuff like this and have never given any indica-
tion that it bothers them. Neither seem to care what anyone says
about them or their family.

"Fine," she says, laughing, "but just in case. Let's not put a
downer on the weekend, yeah?"

"Got it," I reply, shining the light across the wall. Each message
is very personal and very angry, the writing messy as if written in a
hurry. I want to protect them from this if they haven't already seen
it. Red spray is splattered haphazardly on the brick, mold crawling
alongside it. Two cans have been left on the floor.

Who leaves the evidence behind? Mr. Beaufort should have the cops come in here, I bet there's some DNA. Oscar's group won't be quite so smug if that happens.

"Bessie, look," Kash says, crouching down in the corner. "The dust has been disturbed."

I shine my flashlight across the floor in front of her. That's not surprising, since someone has clearly been down here, but the weird thing is the long rectangle shape in the dust.

"It looks like someone's been sleeping here. It's the size and shape of a sleeping bag," I say. "Or at the very least they've rested. Perhaps while they were planning all of this."

"Would you turn the site of your vandalism into your Airbnb?" she asks.

"Well, I wouldn't vandalize somewhere in the first place. But you're right about someone staying here. This must've taken some time. Do you think they're still here?" I ask, mentally kicking myself for even bringing up the possibility.

"Doesn't look like it. There's nothing left behind but the mark from the sleeping bag or blanket," she replies. "Speaking of sleeping bags, we should set up our beds before tonight."

"Sharing a room with Allegra and Jia." I turn my nose up as she stands. "I love them, but they both snore and Jia talks in her sleep."

"It's going to be a *long* weekend," she says, laughing. "But we're in a castle! How epic is that?"

"Very." I take one last look at the wall and confirm my decision to leave this discovery underground. I link my arm with Kash's as we head toward the stairs, the thin panes of glass rattling as the wind outside picks up, whipping at the castle.

This time she leads the way, knowing the layout of the castle from memory. I follow her up a much grander set of stairs, this one mahogany wood with gold carpet bars and a sweeping banister with flowers carved into it. Signs of previous owners' footsteps are etched into the worn carpet.

"Here we are. The girls' room," Kash says, pocketing her phone because the three long windows let in enough light, even with the storm outside.

It's a huge, nearly empty room, with a large redbrick fireplace, soot staining the tile under the iron grate, and pretty sage walls. There are deep indents in the dark carpet where a bed and wardrobes used to be and thick sage curtains hanging either side of the windows, every single one sun-bleached at the edges.

Along one side, rather randomly, is an oak chest of drawers. The wood has aged, faded, and the delicate white metal handles are all hanging loose. Whoever took the rest of the furniture didn't want this.

"Our things are already here. How did our things get here?" I ask, noticing the four backpacks that sit near the fire.

"Allegra sent Jia on a bunch of errands when we first arrived. I think she brought them in."

I walk over to one of the windows and watch the rain pelt the ground and the wind knock trees sideways. I can't see anything but forest stretching out for miles. We're in the middle of nowhere.

The rain bounces off the water in the moat, making me want to open the window so I can listen to it. But something else quickly grabs my attention. "Kash, come here. Does the moat look higher to you?"

"What? I know the rain is coming down, but it's only been about fifteen minutes since it started. It's not possible—" She snaps her teeth together and turns to me. "Oh. Okay, that's definitely rising."

"I can't see properly, the rain is too heavy, but does it look like the field past the moat is flooded?" I ask, pointing to the area I'm pretty sure is waterlogged. It must be a nearby river. There's one near my hometown that bursts its banks every time a storm hits.

"Maybe. We should tell the others. If the storm keeps up, no one will be able to get here, Bessie. It'll just be us seven the *entire time*."

I take out my phone mid-rant and check the weather report. The seven of us being alone isn't usually an issue, but Kash is right, our group is fractured, and we haven't spent that much solid time together since last year.

It might be difficult.

Kash shakes her hands out. "I mean, I love my friends, but four solid days with them is going to be a challenge. Allegra is going to ..."

I zone out because the storm is more important than yet another Allegra moaning session. Kash's secret crush on her isn't something we're ever allowed to vocalize anyway.

"Er, Kash. There's now a *severe* weather warning for wind and rain," I say. "Lasting until Sunday. Strong possibility of flooding. Well, we can see that. *Threat to life*."

I look back at the trees bending in odd directions, one teetering precariously over an old wooden shed out on the grounds. So many of the trees out there are nearly sideways.

"Wait, someone's outside," I say, leaning closer to the window.

"Where? I can only see rain."

"The shed." I squint, trying to focus in on whoever is walking around. It's hard to tell through the waterfall of rain, but I recognize the silhouette and the dark hair. "I think it might be Jia?"

"Why would she be out there?"

"That could be the woodshed. Allegra and Fergus said we need to light the fires. Not very chivalrous of the guys to send her."

Wind blows viciously at the trees, some of them barely clinging to the ground, about to succumb to the storm. This is not good. No one should be out there.

I bang on the window, trying in vain to get Jia's attention as the tree looming over the shed splinters, the trunk snapping and bouncing back toward the sky. It's only a matter of time before it comes down completely.

"Jia!" Kash screams, but it's useless. "Keep trying, I'm going down!"

I whack my palm against the glass and grab my phone to shine the light and make her look over. "Jia! Up here!"

Kash knows the layout of the castle, so she'll be quick, but I'd feel better if Jia would get the hell away from that shed right now. *Come on, Jia, move.*

The sky lights up above me, a fork of white scattering over the castle before disappearing. *Shit.*

I hold up my flashlight, waving it around in the window in the hope that she'll be looking up after the lightning and notice me. "Jia!"

She turns around but it's too late—the tree comes down hard, flattening the shed with her beside it.

My eyes widen. "Jia!" I scream, and spin around.

I run from the room and thud down the stairs, my heart slamming against my rib cage. At the bottom, Allegra and Fergus peer through the door.

"Bess, are you okay?" Fergus asks, his face morphing into his signature look from last year. The one where he was constantly worried about me.

"A tree fell on the shed. Jia's under it!" I say breathlessly, heading for the door.

"What?"

"Oh my god!" Allegra shouts. "Shen! Zeke!"

Kash left the door open, rain already making a puddle inside, almost causing me to lose my footing.

I sprint into the rain toward Jia, with my friends behind me. Kash is ahead, and I can just about make her out through the blanket of water. My clothes are soaked through already, bitterly cold and sticking to my skin. The wind is making it feel like I might freeze on the spot.

The warmth of the sun when we arrived has been whisked away.

"Kash!" I shout, wiping rain from my eyes. "Kash, where is she?"

The shed is buried under the huge bushy tree, only partly visible through leaves. The ground is a mess of wood, splintered bark, and new leaves.

"I can't see her. Jia!" Kash yells, pushing her hair back from her face. "Jia!"

"Where was she?" Zeke asks, stepping over a branch. Shen and Fergus join him, sifting through branches and broken planks of wood.

"Does anyone see her? Where was she, Bessie?" Zeke shouts over the howling wind.

"Right by the shed the last time I saw her. She turned around to look at the lightning, and then the tree fell."

I crouch down, wiping rain from my face and sheltering my eyes. The tree almost completely covers the small woodshed as if it was trying to eat it whole. Why the hell was she out here alone, anyway?

"Over here!" Fergus shouts. "She's breathing but, shit, she's bleeding!"

The sky lights up again, thunder roaring directly above us.

Zeke grabs my arm. "We need to get Jia and get inside. It's not safe out here." He tugs me, getting hold of Kash too in what I think is an attempt to keep us all together.

We stumble as we climb over the trunk, hands and feet slipping on the wet bark. Zeke lets go and I drop down the other side, almost knocked sideways by a strong gust of wind.

"Oh god," I mutter, my hands hovering over a branch that's trapped Jia against the ground. She's lying on her side, eyes closed, with a wound on her head that's trying to bleed while the water washes it away.

"We have to get her inside. We can't wait."

"Bessie, I need you to move her in a second. Everyone else, grab the branch and lift," Fergus instructs, positioning himself on the other side of the branch. "Lift!"

I hold my arms out, ready to pull Jia away from the tree. The rest of my friends groan as they raise the heavy branch. Before they get it high enough, something catches my eye in the window of the castle.

It's gone in a flash and could just be my imagination, but for a second I thought I saw someone watching us.

6

Allegra runs ahead to grab some blankets while Fergus picks Jia up and carries her, stumbling awkwardly on the uneven, soggy ground. I run beside him, my eyes half on where I'm going and half on Jia, searching for any sign that she's breathing.

It's impossible to tell with all the chaos. All I can do is pray.

Shen closes the door behind us, slamming it the second we get inside. The lack of wind and rain does nothing to warm me up, not even a fraction. I push my wet hair out of my face and focus on what we need to do now.

"Lay her here," Allegra says, gathering blankets and putting them on the floor beside the crackling fire.

"There's plenty more wood. What was she doing?" I ask, spotting the massive pile in an old iron basket near the fireplace.

Fergus and Zeke lay her down, being extra gentle with her head. The wound doesn't look too bad at all, a small amount of blood gathering on the surface and a drip or two rolling into her hair.

She's breathing, her chest very steadily rising and falling, so I think she's going to be fine . . . but why are her eyes still closed?

"She didn't go for wood," Shen replies, checking the pulse on her neck. "She said she was exploring. I thought she meant inside, or I would've stopped her."

"We need to get her clothes off so she can warm up," I say, gathering the blankets that Zeke has dropped by her side.

Allegra unzips her drenched coat. "You're right. Boys, out for a minute."

She waits until they've left, and then Kash and I help her to take off Jia's soggy top and jeans. She groans but doesn't open her eyes. *Thank goodness.*

"It's okay. We're just getting you dry and warm," I say, then add to Kash and Allegra, "We'll need to get her some clean clothes once she's warmed up."

Allegra nods, covering Jia with the pile of blankets. "You really scared us for a second."

Kash holds Jia's wrist, taking over checking her pulse from Shen. "She's all right."

"Shouldn't we call for help?" Allegra asks. "Get her seen by someone professional, no offense."

Jia groans, gently shaking her head at Allegra's question.

"I'm not sure," I say, looking at Jia. She'll be worrying about all of us; once it's known we're here, we could get into a lot of trouble. But she's hurt, and although I like that she's breathing and somewhat replying to us, and that her pulse is good, I don't love the idea of not getting her checked out properly.

"She seems okay," Kash says. "Let's get her warm and then see."

"I'll let the boys know they can come back in," Allegra says once Jia is covered from her toes to her chin. Jia's color begins to return to her cheeks. "Shen and Kash should be the ones to decide if we need to call, because Jia's not going to agree."

Jia groans again, her eyes still closed.

"No arguments," Allegra says, getting up to let the boys in.

"You okay with that?" I ask Kash when Allegra is out of earshot. "It's a lot of responsibility."

She nods. "We're the ones who want to go into the medical field."

"You're also both teenagers," I say, rubbing Jia's hair with a towel while being careful of the cut on her head that appears to already be healing.

"We'll be fine. Her pulse is strong, and the cut is superficial. She's responding. Those are all good signs. I can see why she doesn't want us to call anyone. I wouldn't."

I don't think I would either, but that doesn't mean we shouldn't.

Allegra comes back in with the others and, as if she'd been waiting for a bigger audience, Jia groans and lifts her hand to her head. *Thank god she's moving.*

"Jia, hon. Can you open your eyes?" Allegra asks, kneeling beside her and stroking her forehead.

"I . . . ," she whispers.

"It's okay. Don't move, you might have a concussion. She doesn't feel too cold anymore."

Jia blinks heavily a few times and then opens her eyes. "No, I'm okay . . . I think. I do feel cold still. What happened?"

"You were outside in the storm and a tree fell on you," I tell her. "Do you remember?"

"What do you think about the hospital, Shen?" Kash asks him.

Jia's eyes widen, now fully alert. "Oh, absolutely not. No. I hate hospitals, and I'm fine now. You said I'd be fine. And yeah, I remember. I don't have a concussion."

"I think you do, Jia, but I'm not a doctor," Kash tells her.

"I agree," Shen says, but it's not clear who he's siding with.

Zeke pats her shoulder, holding his phone. "Thank god you're okay, because the cell service has just gone out, and the storm is worsening. What were you doing out there?"

We might still be able to make an emergency call or drive her ourselves.

"I was just looking around. Then I thought I saw one of you . . . maybe more than one . . . out there through the window and went to see."

"As in, you actually saw someone out there?" I ask. "We were all inside."

Jia's eyes slide to me and she blinks heavily. "Yes, but there was no one there. I don't know, maybe it was something else, pretty hard to see properly with the wind and rain."

"Right, it's just that you were out there for a while. Didn't you hear the tree?"

"Oh wow, Bess, way to victim-blame," Allegra says, turning her nose up as if I'm really saying Jia is at fault.

"That's not what I'm doing! I'm just trying to figure out

what's going on. Obviously I don't think it's Jia's fault a tree fell on her."

"Stop arguing. What are we going to do?" Shen asks. "I think you should go to the hospital, Jia."

"I don't need to go to the hospital," Jia says. "Kash will check me over."

Kash startles, her dark eyes widening at now having sole responsibility. "What?"

Fergus points at Kash. "Yes, your parents are doctors and—"

"Fergus, you don't inherit medical training," she tells him.

"I know that, but you want to be a doctor too, and I also know that you're already halfway through the first uni year's textbooks."

They were always going to check her over as best as they could, but Fergus is making it sound like Kash will be as thorough as a doctor. I trust her, but it's *not* the same. The wrong call could have a devastating effect.

"Yeah, Kash, I trust you more than anyone in any hospital," Jia says. "Allegra, I need some clothes. I appear to be naked under these blankets and I'd like to not be, please."

"Allegra, Kash, and I undressed you so you'd dry. The boys weren't in the room," I tell her.

She glances up at me. "Thanks. I vaguely remember, but it feels like a dream."

We all need a change of clothing. With the adrenaline wearing off, the cold has seeped deep into my bones, causing goose bumps to pop up all over my skin. I'm still dripping.

"Trusting me more than a doctor is a terrible idea, Jia," Kash replies. "Do you have any pain?"

"My head and chest a little. Neither too bad, more like an ache. Honestly, I feel fine. I'd get up if I had anything on."

"Your vision. Is anything blurred, or are you seeing double?" Kash leans closer, taking her role as doctor very seriously. While she's asking questions, Shen takes her pulse again and touches the area around her head wound.

"My vision is fine."

"She was out of it for a while," Fergus says. "I was there first, and she was unconscious."

"Yeah, it was, what, a minute or two?" Zeke replies, watching Shen clean and dress Jia's wound.

"Probably more like four or five," I say. "It took a couple of minutes to get her inside, and she didn't regain consciousness properly until we got her under the blankets."

"I am here, guys," Jia says. "And I'm *fine*."

Allegra dumps a bag down beside Jia and holds up a soft pink loungewear set. "This will warm you up. Boys, clear out again, please, we're not putting on a show."

Zeke, Fergus, and Shen grab their bags and leave, all of them soaked through and in need of a change too. Fergus's lips are turning an alarming shade of blue.

"Do you need help, Jia?" I ask.

She pushes herself up so she's sitting and touches her head. The wound wasn't bleeding at all before Shen put the small bandage on, but she'll likely be left with a headache.

"I appreciate you undressing me, but I'm awake now and can handle it," she replies politely, her eyes a fraction too wide at the thought of being dressed like a toddler. She takes the clothes from Allegra and smiles to convince us that she's fine.

We give her a second, making sure she doesn't faint, and then get changed ourselves. I peel the soggy clothes off my body, my skin breaking out in another round of goose bumps. The clothes hit the floor, landing hard in a puddle on the beautiful, hundreds-of-years-old flooring.

I rip open my bag and wrap a towel around my frozen body, and then pull on a new outfit, the warmth instantly comforting. "Do we think the party will still happen tonight?" I ask.

Allegra spins around, the towel wrapped around her head almost dropping to the floor. Her mouth pops open as if I've just asked her to never hold another gathering ever again. "Jia's fine, so why wouldn't it?"

"Look outside, Allegra," I reply, pointing to the window. "Do you think anyone will risk driving in this? They wouldn't have left yet."

Kash pulls on an oversize sweatshirt, wrapping her arms around her waist as she tries to warm up. "Have you checked the weather report recently? Because Bessie and I have. There's now a severe warning for rain and wind. We've all seen how quickly those trees can come down and we're surrounded by a whole forest of them."

"But we're only two hours from school." Allegra sounds like a petulant child who's about to throw a tantrum. She doesn't cope well when things don't go to plan. *Her* plan. But I don't understand how she can think her party is more important than the safety of our friends.

"Right." I'm not sure it matters if school is two hours or ten minutes away. It's still dangerous. "But the weather warning says not to travel unless necessary. I don't know how many people in our year are going to think this party is essential."

Actually, it's probably all of them.

"Well, it is! Stop looking at me like that. We're nearly in our final year, and then we'll all go our separate ways. We have to make the most of the time we have left. Plus, we're in a *castle*. No one else has had a location like this before. Everything is going to be *perfect*."

I take a step back because her eyes are wild and her hands are waving around like she's landing planes. She sounds unhinged.

Jia sits on her makeshift bed of blankets, watching Allegra in the way she does when she's about to pacify her best friend. "This weekend is going to be awesome, Allegra. Not even a tree crushing me is going to stop it. People will come, so don't worry."

She's saying all the right words, exactly what Allegra wants to hear, but I can see the hesitation in her expression.

Kash and I towel-dry our hair, not getting involved because frankly it's pointless.

"You're right. No one is going to drive in this," Kash whispers when Allegra and Jia start a conversation about whether they should pre-open some bottles of beer.

I don't think that's a thing unless you're a bartender, but I realize that neither of them usually serve the drinks. Jia should stick to water.

"The moat is still flooding over," I say, looking out the window. The bridge is almost level with the water.

Kash smiles. "A party for seven will still be fun. . . ." It sounds like she's trying to convince herself more than me.

Kash, now dressed all in black, channeling her inner ninja, as she puts it, hovers by Jia as she stands up. I hang my towel over a chair, my hair as dry as I can be bothered with. It's wavy and kind of messy, but it'll be fine.

Jia seems remarkably steady on her feet considering she was just flattened by a tree, but I don't miss the wince as she straightens her back. I'm hoping it was more shock than injury because other than looking a bit uncomfortable, she does seem fine.

"Jia, we can probably still get to the hospital if you want to go," I say, not happy with her discomfort. "I can borrow Fergus's car and take you myself. We don't all need to go."

I ignore the death stare Allegra is shooting at me.

Jia tilts her head. "I appreciate it, Bess, but I *promise* I feel fine. It would just be a waste of time to sit in the ER for ages."

"But—"

She holds her hand up and cuts me off. "No. I'm okay. Just a little achy still."

I look to Kash for help, because Allegra is going to side with Jia without a doubt.

Kash shrugs again. "I'm with Bessie. While I agree you look fine, we can't be certain."

"I can," she says stubbornly. "I know how I feel, Kash. My head is clear. I'm just a little sore from the accident."

"All right," Kash says, and turns back to me. "We can't force her."

"Promise you'll tell us if anything changes."

Jia laughs, waving her hand as if to bat our concerns away. "Promise. Let's move on now. Please."

"All right. So, do we finish decorating or just stop where we are now? Maybe we could add more for tomorrow if people arrive," I suggest.

Allegra stops short of stomping her feet, but she does put her hands on her hips. "We have two hours before the party starts. It could still happen. Let's stop being negative."

"Sorry," I reply. "I'll go hang our wet stuff on the radiator. It doesn't get hot, but they'll dry faster on there than on the floor. I'll tell the boys they can come in. We'll prep for the party, Allegra."

"I'll come with you," Kash says. "I have some ibuprofen in my other bag, and I think it's a good idea for Jia to have some."

"I second that," Jia says. "Don't get me wrong, I'm *fine*, but my head and chest could use some relief. A tree falling on you will do that."

"You're able to joke about it. Good sign," I say, gathering my heavy, waterlogged clothes.

Kash and I leave Allegra digging through her suitcase.

"It's safe in there now, boys!" I shout in the empty hallway. Who knows where they went. "Kash, I need to tell you something."

"You're whispering. Sounds secretive."

I look over my shoulder to make sure we're not overheard as we walk upstairs. "If you think it's secretive, why be so loud? Anyway, Jia thought she saw someone outside."

Kash quickly catches on and says, "You thought you saw some-one too."

"Uh-huh. I'm fairly certain I saw someone watching us from inside."

"We were all outside, Bess."

"Uh-huh," I mutter again.

"Nope." She stops and grabs my arm. *"Absolutely not."*

"What?"

"We're alone in this castle all weekend, and no one knows we're here. There's a massive storm that's knocked out the phone signal. If you think for one second I'm allowing you to start freaking me out about someone else being here, you are——"

"All right, calm down. I'm not saying that's what's happening. You saw the graffiti in the cellar. Maybe someone from that group has been hanging around, and that's who Jia saw."

"But you saw someone too, right? *Inside* the castle. I think I'm going to throw up."

Yeah, I never should have said anything to her. Horror movies are her favorite, but we can only watch during the daytime. Kash spooks easily. To her, every bump in the night is a serial killer.

"No, it's okay. I mean, I was super-stressed and panicking that Jia was dead. The rain was pouring. It could've just been something that blew past the window."

She makes a strangled sound and follows me up the rest of the stairs. "Do you seriously expect me to believe that bullshit expla-nation?"

"Not really, but it was worth a shot."

"We know someone was staying here," she tells me, her mind working overtime to freak her out. "That person is still here. I know it."

"You're giving me whiplash. What happened to not freaking out? Besides, they might not have stayed long."

"I'm giving *you* whiplash?"

"I'm sorry. I just needed to tell someone."

Granted I chose the wrong person to tell, but I trust Kash more than anyone else in the world.

"You can tell me stuff. I want you to. Just . . . can you not tell me that a creep is hiding in the castle again? Please."

I laugh and am just about to reply when something or someone makes a thudding sound. Kash screams, throwing her wet clothing down in front of her.

"What was that?" I ask her, eyeing the pile of clothes on the floor.

"No, what's *that*?" She waves her hand toward the noise.

"I think it's footsteps." It's definitely *someone*. "Zeke? Fergus? Shen? What are you doing up here?"

"Shh! Bessie, have you lost your mind?"

"Kash, it's probably one of the guys. We have to relax. Hello? Guys, who's there?" I take a step forward, my heart thumping against my rib cage. The long red hallway seems to stretch for miles, growing with every eerie second of silence.

What if it *is* someone from the save-the-castle group? They wanted to burn it down. But surely they wouldn't now. They know we're here. Maybe they just want to scare us. Oscar might have figured out who we are. It's creepy how easy it is to convince yourself that you're in danger.

I'm not thinking straight, but my logical mind has been kicked to the background. Fear curls around my stomach and squeezes. All I can think about is these people setting fire to the castle while we sleep.

I take another step. Kash is right behind me, breathing heavily.

Being brave *sucks*.

The footsteps start again, growing louder, whoever they belong to getting closer to us. I clench my hands, making fists as if I'm about to get into a street fight.

"Who is it?" I ask, stepping back because my bravery is short-lived. My hands are still ready, though. That is if I don't run away in about three seconds.

"Bessie, let's go. There's another staircase along the hallway," Kash says, her voice low. She pulls my arm to get me to follow, but if we go we'll still be thinking the worst.

My breath catches as someone steps around the corner.

I jump back, bumping into Kash. But after a second, I recognize him. "Oh my god! Hugo! I think I'm having a heart attack, Kash. Is it possible to still talk while you have a heart attack?" I ask, placing my hand to my chest, feeling the erratic beat under my palm. "What the hell are you doing sneaking around, and when did you get here?"

Hugo smirks, leaning against the wall with his ankles crossed. He's enjoying this. "You two doing okay over there?"

"Seriously, when did you arrive?"

Kash lets out a long sigh and drops my arm. Her eyes shoot daggers at Hugo.

"Just now. Couldn't find you guys but saw your things in that *massive* room. I went to check out the place," he replies, ruffling the curls on top of his head and dripping water on the worn carpet. "Abbas and Odette are with me . . . somewhere. Odette wanted to see if she could find the room where servants had to sleep. Something about it being worse conditions than a prison, but I don't know."

"You made it through the storm?" I ask, my heart finally beginning to slow down.

"Looks like it. We lost signal on the way. Almost went past the turn for pothole alley. The road leading up here is terrible."

"Is anyone else coming?" I ask.

"I can't be sure. We were the first to leave school, after you lot. I'm thinking the others won't risk it now. Two roads were flooded; one had a tree down across it, crushed a car. Police and paramedics were everywhere. We had to turn back and take another route. I'm sure we only made it because Abbas drives a monster truck."

"Oh god."

He shakes his head. "The car looked bad, but hopefully they're okay."

"Hopefully," Kash says. "Oh no. Allegra is going to be *impossible* if no one else comes."

At least we have a few more people. She'll like that it's Hugo and Abbas, being hot older guys.

"We should get back downstairs. I'm just grabbing the things we need," Kash says, ducking into the bedroom after scooping up the wet clothes and taking my load, forcing me to release my death grip.

"Did you not see us outside?" I ask. If they had arrived not long ago, wouldn't they have seen us? It takes a little while to cross the bridge and walk up to the castle. Or if they arrived before that, why wouldn't they have seen or heard us inside?

"I saw rain, Bessie. Lots of rain. Abbas almost got hit in the face by a branch. It was comical, actually. He ducked, slipped, and fell on his ass. Had to change his jeans when he got inside. What's going on? You look on edge. I am sorry for scaring you."

I shake my head. "It's been full-on here. A tree came down on Jia. Almost a shed too. She seems fine, just a sore head and chest, but she's refusing to go to the hospital. Weird thing is, I thought I saw someone in the window when we were all outside. Then we come in and run into you. . . ."

"Back up, love. You saw someone else in the castle?"

"Thought I did. Pretty sure. Could've been you guys, though. If you went off to explore, we could've just missed each other."

He shrugs, and it makes me so jealous how casually he can let things go. "Makes sense—I've been all over the top floors so far. How's it going down there?"

I fold my arms and roll my eyes. "Allegra turned into the party-zilla again, but Jia's accident kind of put a stop to that. Temporarily, anyway. She's hoping everyone will still come, but after what you've just told me that's massively unlikely."

"So it's a party for ten tonight."

"I hope you brought your dancing shoes."

He smiles, his eyes glowing. He's not as wet as I thought he'd be, considering he just recently arrived and would've had to walk through the storm, but maybe he changed clothes like we did.

"Fergus wasn't joking when he said it was a castle."

"No, he was not." I look up. "It's amazing . . . and kind of creepy."

"The castle or the fact that we're stuck here?"

I hold a finger up. "We're not stuck here. Others just can't get here."

"Erm, you haven't seen the bridge, have you?"

"What about it?"

"It's almost underwater."

"I saw a bit of it, but I don't understand how that's possible? It's higher than the moat, even with it flooding over."

"Yeah, you should see how high the moat is. We found the edge of it walking over, had to walk through water when we got off the bridge. I didn't realize this was a pool party."

Oh, I could whack him for being so nonchalant.

"Hugo, this isn't funny. That bridge is the only way to the road."

"Not laughing. Much. There are two rivers nearby that've burst their banks, according to the cop at the roadblock. The flooding has affected most of the village. Castle's higher, so hopefully the water won't reach inside. Odette said the weather warning ends on Sunday evening, so we'll be fine."

"You think if the rain stops Sunday evening the flood will have subsided by Monday?" I ask, my voice embarrassingly high. My parents will freak if I'm not home on Monday evening.

He pushes away from the wall and steps closer to me. "Yes, I do. Please don't panic. How are you, Bess?"

I tilt my head as he approaches, my heart fluttering for another reason as he gets a bit too close. "Freaked, Hugo. How are you?"

"Ready to party. I have beer, so you don't need to freak for long."

Kash walks out of the room, her brows nearly touching her hairline. Hugo steps back. "I'm sorry, did I hear that the flood means we can't leave?"

"You sure did," I reply.

"Don't worry, girls, once the storm passes, I'm sure the water will drain fast."

"Forget it. Let's just get the pain meds to Jia and try to have fun," I say, shaking my head to physically rid myself of the worst-case scenarios. "I'll be right back."

I dash into the room to hang up my wet clothes, listening to Hugo relay what he told me to Kash.

When I come back out they both turn to me, Kash looking scared and Hugo like he's just been to war. I almost laugh because I'm sure she's been chewing his ear off.

Meanwhile I feel calmer. The person in the castle was Hugo—someone who's supposed to be here—and Jia is fine. I'm sure if the water takes a little longer to subside, we can make an excuse to stay away from home.

"You're sure about staying? Because he told me everything," Kash asks, looking between me and Hugo.

"I am. We should go downstairs," I say, walking away because I can't keep going over this. Besides, we don't have a car, and I don't want to leave Jia with Allegra, since she doesn't seem concerned.

We take the stairs together, Hugo whistling as he looks up at the high ceiling and chandelier.

Kash glances at us when she's at the bottom. "I'm so not sure about this. Maybe we can borrow a car for the weekend, Bess."

Hugo slings his arm around my shoulders as we reach the foyer. My eyes widen. Oh, I so don't need a new crush. "You said Jia was okay now, right, Bess?"

"Seems to be—says she's just a little sore and achy. Not sure we should count on that, as she always wants to please Allegra," I reply.

"See, Kash. Jia is okay, she's had painkillers."

I'm not sure that's what I said, but this is likely our only opportunity to be here. If planning is granted, I bet the Beauforts will get work started straightaway. Considering they're already having things done. We can survive one weekend.

Over in the ballroom, Fergus is playing around with the speakers and Shen is connecting his phone, where he has the playlists for the weekend. Everyone has contributed, so there's a wide range of songs.

Fergus looks at Hugo's arm around me and quickly blinks away his irritation. I feel my face heat up despite having done nothing wrong.

Zeke is eating chips, sneaking some in before Allegra catches him. She's actually made a cute charcuterie board with meats and cheeses. There's no way of keeping that refrigerated, so it'll have to all be eaten tonight.

With Zeke and Fergus that won't be a problem.

Hugo wraps an arm around Kash's shoulder, the other *still* around mine. "See, we're going to have a great weekend. Hey, Zeke, that better be guacamole."

Kash rolls her eyes as he walks off toward the food, fist-bumping Zeke.

"I swear all he thinks about is food and beer," she says, wandering off. "Odette!"

I make my way to Fergus and Shen. "Hey, did you guys hear about the roads?"

"Abbas filled us in. I didn't think it'd be that bad," Fergus says. "But we're safe here. Castle's on high ground. Flooding isn't uncommon when the rain is heavy, but it always clears fast. I can see you stressing, Bessie. It'll be fine by Monday. I promise."

He's as confident as Hugo.

"If it isn't?" I ask.

"Then we'll stay an extra day," he says. I'm not sure my parents will be home, but they will know if I'm not with all the security cameras we have. I guess it wouldn't take much to convince them I'm staying at Kash's, though. "We have plenty of food and plenty of beer."

"Yeah!" Shen cheers, picking up his bottle.

Well, isn't that a relief. . . .

What I don't understand is why neither Fergus nor Allegra warned us of this before we came. We all knew about the storm— minus the severity of it—but didn't worry too much. I certainly didn't know the castle was liable to bloody *flood*. We could've come here at the end of the weekend.

"No one can know we're here," I say.

"I completely agree, and they won't." He plugs a wire in and the speakers crackle, the sound echoing noisily in the large room. "That's it, Shen."

Taylor Swift's "Shake It Off" drifts through the room, and you can't be unhappy when Taylor's playing. I find my stress levels lowering and my smile growing. That's the power of Swift.

"I'm getting a beer," I say, leaving them to it.

I grab a beer and dip a Dorito in salsa.

Hugo clinks his bottle against mine. "Nice to see you've joined us, Bess."

"We're stuck until the storm is over. Might as well enjoy it."

"Damn straight we should."

7

Two hours later, when the party was supposed to start, we're in the pitifully decorated ballroom. Allegra doesn't seem to care. I'm not sure if that's because she's over it or because she thinks the room looks good.

Odette and Abbas are sitting in a circle with Shen, Zeke, Jia, and Allegra. Everyone is slightly buzzed and incredibly happy.

Jia, against nearly everyone's argument, has been drinking beer. Two beers—I've been counting and trying to stop her. Kash shoved a bottle of water at her after the first one, knowing we can't actually stop her. She does seem to move more easily now, but I'm not sure if that's due to genuinely being okay or the alcohol.

The floods and storms have been forgotten, the beer making the world brighter. We have to make the best of the situation. Or at least that's what Fergus has said a few million times.

"Hey, you doing okay?" Kash asks, sitting beside Jia.

"Yeah," Jia replies.

"It's time for ibuprofen, and maybe this time try it with water and *not* beer. In fact, you should lay off the beer now."

She smiles and taps her head. "Thanks for these . . . and beer makes them work faster."

Kash rolls her eyes as Jia knocks the pills back with a large swig. "Yeah, Jia, that's not right. You shouldn't be drinking."

"Kash is right. Switch to water and drink again tomorrow if you wake up feeling fine," I say, trying to reason with her.

"I'm fine now. Seriously, stop with all the stressing, guys. There's nothing wrong with me but a bit of an ache now."

"Then why did you just take more pills?" I ask.

"Because I don't want to ache!"

Kash and I look at each other and then at the rest of the group for help. They were vocal with the first beer and quieter with the second, and now they're silent.

That's just great.

"Just be careful," Kash sighs, relenting because Jia is clearly not going to listen to us.

"Okay," Allegra says, raising her hands. "I know this isn't exactly what I had planned, but we need to roll with the changes. We can't control the weather. We're lucky that Jia is totally fine. We're all having fun, right?"

She stares directly at me and then Kash when she says that.

"Definitely . . . but, Allegra, before you do the motivational speech thing, we need to discuss leaving in the morning," Kash says, her eyes finding the window again.

I do a double take because she mentioned this before but never said anything further. I thought she'd decided we were fine. Sometimes her brain works too quickly for me to keep up. Sometimes it works too quickly for her to keep up too.

"What? No way, we're not going anywhere. Ten's a party, Kash, so jump on board with the new plan."

"Your best friend was knocked out and the flood is going to keep us from being able to leave soon."

It probably already has. I'm sure we're too late.

Allegra stares, deadpan. "On Sunday the water will be gone, and you'll feel silly for overreacting."

I smile at Kash as Allegra walks off, not bothering to wait for a response. She's over anything that could ruin her weekend.

Kash huffs and heads over to Zeke, Hugo, Odette, and Abbas, who are playing poker and clinking beer bottles while laughing loudly.

I spend thirty minutes watching poker and sipping a beer, then another thirty chatting with Fergus about the house in Scotland he's inheriting. It's not a castle, but it is a stately home.

"We should have a party there next," I tell him.

Fergus laughs. "I'll do my best. I'm going to get another drink. Do you want one?"

"No, I'm good, thanks," I tell him, my eyes drifting to Jia, who has been sitting down for the last ten minutes. She has a fresh drink in her hand that I want to rip from her fingers.

I go and sit beside her on the pile of sleeping bags the boys have left here as makeshift sofas.

"Hey."

She winces, holding her rib cage. "Hey."

"Okay, what's going on?" I ask. "And don't tell me you're fine, because I can see that you're not."

One minute she's partying and the next she needs to sit down.

She glances up at Allegra, who's far too busy kissing her boyfriend to notice that her bestie is suffering. "My chest hurts, but it's okay."

I narrow my eyes. This is exactly why she shouldn't have alcohol. "Where exactly in your chest?"

"It's rib pain. I'm pretty certain."

"Do you have any swelling?" I ask, ignoring her trying to brush it off again.

"Not really. Maybe a touch, but there is light bruising. Please don't make a big deal out of it, though, it's not *that* painful. I can still move around. I've been dancing."

"You could have fractured ribs or internal bleeding."

"I'm pretty sure it would hurt more than this if they were fractured. It's just a bruise." She takes a slightly ragged breath. "Promise I'm okay to stay. Besides, it's not like we can leave anyway."

"We'll find a way if you need it. Phones don't work, but we can still call emergency services."

"Oh yeah, let's risk their lives for a bruised chest. It's hardly life-or-death, Bessie. We can't call anyone; you know how much trouble we'd get in. We've lied to everyone about where we are."

"What about getting you out of here?"

She winces, holding her chest. "You can take me when it's safe to. Go have a drink and chill. You're more tense than me, and I'm the one with bruised ribs and a possible concussion."

"Yet you're drinking beer!"

Kash has been checking her closely for signs of a concussion, and so far she doesn't have any. With a headache being Jia's only symptom, Kash and Shen think it's unlikely. That doesn't mean she's okay to drink.

"I'll make this my last one. Okay?"

"Good."

"Stop stressing!"

"I'm just worried about you."

"I appreciate the concern, Bess," she says, her expression softening. "*Don't* look up, but Hugo keeps staring at you. You should go talk to him. He's gorgeous."

I blush involuntarily. "Yeah, he thinks I'm a child."

"He does not."

"I ran into him this morning. *Literally.*"

She laughs. "It didn't go well?"

I shake my head. "I mentioned Raif and he practically ran away. Not the smartest thing to do, since we've avoided that particular subject like the plague."

Jia dips her head, chewing on her bottom lip. "How is Raif?"

"Hugo said he's okay. Not coming here, clearly. I just don't think he's going to talk to us again."

"We can't do anything about Raif," she says, raising her eyes. "Go talk to Hugo. I'm sure he could use some fun."

"He's at a party with his best friends. I think he's having fun."

She holds her beer up, waiting. I clink my bottle against hers, laughing.

"Promise me that's the last."

She ignores me. "Cheers to us and to this party. Nothing is going to stop us having the best weekend. We have enough pain-killers and beer and snacks to last. Live it up, Bessie." She rolls her eyes at my pointed expression. "And yes, I promise."

I finish my drink with Jia, using the time as an opportunity to check that she doesn't seem confused or disorientated, and then I need the toilet again because the beer is flowing a little too freely.

The bathroom along the hall is the one we're using, so I make my way out; I leave everyone behind, including Allegra and Shen, who are now dancing in the middle of the room.

Hugo and Abbas are standing around near the door, and I suddenly wish I could hold my bladder indefinitely so I won't have to walk past them.

"Hey, Bess," Abbas says as I go to pass.

"Hi."

"Hugo and I were about to check out the castle. Want to come?"

"All of the rooms are empty. Some have a piece of furniture or two. Nothing much to see."

I'm not really up for snooping around in the dark. Some rooms were creepy the first time around this morning. The damp graffiti cellar.

"Come on," Hugo says, throwing his arm around my shoulder.

Again? I don't hate it, but it makes my stomach feel . . . weird. I'm not sure if that's in a good way or not, but something is off.

"Where's Odette?" I ask, clearing my throat.

Abbas laughs. "She and Fergus have gone to see if there's anything in the kitchen."

"What?"

"Odette said people always leave food behind when they move."

"Right."

"I think she wants to see the oldest-dated food. I'm sure she'll move on to looking through the drawers soon."

"That's odd."

"Correct."

"And you two want to go where?" I ask.

"Everywhere," Abbas replies. "You must've taken a tour when you arrived."

"I did. In the daylight. And didn't you already tour? Also in daylight?"

Abbas shrugs. "We did a quick sweep but ran into the others. I haven't seen the top floors."

"Have you seen the cellar?" I ask.

His jaw drops. "I didn't know there was one. Take us there."

"It'll be too dark." It's a ridiculously pathetic excuse.

"If you have a phone, you have a flashlight," Hugo says. "You in or not?"

I shrug, not really wanting to sit around and drink more beer anyway. I can't relax. We have three more days of this.

It's not like we can even entertain ourselves with capture the flag, since it'd be no fun in a storm, and Zeke left his playing cards in the car. I'm kind of grateful for that one, to be honest. It would only be a matter of time before someone suggested strip poker.

"I'm in," I tell them. "Cellar first."

"Is it creepy?" Abbas asks.

"No bodies in there," I reply, leading the way.

Hugo punches the air. "Damn, I was hoping for a murder mystery weekend."

I've been on a lot of those with Kash, Allegra, and Jia. So much fun. We have a sixty percent success rate.

"So anyone find it weird that this is the venue for the spring party weekender?" Abbas asks.

"Isn't Juliet having one at her parents' house in the Cotswolds?"

"Yes, but her parties are never as good as Allegra's." Abbas holds his hand up and lifts a brow. "You take that to the grave, all right?"

They follow me into the servants' kitchen. In the dark it looks even bleaker.

I open the door to the cellar and gesture for them to go ahead. "I promise I'll never tell that you prefer hanging out with the younger-year group."

Abbas coughs as we reach the bottom. "It smells awful down here."

"That'll be the damp and the mold. Hey, take a look at this. What do you guys think?" I ask, shining my light on the graffiti.

"Whoa," Abbas murmurs, moving closer to the wall. "I think someone is in desperate need of a spa day."

Hugo moves along the wall, reading every threat. "Kash mentioned a Facebook group trying to save the castle from development. I can't believe they've broken in." He looks over at me. "We won't mention it, by the way."

"Kash and I met one of the members in a weird little grocery store just out of the village. This guy, Oscar, said a couple of them are hard-core and would rather the castle burn than become apartments for the rich."

Abbas scoffs. "Ugh, I hate the rich."

"Shut up, mate," Hugo says, nudging his friend. "Are you worried about this, Bess?"

"I don't know," I say pathetically, not wanting to seem like a massive baby in front of them. In front of Hugo. I've just had a weird vibe, despite how stunning the castle is and how much I want to enjoy this weekend.

"Forget them. It's not unreasonable for them not to want this place changed, but it's nothing to do with us. We are here to *party!*" Abbas cheers like a drunk soccer fan.

"We should move on before he takes his shirt off," Hugo says.

"Wait . . ." I shine my light at the lower left side of the wall. "Oh my god," I whisper. "This one wasn't here earlier."

Freshly painted words read *Leave while you can.*

"What?"

"This is new!" I crouch down and touch the black paint, smearing it and making my fingertip look like I've just been processed at the police station. "It's tacky but not set."

"The damp down here wouldn't let that dry," Hugo says.

"Yeah, but it wasn't here when Kash and I were exploring earlier."

"Are you sure?"

Am I?

"Yes! Fairly." At least I *think* I am. I should've taken a photo. I rub my temples, feeling a pressure headache building. "We were spooked by it, didn't expect that group to be able to get inside."

"The state of the windows up there. Anyone could get in," Abbas tells us. "Maybe the grocery guy was doing the rounds, trying to make the Beauforts feel unwelcome."

"I didn't tell Oscar we were coming here."

Oh my god, I wish I could remember if this was here before.

"You think he didn't know you have money?"

"No, I think he wouldn't know I was coming here," I reply, and Abbas tilts his head, knowing I'm right. "I don't like this."

I'm glad I can't see their expressions clearly, because they probably think I'm a paranoid freak.

I look at the message again. I'm sure it wasn't there.

8

After the creepy cellar incident, Hugo and Abbas lead me back to the ballroom. I'm not sure if they just don't want to continue the tour with a buzzkill or if they're concerned as well. Either way, no one mentions the tour fail.

Abbas breaks off, heading straight for Odette, who's now back with Fergus. Hugo grabs a couple of beers and hands me one, smiling as if he thinks I really need it.

"Are you okay?"

There's no hint of trepidation in his tone, so I'm left wondering if I'm overreacting and questioning if I'm right about the paint. Could it have been there before and I was too freaked to notice? It might not have dried because it's so damp down there.

"Yeah, I'm fine," I reply with no way of knowing if I am or not. "I think it's the fact that we can't leave that easily that's messing with my mind."

"Makes sense. Do you really think someone else has been here since we arrived?"

"It's not out of the realm of possibility that I missed it or forgot about it."

It's just . . . I was sure I hadn't read it before.

Odette holds a drink in one hand and a bag of flour in the other. "Here I have an ancient artifact. Flour that went out of date in September *1994*."

Abbas shakes his head. "Your quirks are getting weirder."

"Ignore her. I think she took a hit to the head at some point too," Hugo says. "Jia looks well, though."

"Yeah," I say, feeling slightly lightheaded as I take a sip of yet another beer.

I'm still convinced that taking pain meds with beer is a terrible idea, but she's on her feet now, laughing with Allegra, Zeke, and Shen. Maybe she really is okay and I've been worrying for nothing.

She might not have fractured anything, but even if we got her to a hospital there's nothing that can be done for a broken rib.

"It's getting even worse outside," Hugo says, tipping his chin toward the window. "Zeke still thinks we should have a kickaround in the morning. Said the wind would make it more interesting."

"If by interesting he means dangerous, he's absolutely correct."

Jia's accident happened outside in the wind. Who the hell thinks it's a good idea to go out there?

"I'd say what's the worst that could happen, but we already

know." He laughs and points the neck of his beer Jia's way. "Though you'd never know it by looking at her. Other than the bandage, that is."

It's already started to peel where she keeps playing with it. I'm surprised she hasn't taken it off yet.

In the middle of the room Allegra, Shen, Jia, and Zeke are dancing. Abbas joins in, leaving Odette and Kash laughing and taking photos of them. Jia is slower than usual, no sign of twerking, but she's not exactly taking it easy.

Even Shen and Kash don't seem at all worried anymore. Shen especially, since he's swinging Allegra around like they're on *Dancing with the Stars*.

I laugh as Abbas does the robot. "He is the worst dancer I have ever seen in my life."

"His mum owns a dance studio in Edinburgh. She would be ashamed of this spectacle."

I want to reply, but a thud above us stops me. "Did you hear that?"

"The thunder? It's been on and off all evening, Bessie."

"No, above us. Footsteps. Or something dropping."

"What room is directly above this one?" Hugo asks.

"Um, the room us girls are staying in."

"Want me to check it out?" he offers. "If it'll make you relax and enjoy the party we're *supposed* to be having."

I shake my head because at some point I need to lighten up, right? "No. Jia loaded her bags up on this tiny broken chair. It's probably just her stuff that's fallen."

"Oh, logic, Bessie. Nice."

"Very funny."

"Sorry. I get it, you're freaking without adults present."

"Way to make me sound like a seven-year-old."

Hugo laughs and sits down on the makeshift sofa that Jia seems to have no intention of taking over again. I take a seat beside him.

"I apologize again," he says, smirking and showing no sign that he's sincere. "Nothing bad is going to happen. We can take care of ourselves."

"Yeah, I know. I'm all good." Or I will be tomorrow when we have better light.

Most of the castle is in darkness because of the bad wiring, and everyone knows that even your own home is scary when you're alone in the dark.

"I'm glad you guys came," I tell him. "We haven't seen you at a party since . . ."

"Since before the accident with Raif," he says casually. "We can talk about it, Bessie, you know."

We've spoken about how everyone's been doing. But we've never delved deeper into what happened and why. We haven't spoken about why Raif disappeared off the face of the planet.

"Right . . . I just feel awful about it," I say. "Physically too. I get this heaviness in my stomach whenever I think about it."

"*You* are the one who almost died. What do you have to feel bad about?"

His voice is heavy, loaded with questions he's holding back.

We've danced around this subject before, neither one of us getting too honest. It's something I believe we would all benefit from, but Raif won't even reply to us.

There's so much about that night I don't know and don't understand.

"I feel awful because Raif's gone," I begin.

Hugo lifts a brow, his eyes alight with amusement. "That was rather dramatic, don't you think? He isn't dead."

I lower my beer bottle, setting it on the ground. "He isn't coming back to school, is he?"

"He's at St. Sebastian's. Seems to be doing well there."

All the schools in the area seem to be Saintly. I've partied with students from a lot of them and can say with absolute certainty that they are not.

"Oh. I'm glad he's doing well." Disappointment is heavy in my tone.

"You were hoping he'd come back. I'll tell him."

"Do you think it'll make a difference?"

He shakes his head, glancing off into the distance. "No, I don't. Nothing we've tried has worked. He's drowning in his own guilt."

I've never understood that. He was behind the wheel that night, the dangerous driving charge made to disappear with a flash of their dad's credit card, but thankfully no one was killed.

We were, *are*, willing to forgive his mistake. I already have.

"I'm not saying that he shouldn't be held responsible, but I don't think he needs to run away."

Hugo's hand grips his bottle harder. "I agree. He doesn't."

"Your parents can't make him come back?"

"They tried," he says.

"Did he talk to you about what happened that night? Fergus doesn't remember anything."

"You don't either, huh?"

I frown. He knows I don't. "Just a big black hole where that night was. It's *so* frustrating. I even tried hypnosis, but it didn't work."

At first I was obsessed with knowing, because Raif had never been a reckless driver. My parents made me go to therapy, not because they wanted me to recall the events of that night but because they could see how it consumed me.

"My therapist said sometimes your brain protects you and that's why you forget. I remember thinking that's the weirdest thing I have ever heard, but it also makes sense, right? Something's going to harm you and your brain just severs the link to that memory."

He takes a swig of beer. A long one. "What's the last thing you remember?"

I rub my forehead as if that's going to repair the lost link. "I remember being at the party. People drinking. Then I woke up in the hospital."

"Raif wasn't drunk."

"I was told. He didn't arrive until late either."

"That's right. We had family dinner before, and my parents wanted him to stay. The party was about an hour-and-fifteen-minute drive, but he was insistent. We received a call two hours after he left, telling us there had been an accident."

I frown. "He was only there for forty-five minutes?"

"Yeah."

That's not like Raif. We usually have to drag him out of a party.

"I knew he was coming later, but I didn't realize. Fergus doesn't know why we left so early either," I tell Hugo.

"Now, Fergus *was* tanked, according to a couple other people who were at the party. None of you told anyone you were leaving, but they all assumed Raif had taken Fergus home and you went along with him."

I nod. "Raif was always great at being the one to take care of people at parties. I think he'd like this one."

Hugo nods, staring into his bottle of beer like it has the answers. Fergus gave that one a go after the accident. His parents shipped him off to rehab for two weeks in case the drinking became a problem.

The Beauforts having an alcoholic teenage son isn't a good look. After his stay, he became obsessed with protecting me and helping me through my anxiety.

"Seems like you know a lot more about the accident than I do," I say, maybe not as casually as I'd hoped, so I run with it and add, "Care to tell me what you're hiding?"

His eyes slide slowly toward me. "What do you mean?"

"Don't pretend you don't know what I'm talking about. I can tell when you're lying."

"I'm not lying."

"Fine. I can tell when you're holding something back. Hugo, please, what else is there?"

He shrugs. "I don't know, Bessie. That's as much as I can figure out, because you and Fergus *don't remember* and I'm not sure Raif would tell me even if he did."

"Why did you say it like that?" I ask, sitting straighter. Does Raif have his memories back?

"I'm just saying, he doesn't talk about it to anyone."

"Bessie!" Kash appears and reaches out for me. "Come dance."

Hugo takes the opportunity to stand and walk away.

I'm left alone with more questions than before.

9

I rub my eyes to wake myself up. Dull light streams through the windows because we forgot to draw the thick curtains; rain is still pelting against the glass like it's trying to smash its way in.

Allegra's snoring coupled with the storm meant that I only got about three hours of sleep last night. I'm thinking most of us will sleep in, ready to party again this afternoon.

I groan, sit up, and stretch out, my muscles aching from the glorified camp bed. You probably can't call two sleeping bags a bed. My stiff neck and aching hips will attest to that.

Kash is beside me, her dark hair a knotty mess from fidgeting in her sleep. I'm used to her restlessness, since we've shared a dorm for five years.

Allegra is on the far side, sleeping soundly, and Jia is sandwiched between them. The little fire we had in our room was out by the time we went to sleep, so it's quite chilly now. Thankfully not as cold as I expected, though.

I tilt my head, rubbing my eyes again. Huh. Jia comes into sharp focus, and something looks . . . wrong.

What is that?

My smile fades as I take in Jia's milky-white complexion, several shades paler than usual.

"J-Jia," I say, curling the sleeping bag in my fist. "Jia, wake up." My voice is as weak as I feel, the air leaving my lungs as I try to figure out exactly what I'm seeing.

What the . . .

She doesn't budge. Not a centimeter. Not at all.

Her chest isn't moving.

"Jia," I mutter, pushing the sleeping bag down and clumsily wriggling out of it, my body frozen from the inside. "Jia!"

I crawl across the floor as Allegra and Kash start to wake, panic wrapping around my throat and squeezing like a boa constrictor about to kill.

"What're you doing?" Kash asks.

I reach out when I get close enough, my hands trembling. "Jia, wake up. *Wake up!*"

The tips of my fingers feel like they're touching ice as they brush against her neck. I retract my hand as if Jia has shocked me. "Oh my god." I press down on her cool flesh but there's nothing there. No thud of a pulse. Absolutely nothing at all.

"What the hell are you doing?" Allegra demands. "Leave her alone, Bessie. She's sleeping."

"She's not sleeping. She's dead," I say, looking up at Allegra's wide-eyed expression.

"No. Shut up, Bessie. That's not funny," she snaps.

"I-it's not a joke."

She scrambles to get out of her sleeping bag the way I did, desperate to get free. "Don't be ridiculous. She's my best friend, I can wake her. Jia? Jia, get up!"

"She c-can't." I stand so fast my head swims, almost knocking me off-balance. I stumble and have to hold on to the drawers to steady myself. "We need to get help."

Kash shouts out, a scream of fear and frustration. "No! No, no! My phone's gone. What the hell! Where is it?"

"What?" I stumble back to my makeshift bed, where I left mine by my pillow, because there is no time to waste if she's lost hers. "Oh my god . . . mine is gone too. It was *right here* last night. Allegra?"

"Same," she replies, her voice monotone, hands trembling. "Someone has been in here while we slept and taken our phones. Why would they do that?"

"Did they take Jia's?"

"Yes, it's not here! Do you think she was dead when they came in?"

Kash jolts. "What if they killed her?"

Allegra gasps, flinging her palms out as if she's trying to bat Kash's words away. "No. Absolutely not. You back the hell up right now. No one has killed anyone."

Kash crawls to Jia, pressing her fingers against Jia's neck, her gasp audible over Allegra's dramatics. Cold. Rigid. Gone.

Kash slowly shakes her head, reaching the same conclusion that I did. Jia has been dead for quite a while.

"She was fine last night. Didn't you see her dancing and drink-ing beer?" Allegra asks, desperate for a loophole in death.

"But she was in pain while doing that. You know she was," I tell her, clenching my hands as my fingers tremble.

"No, but—"

"Stop it," I snap. "You're not helping. Jia wasn't fine yesterday. She had chest pain as well as a headache. Look, I think there was something wrong with her ribs. She said she was okay, just bruised, but what if it was more serious than that. Or her head, she was knocked out for a while."

"That's it." Allegra points at Jia. "Bessie's right. She had a tree fall on her. A head wound. Probably broken ribs too. We don't know what was happening *internally*. No one killed her."

Kash takes a breath. She drops her hand from Jia and stands. "So it's a coincidence that the phones were stolen the night she died? We don't know anything for sure and it would be silly to assume nothing sinister is going on."

"We know our friends!" Allegra screeches, dropping back to the floor beside Jia. She reaches out to touch her but hesitates, her hand hovering inches from Jia's face. "Who would do this, Kash? Come on, if you think a person is responsible, tell me who!"

"I don't know who! You think I'd be standing here if I did?"

"Stop arguing," I tell them. "Look at her."

Jia's cold body lies still in the middle of our circle. I need to know when exactly this happened. *What* exactly happened. Because Kash is right about the timing. It does seem like too much of a coincidence.

But Allegra is right about our friends too. No one hates Jia. She's too nice. *Was.*

We need to slow down, calm down, and think.

It's a pretty big leap to assume Jia was murdered, coincidence or not, but we're all on edge. That does not aid rational thought. I get it too, and if Jia hadn't been hurt yesterday I would be quicker to assume.

"We all love Jia," Allegra says, finally touching her. She takes her hand away. With tears in her eyes, she smiles. "We all love her. You know *this* isn't something anyone has done."

No, maybe it isn't, but the phones didn't walk off on their own. We can't explain that one away.

"What if we're not the only ones in the castle?" I ask. "We know that others have come here. We know that builders have been in and out."

"You think the builders stole from us?" Kash asks, as if that's a genuine lead.

"No, I'm just saying that people have been here recently. I don't suspect the builders, obviously."

"They're not even due to properly start work on the exterior for another three months. They've just been in patching up things that need doing no matter what the castle turns into."

"Yeah, no one thinks it's them, Allegra," I repeat. "But it was *someone*, and I think maybe it was one of the guys."

"A practical joke. Zeke or Shen, maybe?" Kash asks, her big eyes flitting from us to Jia.

"Maybe. We need to go find the others. We need to get help and we need to get out of here."

It's been a few minutes since I woke, and I'm still in a room with Jia's body. But it feels wrong to just leave her alone.

Kash gets to her feet and I help Allegra up, pulling her when she makes no effort to stand.

"She's my best friend," Allegra whispers, her lips trembling. "She's my best friend. Oh my god. What are we going to do? Jia . . ."

I nod, tears pricking my eyes as I step around Jia's lifeless body. She looks just like a mannequin, so still and pristine. *Don't think about that. Hold it together.* "I know, Allegra. Come on, we can't stay in here."

"Leave her alone, you mean? Shouldn't we at least cover her?"

Kash moves closer, crouching in front of Allegra. "We shouldn't touch her again. The police will want photos."

If there is foul play, covering her could potentially disturb any evidence.

"Oh god," Allegra sobs, pressing a hand to her mouth as if she's about to vomit.

"She'll be okay here. We'll make sure of it," I tell her, taking her hand and trying to be brave. "Now come on."

Allegra lets me pull her up. She doesn't take her eyes off Jia, and it makes her unsteady on her feet. I let go when she feels stable and take a long breath. We have to go tell everyone else what's happened.

I still feel like I'm in the middle of a nightmare and will wake up any moment to find Jia munching on one of Allegra's breakfast bars.

Kash and I lead the way, with Allegra trailing us. Her eyes are vacant when I glance back. I don't think she has much awareness that she's even moving.

We walk downstairs, the sound of conversation and laughter drifting along the hallway as we make our way to the ballroom.

Most of the guys are awake. Zeke, Shen, Fergus, and Hugo are sitting around drinking coffee. They turn to us as we shuffle toward them. Abbas and Odette are the only ones missing.

"G-guys," I mutter.

"Oh, look who decided to get up," Fergus says, laughing.

"We were going to send a search party," Shen adds, holding an arm out. "Come here, Allegra."

I watch as one by one the smiles fade from their faces, finally reading the room. They look so small in the ballroom now, as if the castle grew while we were asleep.

"What's going on?" Zeke says, standing as he notices the look of horror on my face. I'm sure it's mirrored on my friends' faces too. "Bessie, what's going on?"

"It's Jia," I say. The words feel impossible to voice, as if my throat wants to hold them in. I don't want to say them out loud. "Something's happened. She's upstairs, and she's not . . . she's . . ."

"Dead," Allegra adds, sobbing into her sleeve. "She's dead. Oh my god. She's dead! She's dead!"

Kash turns just in time to catch Allegra as her knees buckle and she folds in half. She almost dropped to the solid wood floor.

Silence falls in the room and Shen stands sharply. "Allegra?"

No one says anything else. I feel time ticking by when it's supposed to stop for moments like these. No one moves again.

I wait. Five seconds. Ten.

Do something!

None of us know what to say or how to act, stuck in a state of shock and disbelief. We were partying with her last night. She was happy, laughing and dancing. How do you go from that to oblivion?

It doesn't make sense.

"What?" asks Fergus, the first one to break the spell. He pushes himself up and stomps noisily toward me. "What did Allegra say?" he says, grabbing my wrists and pulling me closer to him. "Bessie! What the hell is going on? Where is Jia?"

"In bed. She's in bed . . . and she didn't wake up. It's true, Fergus, she's dead. I found her just now."

His hands tighten around my wrists. "But that doesn't make any sense. Are you sure?"

"I'm very, very sure. Kash checked too." I turn to the group. "Do any of you have your phones? Ours are gone."

"Mine's gone," Zeke says. "No! I usually check it first thing, but we got talking. Shen was—"

Shen slaps Fergus on the shoulder, his fingers gripping him what appears to be a touch too hard, as if he's trying to grasp something tangible so he doesn't spiral. "Yours is missing. Mine too."

"I have nothing," Hugo adds, gesturing to his makeshift bed. "It was right here as well. What the hell is going on?"

"Really, none of you guys noticed this morning?" Kash asks.

"That's what I said," Zeke replies, his tone snippy, shoving his hands in his hair and turning back as if he expects his phone to reappear.

"Did you check?" Shen asks Kash.

"Briefly, and then I was busy trying to find a pulse in our friend!" she snaps back at the accusation.

Hugo steps between them, holding his palms up in an attempt to calm the situation before it escalates. "Like we said, we've not been up long and got talking as soon as we woke."

"So not what we need to worry about right now! My best friend is dead!" Allegra says, gasping and shaking her hands. "What's wrong with you people? I don't care about the phones. We need to leave and get help."

"She's right," I say. "Where are Abbas and Odette?"

"Sleeping in that blue room up the hall," Hugo replies.

Allegra raises her brow. That wasn't one of the rooms on the preapproved list, but it pales in comparison to the current situation, so she lets it go.

I move away from Fergus and he drops his hands. "Okay, I'll go get them."

Hugo walks with me. "Not alone. I'll come with you."

"You don't think I'm safe?"

"I'm not taking any chances."

I watch the shock in his eyes turn to fear. I think he's beginning to understand why I was so freaked out yesterday.

The castle feels alive . . . but it wants us dead.

10

Everyone is jumping to conclusions pretty darn quickly, trying to make sense of something so shocking. Myself included. It's putting me on edge, making it harder to work only with the facts.

"I don't want to find out how safe we are by letting you wander around alone," Hugo says, and nods his chin toward the door. "Come on."

He has a point there, so I follow him past Allegra. Shen is finally making his way to comfort her. Jia was his friend first, so he must be just as devastated. I can't think about that right now.

"The rest of us need to figure out if we can get to the cars. I know the storm's bad, and there's a no-travel warning, but I think this counts as an 'unless necessary' situation," Kash says.

The growing moat is doing everything in its power to keep us here, but we have to try. We can't stay here until Monday with Jia's . . . *body.*

"What about Jia?" Shen asks.

As Hugo and I leave, I hear Kash reply that she'll take him to Jia. It's understandable if Shen doesn't want to go for help before he's seen her, to witness the scene for himself. Maybe someone should stay behind too rather than leaving her alone. Who wants to be here alone, though?

"It's along here," Hugo says, his voice icy, hands balled into fists. He looks like he wants to run, swim, do whatever he needs to get out of here and away from us.

This was supposed to be a fun party weekend. That's what he was promised.

"Hugo, I'm seriously freaking out here," I tell him, trying to breathe evenly; I'm still half in denial about Jia, though I've seen her for myself.

"I understand that completely, but we're going to be fine, Bessie. We'll get out, get help . . ."

Then what? That's only the end of *this* nightmare. There's another one waiting for us on the outside. He doesn't even sound convinced of his own words.

"And Jia?"

"You said she's gone. There's nothing we can do for her now. As callous as this is going to sound, we need to focus on us."

Hugo is speaking as if he's made up his mind and we're in immediate danger. It's easy to make that jump with the missing phones along with Jia . . . but there is no evidence that Jia was killed or that someone else is here.

It could be Abbas and Odette playing a prank with the phones. I have to believe that or I'll completely panic.

"I understand . . . but I don't like leaving her up there. If we leave and she's just here, what does that say about us?"

"We're not forgetting her, Bessie. We're leaving to find help."

I take a ragged breath, my lungs refusing to work properly, and mentally prepare to tell more people that Jia is dead. There will be lots of questions when we contact the police. Then many more after that.

What the hell do we say to people at school?

We should've insisted she go to the hospital, picked her up and carried her kicking and screaming. Her life was more important than keeping quiet to stay out of trouble . . . but now it's too late. We don't get to reverse time and make a better decision.

Hugo opens the door and the creak wakes Abbas and Odette.

They're in a room with a huge fireplace, too big for the wall it's on, almost engulfing the whole thing. There is nothing else at all in here; the room is stripped bare, wallpaper either ripped away or hanging in shreds.

The one tall window on the narrow wall is covered by a blanket that they've hung from the gold rod, and the floor is a road map of scratches in the wood.

Abbas groans, covering his eyes with his forearm as if we've let in light. "What's with the wake-up call, mate? I'm knackered after last night. Could barely sleep with the storm too, so—"

Odette nudges him and sits up in her sleeping bag. "Shh. What's going on? You two look awful."

"We have to leave," Hugo says. "Now. We have to leave now. Get dressed and come to the ballroom."

"Why? What's going on?" Odette asks again, her expression

falling as she gets out of the sleeping bag and grabs a hoodie to put on over her loungewear. "Hugo, you're scaring me."

"Shit, have we been caught?" Abbas asks, his dark eyes nearly popping out of their sockets.

"Um," Hugo mutters. "It's, er, Jia. It's Jia. She's . . ."

"She's dead," I say, saving him from having to speak the words when he's clearly struggling. They don't get any easier.

Odette side-eyes us, tugging the hoodie over her head.

Abbas coughs, looking our way. "As far as jokes go, guys, this is—"

"Stop, Abbas." Hugo runs his hands through his hair and sighs. "She's dead."

Odette shuffles backward, almost tripping over the sleeping bag. "She's dead? How? Are you sure?"

"I'm sure. I found her just now," I tell her. "We think maybe something happened to her, internally, when the tree fell on her, but we've only had a second to figure it out, and then we came to find you. Here's the weird part—none of us have our phones."

They move in unison, both bending down beside their floor beds to where they left their phones. Abbas throws a blanket out of the way and slings a pillow. "What the hell!" he snaps.

They didn't take the phones, then.

Odette looks up, her face pale and jaw slack. "I don't have mine. Okay, I'm getting scared now . . . and Jia's . . . Where are our phones?"

"All things we're trying to figure out, and that's why we've woken you," Hugo replies. "Let's move. The others are in the ballroom trying to find a way out."

"Is the bridge still underwater?" Odette whispers.

I nod, trying to be patient as they gather up their things. "Yeah, I glanced at it briefly. There are a lot of trees down. We have to try, though. We can't stay here, and we need someone to come for Jia. The storm isn't due to end until tomorrow."

Hugo wraps his arm around me, sensing I'm not doing well. "It's going to be okay, Bess. We're getting out now, and we'll get help."

I shrink into his side, wishing I could disappear because everything feels too big right now. I can sense the panic and anxiety from last year beginning to resurface no matter how hard I try to push it away. It can be stronger than me, and I'm scared to have to work that hard to fight it again.

"This was such a bad idea," I mutter. "We never should've come. After the incident at the supermarket with Oscar from that group, we should've turned around and gone home."

"What incident?" Odette asks.

"Some group in the village. They're trying to stop the development. Kash and I met one of them, Oscar, and he was kind of intense. Then there's the graffiti in the cellar. You saw it. You don't think one of them would be doing this?"

The three of them turn their attention to me. Odette lifts a brow. "You think a group of, what, vigilantes came here and killed Jia?"

"That's not . . . no. I'm speculating because I don't have a clue what happened. No one can get here, same as we can't get out."

Only that's not true, because someone has. There's graffiti all over the cellar, so there's a way in without a key. But the grounds probably weren't flooded when they did that.

Abbas pulls on a sweatshirt. "Can we go find the others? Safety in numbers and all that."

"That's what we're trying to get you to do," Hugo replies.

Kash and Shen are walking down the stairs as we pass. Shen's face is deathly pale, and the light has dimmed in his black eyes. Bile travels up my esophagus, a physical reaction to realizing where he's just been. Looking at his oldest friend's dead body. He's so brave. I'm not sure I could do that if it was Kash or Fergus.

"Are you okay?" I ask him when he reaches the bottom.

He shakes his head, mouth falling open, breath coming out in short, sharp pants like he's barely holding on. "What am I supposed to tell her parents? I know them. I told them I'd watch out for her when we moved here."

I touch his arm, hoping it'll offer him some comfort, and find him tense. "This isn't your fault. No one could have done anything. I'm so sorry."

He rakes his fingers through his tangled hair, ripping strands out as he pulls away. "I need to get out of here. I can't stay."

"We have Odette and Abbas. We're going now."

Abbas squeezes Shen's shoulder. "We'll get out, mate."

The front door opens and Fergus walks back in, shaking his hair, raindrops scattering all over the floor. Rain pounds on the windows, coming down sideways like bullets.

"There's a tree fallen near the edge of the moat, more all around the grounds. It's crazy out there." He strips off his coat, throwing it on the floor like it's personally done him wrong. "Bridge is underwater. I can't see if it's damaged, but I'm not sure if we're going to get across it until the storm has passed."

Allegra joins us in the foyer, opening her arms for Shen. "It's okay. We're going to leave," she whispers.

"We're working on it, Allegra," Fergus tells her. "It's not that simple."

He's right. I can see through the window just how bad the storm still is. Branches are scattered all over the lawn, and the trees that are still rooted are bent almost ninety degrees.

How are we going to get across the moat safely in these conditions?

"Okay, none of us have our phones, right?" I ask.

"Obviously, Bessie!" Allegra snaps.

I ignore her outburst, because if my best friend had just died I wouldn't be worried about being polite either.

"So who does? If the bridge is underwater and it's too dangerous to cross the moat, there has been no way in or out since yesterday. We all had our phones last night. The person who took our phones is probably still here."

There's someone in the castle.

"You're right," Hugo says, turning to face me. "But I'm not sure we should be looking. We don't know what this person is capable of. We need to focus on getting out."

"I'm with Hugo," Fergus replies. "Screw whoever's playing hide-and-seek with our things. We just need to get across that moat."

The elephant in the room is the suspected murder. Fergus and Hugo are behaving as if they don't believe Jia died of natural causes, but neither of them is admitting it. Murder makes absolutely no sense. Who would want to kill Jia? She never did anything wrong and never hurt anyone. She raised money for charities and volunteered at dog shelters.

I shake my head and Fergus drops his grip on my wrist, the world appearing infinitely darker. "You said yourself it's hopeless, Fergus."

"No, I said I don't think we'll get across it, not that it's hopeless. Everyone grab a change of clothing and a coat if you have them. We'll put them in my bag, it's waterproof," Fergus instructs, waving his hands as he comes up with a plan on the spot. "We'll swim across and—"

"No! Look at it out there. It *is* too dangerous," Odette says, staring out the window. "The wind is knocking trees sideways or snapping them in half, Fergus. I don't think an Olympian would make it."

"There's no tide. It's a moat."

Odette throws her arms up. "It's not the water that's the problem."

She's right. The wind is how Jia was injured; she wasn't even in an open body of freezing, rising water.

"So what do you want to do? Stay here with Jia's dead body upstairs?" Fergus asks.

Odette winces at his words. "Once the storm has passed tomorrow, we can get help."

"We need it now!"

"Okay!" I snap, barging in front of them before things escalate further. "That's enough. Fergus, she's right, we can't risk it. What if someone else gets . . . hurt? We could end up in an even worse position than we're in now."

Wind howls outside, taunting us. It's already claimed one of us, and it wants more. This castle feels haunted, rotten, the pretty building a cover for its true face.

But I know, logically, that's total bullshit. The castle isn't evil, and the weather isn't trapping us here.

It's just a horrible accident.

"I'm not staying here with her!" he shouts, closing his eyes and rubbing his temples. "She's dead."

I take a step closer to Fergus, not quite understanding what's going on with him. He's usually the guy you want around in a crisis. Fergus is calm and so laid-back, almost to a fault.

"Fergus," I whisper, taking his hands in mine. His chin drops to his chest when I squeeze his hands. This defeated side to him isn't something I have ever seen either. "Hey, it's going to be all right. We'll stay here, in the ballroom, all together."

He looks up at the ceiling with wide eyes as if he can see through it to Jia. "How can she be dead?"

"How did she die?" Hugo asks. "Are there any indicators? We should figure that out."

"Yeah, anyone here a freaking forensic detective?" Allegra asks sarcastically, her sharp tone telling of her pain and confusion.

"You don't need to be a forensic detective to make an educated guess."

"Why are we just standing here?" I ask, dropping Fergus's hands. "Fergus has already checked outside, and we know we can't leave yet. So that means we're stuck here for a while. Does anyone know when exactly the storm is supposed to let up on Sunday? I can't remember what it said."

"It's supposed to last until tomorrow night. I'm not sure if it's going to be severe the whole time," Odette says.

"We could be stuck here for over twenty-four hours?" Allegra asks. "No. That's unacceptable. We can't wait that long."

Odette straightens her back, a telltale sign that she's had enough of Allegra already. "I said I don't know the severity. It could ease up enough."

"Let's split into three groups," Zeke says calmly. At least one of us is still able to think straight. "Group one is going to see if there's a way out. Fergus has been out front but not all around the castle. Group two, which needs to include Kash and Shen, is going to see if they can figure out exactly how Jia died. Group three is going to set up the ballroom, because in case we're not getting out we need to stick together."

"I'll take Hugo with me too," Kash says. I think it has more to do with his brawn rather than his brain. Kash is worried.

Zeke nods. "Fergus, Abbas, Allegra, and Odette, you set up the ballroom. We're going to camp in there. We need all of our bags and bedding. Bessie, you're with me."

"I'm not falling apart, Zeke. I'm coming with you and Bessie," Fergus says, holding his hands out to the sides. "Besides, I'm already wet."

I zip up my hoodie. "All right, everyone knows what they're doing. Let's go."

11

Zeke opens the front door and the rain comes pouring in, wetting my clothes. I'm getting déjà vu, only this time we're going out to get help rather than to rescue Jia.

Why did I get stuck with his group? I'm still in my loungewear and hoodie, so I'm probably going to freeze. How great would it be if that was my biggest problem right now? Stressing over something as mundane as being chilly for a little while.

Then I hear Kash, Hugo, and Shen's footsteps up the stairs, walking slowly to put off what they're about to do, and realize that I would take the rain any day. Their job is much worse than mine.

I shelter my eyes with my arm as wind whips rain at my face. It doesn't do much good—water still sprays in my eyes until I can barely see. Fergus has my free hand, holding it so tight I'm afraid he might crush my knuckles. Zeke is behind me with his hand on my back, the three of us making a chain so we won't get separated.

The moat is barely visible ahead of us, rain creating a barrier, another obstacle for us to fight through. The weekend feels like one massive test, pushing us to the limit of what we can handle. Jia has already paid the ultimate price.

What else could go wrong?

I scream, almost dropping to the ground as a gale shoves us all backward.

Fergus doubles over, his hand slipping out of mine. Zeke has more balance and uses it to help me stay on my feet. I lean into the relentless wind, my body at an unnatural walking angle to stop it from happening again.

My clothes are drenched, sticking to my skin, and water drips uncomfortably down my neck. I slide strands of hair out of my eyes.

The sky is almost black, clouds having taken over. Even the weather is against us, or that's what it feels like, anyway.

"How far away are we?" I shout.

Fergus looks over his shoulder, squinting his eyes, and points. "Nearly there."

We push on, walking against the wind. I keep my focus on the trees, watching them bend ninety degrees. My skin is frozen to the point where I'm worried for my toes, but I shove that thought to the back of my mind.

At the edge of the moat, which is much closer to the castle than it was yesterday, I drop to my knees. Half on purpose and half because the wind is too strong.

I can't tell where the moat used to start; the water has crept along the grass and is slowly moving toward us. I also can't see the bridge at all, only the tops of the posts where the handrail begins.

"How high has the water risen?" I ask, holding my hands over my eyes so I can see better. "Where is it?"

"The bridge is … well, part of it is over there," Zeke says, squinting into the distance and pointing.

I follow his finger and spot a couple of floating planks of wood being swept away.

Fergus scoffs. "God, I really hope not. It could be from a shed? There are a couple on the grounds. One under the tree that …"

That killed Jia.

"Could be," Zeke replies, rubbing his hands over his face.

"I think it's actually doubled in size," I murmur, my blood running cold because I can't see a way out of here yet.

"What?" Zeke asks, watching the wood like it's our only hope. What does he think he's going to do, nail it back together? Besides, it's more likely to be the shed.

"Width, I mean. The moat. It wasn't this wide yesterday. Hugo said rivers nearby had burst their banks and flooded, but I didn't think it would be this bad so soon."

"Which means it's going to be twice as hard to cross it, and we're doing nothing here. Let's see if it's narrower anywhere else. Looks like it's flooded from this side," Fergus says. "Might mean the road is too, but it's hard to see from here."

That's something to worry about later. We need to focus on getting over there first.

My teeth chatter harder as the cold sets into my bones, my

fingers so numb I can barely move them at all. We need to be fast or we'll end up hypothermic. Zeke and I follow Fergus back toward the castle. The pebbly path that curves around it is about the only thing I can see clearly. The waterlogged grass looks like it'd suck you in as fast as quicksand.

Or just make you slip and look ridiculous.

We walk around the side of the looming castle, the sandy brick so much darker now that it's wet, and stick to the safety of the path to lead us. The turret stretches up to the stormy clouds above us.

The flattened shed that came down next to Jia has mostly disappeared, the tree only trapping a portion underneath it. I can see a few broken planks littered over the waterlogged lawn.

"Looks like it's the shed in the moat," I say, but I'm not sure they hear me over the howling wind and pouring rain. My throat hurts from having to shout to communicate.

We need to find out if the falling tree is what killed Jia, or if it was something—*someone*—else.

Then there's the matter of our missing phones and who the hell took those. If it was one of us playing a prank, it would have ended the second we found Jia.

It *has* to be someone else.

Don't go there.

"Do you think we could get across?" Fergus shouts, nodding at the dirty, rising water. I feel like I could stand here and watch it rise by the second. "We need to get to my car. I can call for help from there."

"The bridge is submerged!" I shout over the rapid-fire rain that bounces off the water. Surely he's seen that.

"Not by more than our height. Look around, the rest of it's just as wide. We need help, and that's our best shot. Come on," he says, leading us back. We're already freezing and drenched, so it's not like getting into the moat is going to make things worse. Unless we swallow some of the water and catch a disease.

The bridge might be the safest place to cross, but that doesn't mean it's actually safe.

I take one last look over my shoulder, wondering if there is another way.

"What about the boat?" I shout, not that I think sitting in a moving object is a particularly great idea.

"It was broken, holes rusted into the bottom, so Dad's having it scrapped," Fergus tells me.

Another brutal gust of wind tries to scoop me up and throw me to the ground. I bend my knees and lean forward until it subsides.

"Keep going," Zeke yells, stumbling as he tries to push through the gale and lead us back to the bridge.

"You can go back inside," Fergus tells me as we stop by the posts and he grips one.

"I can't."

"He's right, Bessie. You can go and we'll continue," Zeke says, turning to me and wiping water from his face.

"I'm not leaving, guys." I want nothing more than to get away from this castle, and I'll happily swim through murky water if I need to. The bridge might not be visible, but it can't be too deep underwater, because I can see a small part of the rope railing. We'll be able to stand on the bridge.

It's impossible to see the other side because of the rain and the fact that the gray clouds have stolen most of the light. We don't know how bad the flooding is over there. I don't want to be negative, but what if we can't move the cars?

Fergus and Zeke take their keys out of their pockets and put them in the hoods of their tops.

Fergus steps up, or rather down, to the bridge first. His feet disappear, legs sliding underwater to about halfway up his shins. Looking over his shoulder he nods, encouraging us to follow.

"Go in front, Bess," Zeke tells me, and I reluctantly step into the icy water. My feet are already soaked, but the cold ring of water slides up my legs and makes me shudder.

Okay, it's worse.

I grimace, keeping my head down as I wade along until I reach the bridge.

Fergus grips the railing, nearly bowling over as a branch whips him in the face. "Shit!" he bellows, flinging his arms in the air.

"Are you okay?" I shout, tucking my head into my shoulders to avoid being hit. The wind is throwing debris our way like it's warding us off this dangerous quest. We should be smart and listen.

"Don't stop moving!" he yells back, keeping his head down and moving faster, one arm now protecting his eyes.

I finally reach out and grab the handrail, my foot finding something more solid than grass to step on. The water is halfway up my thigh. It feels thicker, like it's full of dirt and slimy vegetation.

Zeke puts his hand on my back, nearly bumping into me. "Sorry. Branch. Watch out, there are more flying around."

We're about halfway now and still shuffling slowly, the wind trying to knock us backward. Freezing cold water travels higher up my legs, nearly to my butt. I shudder again at how unpleasant it feels against my skin.

Fergus wades on in front of me, his light hair flat to his head, the hood of his top being used to keep his car key as dry as possible, but the gray material now looks black.

I place my foot down, but it slides out in front of me. Instinctively, I reach for Fergus. With his quick reaction time, he turns before Zeke can catch up and grabs my arm, hauling me back onto two feet.

Always saving me.

"Sorry," I tell him, realizing I could've taken him down with me, his key ending up at the bottom of the moat; I wouldn't fancy our chances finding it again. My instinct has always been to reach for him.

"You okay?"

I nod through the racing of my heart and the stone-cold feeling in my gut. Something else is going to go wrong.

"Almost there," Fergus says, gripping my hand and pulling me along behind him. I feel safer holding on to him.

When we reach the end and the water lowers around my legs, Zeke storms past us, wading quickly through the shallow water and splashing it up around him. It doesn't make a difference to me; the rain is still coming down just as hard.

He sprints when he's completely out of the water, kicking drops up at us, desperate to get the hell out of here and get some help for Jia. I understand the feeling entirely.

Going for help is what we should've done last night, the second the tree fell on Jia. Now all we can do is get someone to take her to the morgue. That decision will weigh heavily on me for the rest of my life.

I take a deep breath and nearly choke on rain as I imagine her lying on a cold slab waiting to be cut. We could have prevented that.

Don't think about it right now.

Fergus must sense where my train of thought is going because he squeezes my hand, silently letting me know that it's going to be all right . . . when it clearly isn't, because look where we are now.

We make our way to the cars, walking like newborn foals with our feet sliding everywhere. The wet, muddy ground makes moving like trying to run on ice.

I lean against Fergus's car when we reach it, my chest heaving with the exertion it took to get here, teeth chattering to the point that it makes my jaw ache.

Zeke goes to his car, but I stick with Fergus, since he's the one with the SOS call button we so desperately need.

I hop into the passenger seat when he unlocks the doors. The rain is louder in here, but thankfully I get a break from water in my eyes. I shiver but know Fergus can get the heat on soon.

"What are you waiting for?" I ask, watching him press the ignition button over and over, each jab harder than the last, as if whacking it will awaken it. "What's wrong? Fergus?"

"Come on!" he snaps, trying the button again, using his knuckle this time. "The key is working, it unlocked the car. I don't understand."

"Fergus . . . why isn't the car starting?"

His eyes meet mine and he looks worried, defeated. "I don't know, Bess! It should."

Disappointment bursts in my stomach and I feel like I could cry. What the hell is going on here? "Is the battery dead?"

He slams his palms on the steering wheel, letting out a growl of frustration. "No. Nothing was left on to drain the battery. It *should* start."

Zeke jumps into the back, literally, and bounces on the leather seats. He slams the door and shouts, "My car's dead! Can't start it, and I know I didn't leave anything on. It was locked."

I glance at Fergus, who takes a long breath, like he does when he's about to lose it and fight, and his face drains of color. "Mine is too. Someone must've tampered with the cars."

"The same person who stole our phones," I say, gripping tight to the side of the seat, panic twisting in my stomach. "Oh my god. What are we going to do? We're stuck here and there's no way out! Fergus, someone is doing this to us."

Fergus tilts my chin to make me face him. "Breathe, Bessie."

"How are you so calm?" I rasp.

He frowns gently at my accusation. "I don't have a choice. Come on, get it together. We need your brain too. I need you."

"We need to know what this asshole has done to the cars. Maybe we can fix it and get out of here," Zeke replies, cutting in to get to the point.

"Allegra's and Hugo's cars too."

Fergus nods, his shoulders losing some of that tension. "We'll check all four cars, don't worry."

"When I get my hands on this guy . . . ," Zeke mutters. I can fill in the blanks and I'll be right behind Zeke, because the longer we're stuck here the angrier I'm getting.

Fergus pipes up, and while they're talking about what a dead man the phone thief and car destroyer is, I take the time to press every button inside Fergus's car, hoping for a miracle. Something must do something. We just need a minute so we can make a call. That's it.

"It's not going to work, Bessie, there's no power."

"But how? What the hell is going on?" I ask, my voice like that of a chipmunk. The question keeps rolling around in my head, annoying me at this point, but it's one that I can't let go of. I need an answer.

"It's going to be okay. We're getting out of this, I promise."

"Pop the hood, mate," Zeke says. "We've sat in here long enough."

I disagree on that, one hundred percent. I feel much safer in here, on this side of the moat, than in the castle.

Fergus keeps looking at me, concern on his face as if he thinks I'm pre-breakdown. The way I was after the accident. He was amazing after that. Along with my parents he was there every day to help me heal, both physically and mentally.

But everything went wrong between us shortly after I started therapy. It was too much, going over everything. My therapist said I had—*have*—PTSD. I chose to deal with what that meant alone, so I pushed him away and told him we were better as friends.

"Fergus, pop the hood!" Zeke repeats, louder to get his attention.

"I can't without the power," Fergus finally says. "You'll need to do it manually."

Zeke mutters a slew of swear words as he opens the door, but he says nothing about the fact that he's the only one going out there. I'm too scared and cold to worry about that.

"I'm dripping. Your car is soaked," I say, trying to keep my mind on something else.

Fergus nods, forcing out a laugh. "You're not the only one, Bess." He ruffles his hair, spraying water all over his dash.

"You love your car."

"True. But it's not the most important thing. Are you okay? You're pale, and not just because you're freezing. I'm getting a little worried about you over here."

I almost hear the "again" he's holding back.

I watch as Zeke lifts the hood.

"I'm scared," I admit. "Really scared. We have no phones and no cars. Jia is dead. Someone is doing this . . . and the last time something bad happened . . ."

"Nothing bad is going to happen to you ever again," he says, as if he believes he has the power to control that.

"What if the person who broke the cars and took the phones *did* kill Jia?"

"Back up, Bess. We don't know that any of this is related to Jia. It's way more likely that her death was caused by her injuries. It's a massive leap from vandalism and theft to *murder*."

"So what? You think someone stole our phones as a prank?"

He shrugs casually, but his eyes are tense. "Could be."

"The cars?"

"They're out of battery. We could've left a light on or maybe a door open."

None of his doors were open, nor was there a light on. He doesn't even believe what he's saying, I can tell by his flat tone. We all know this was sabotage.

"Fergus, I appreciate what you're doing—"

"Damn it!" Zeke shouts, hopping back in and slamming the door hard, rocking the car. "The starter motors are damaged in all four cars."

Fergus shoves his hands through his wet hair. "Shit!" He pinches the bridge of his nose. I watch him try to figure out the next best move. "Okay, let's think . . . think, think, think. The main road is about, what, an hour-and-thirty-minute walk?"

"We can't go all that way, Fergus," I tell him. "Forest surrounds the entire castle, and look over there!"

He does as I've instructed, his eyes widening as he spots two trees down, one with exposed roots and the other broken off half-way. Then there are the dozens of branches covering the road and every other surface out there.

We watch a large branch snap off a tree and fall heavily to the ground. If we were out there, that could have very easily landed on us. There must be thousands of trees surrounding us. We might as well be on a desert island.

"Er, yeah. She's right, mate. It's safer in the castle. The storm's too bad to walk, particularly through the forest."

"How do we go back in there and tell them there's no way out?" Fergus asks. "Everyone is scared and counting on us. How am I supposed to tell my sister that she has to spend another night stuck with her dead best friend?"

"We're still calling her Jia," I tell him, scowling at how heartless his words sound.

"I'm sorry," he says, running his hands through his hair again. "But how are we going back with nothing?"

I squeeze his hand this time, because I can see the fear and desperation in his eyes. Fergus fixes things and helps people. Right now he has completely lost control. "We protect each other," I say. "Okay?"

My words come across as confident as I wanted them to. On the inside I'm petrified, because I know we're going to have to do that walk at some point. Even after the storm it's still going to take a while to get to the police and tell them that our friend's body is back at the castle.

"Is there nothing we can do with the cars?" Fergus asks.

"Not without new parts, even if we knew what we were doing."

"So we go and report back," Fergus mutters. "We tell them we have nothing. We stay there, hunker down in the castle, and wait the storm out."

"We should go help find the phones," Zeke says.

"We have a group on it, but we'll help, pour our efforts into figuring that out rather than worrying about the cars."

I don't know, I'm certain I'll still worry about the cars.

"Whoever has done this wants to cut us off from the outside world," I whisper, my stomach roiling at the thought of being stuck with a killer. Potential killer. "Are we not also worrying about the fact that they're still more than likely in the castle?"

We've touched on that, but I feel like we've brushed it off. Which might be the height of stupidity.

"Don't do that, Bessie."

"Why not?" I ask, looking across at Fergus with my mouth hanging open. "How long are you going to pretend for?"

"None of us are pretending. We understand the threat and we need to face this. But there's no need to lose our heads over it."

"I wasn't."

"Yet. I know you. You're one conversation about a creep in the castle away from a full panic attack."

"I'm fine." I'm absolutely not and I'm speaking through gritted teeth, but Zeke doesn't know how bad I was last year. No one but Fergus and my parents do, and I want to keep it that way. It's embarrassing how heavily I relied on them.

Fergus raises his palms. "All right. I'm sorry."

"We don't know exactly what's going on here," Zeke says, pushing his shoulder between the seats. "Other than being stuck until the storm passes. But that's it. This could just be to scare us, so let's try to stick to the facts and, more important, stick together."

"You think someone in that antidevelopment group is messing with us?" Fergus asks.

"It's possible. Bad press for the castle. They wouldn't know about Jia," Zeke says.

That's a good point. Who would sneak into a room full of people to murder someone because they're angry about a development? Jia has nothing to do with the Beauforts. It doesn't fit.

"Let's get back," I say. "Zeke's right and we just need to wait it out. Move Jia so she's somewhere cold."

Fergus's eyes widen in horror at the thought of moving Jia's body. I have to say, it's not something that I want to do either. We can't leave her in one of the rooms that actually get warm, though. The sun, if it comes out, will be directly on her.

"Of course," Fergus whispers, reaching for the door handle. "Let's go."

The second I'm outside the car, rain pelts my already soaking body. This is bloody miserable and still feels hopeless. But we have a plan now, and that's what I need to focus on.

Jia would understand that we can't get out and that we have to move her, no matter how awful it feels to do so.

Zeke and Fergus catch up with me as I run stumbling toward the bridge, my tears falling with the rain.

12

I go first this time, wading onto the bridge and cringing as the water climbs my body again, my tears still rolling freely down my cheeks. Thankfully they're impossible to see in the storm.

"It's higher!" Zeke shouts. "Getting worse."

He's right—the waterline surpasses the previous one. Only by an inch, but that's still concerning. If it keeps up like this, could it reach the castle? There is no sign that water has breached the castle before, there were no visible watermarks on the walls in the cellar.

"It's what they wanted!" Fergus shouts from the back, his voice barely audible over the wind.

They couldn't have planned too far in advance for this. They didn't know we were coming this weekend any more than they knew just how bad the storm was going to get. This had to be a spur-of-the-moment thing. Spotting an opportunity and taking it.

Oscar must've recognized Fergus and Allegra in the supermarket and known that meant they were coming here. Quite risky, though—their parents might've been with them.

Maybe they hoped for that.

Doesn't matter now either way, I suppose. It doesn't change anything.

It still doesn't fit that it's them. I feel like I'm trying to force a round peg in a square hole.

I shuffle along, placing my feet on the slippery boards beneath me.

"Bessie!" Fergus shouts as I'm thrown backward.

The last thing I hear before I'm dragged under is the unmistakable creak of wood as my feet slide from beneath me. The bridge completely gives way, sinking and taking us down with it.

My mouth opens wide in shock at the freezing cold, dirty water threatening to choke me. I kick my legs, eyes squeezed shut, heading for the surface.

I break through and spit the water from my mouth, spluttering at the disgusting gritty yet slimy texture. The taste is something that I'm certain will never leave me.

When the storm passes, I'm going to the hospital for a shot.

"Fergus? Zeke?" I scream, paddling and barely keeping my head above water.

It's Fergus I see first, treading water. "Come on, Bess!" he shouts. "Zeke's over there. Get out of the water!" He turns as I start to swim, making his own way back to the castle side of the moat.

"Bessie, come on!" Fergus yells. "Keep up."

"I'm coming," I reply, swimming toward Fergus, kicking my legs as hard as I can to get out of this putrid water. Zeke's doing the same from the other side of the broken bridge, splashing wildly as he goes.

My arms and legs whack into debris in the water, and some sort of greasy vegetation wraps around my ankles. It doesn't hold me still for long, breaking off and unraveling. I take a ragged breath and push harder, my limbs working to the point of fatigue.

I reach the side at the same time as Zeke; Fergus, now out, leans over to grab my hand. He pulls me up and I land on top of him, coughing up the gross water still in my mouth. I lie on the soggy grass until I get my breath back, pushing my hand against my heart as if I can manually slow it down.

"What the hell was that?" Zeke pants.

"Bridge snapped," Fergus replies, taking a deep breath as I crawl away from him and the water. "We knew it needed replacing soon but didn't expect the flood."

"That . . . was . . . rhetorical," Zeke replies, breathing like an eighty-year-old smoker. "I know it broke."

I shiver uncontrollably, rubbing my arms to try to get some heat into me. It just feels like I'm touching ice. "We need to go."

I push myself up, the muscles in my legs vibrating with fatigue and maybe a little bit of shock. Zeke and Fergus follow. At least I think they do; I don't look back. All I can focus on is getting into the warmth and changing my clothes.

The grass in front of the castle seems to be stretching, like I'm running on a treadmill and not going anywhere. I never thought I would want to go back inside there.

I manage to sprint the last few yards and slam into the door, reaching for the handle and stumbling inside, trying not to cry again.

The boys come in behind me. We close the door and fall back against it. My chest heaves as I try to slow my heavy breathing, the pumping of my heart scarily similar to the panic attacks I had last year.

You're safe.

It's still morning but I'm absolutely exhausted, so drained I could lie down right here soaking wet and freezing cold, and still sleep soundly.

"Are you guys okay?" Allegra asks, her eyes wide. "God, you're dripping."

"We're fine," Fergus replies, a little snippy. "But the bridge is destroyed. Or part of it. The water has risen so high that the moat has doubled in width, and the wind will try to kill you. Still have our keys after a dip, though, so not all is lost."

"Did you reach the cars?"

Fergus nods. "We're not getting out, Allegra. Not until the storm has passed."

"Why not? What happened out there?"

"The engines of the cars have been tampered with, and the bridge broke as we came back across it," I tell her. "Whatever we do next, it's going to be right here."

"What we do is keep calm and wait it out," Fergus says, standing between me and Allegra as if he thinks we're about to fight.

Allegra's pale brows kick up to her hairline. "I need to process everything you've said later because I'm finding it increasingly difficult to cope. Okay . . . all right, you should all change and then . . . breakfast. We need to eat. Or so Kash keeps saying. Bessie, we've put your bag in the bathroom just down there on the right. The others brought our things down, figured we wouldn't want to go up there."

She's slid straight back into practical mode. I would think it's a little heartless, but it's the most helpful side of her personality.

I nod. "Thanks."

No, none of us want to go and get changed with Jia's body lying between us. I can't ever go back in there.

"Fergus, your clothes are in that room so you can change in privacy. Zeke's is there. Meet in the ballroom when you're done," she adds, pointing to the doors. She's been busy setting up for the night, something we hoped we wouldn't need.

"What did they find out?" I ask. "About Jia."

She shrugs. "Not much. Nothing visible. Her hand is lying on her chest, so apparently they think that means her rib punctured her lung or some other organ."

"Right."

"That's what I said. I don't know why they went up there. Anyway, go get changed, you're shivering and your lips are turning blue. I'll have coffee waiting."

The boys walk away quicker than I do. It takes me a minute to move. I know why they went up there. They want to make sure no one killed her . . . because someone is here with us.

In the bathroom I shed my clothes, goose bumps scattering over my skin. There's a large, ornate gold mirror above the white double sink, one I wish had been removed, because I look horrendous. The floor and tiles are all large and white. The light bulb above my head is dull and hanging on for dear life in an ancient frosted glass shade.

I wring my long hair out and wrap a towel around my body. It's bloody cold in here, so I dry myself as fast as I can, scrubbing the rough towel against my skin. Then I get dressed, putting on my coziest loungewear.

This is the second time I've had to change out of awful cold and wet clothing. I'm so glad I always pack on the heavy side, bringing enough for about a week. At least the rain has showered away the gross moat water, but I'm not sure I'll ever feel clean again.

In the ballroom, Allegra hands me a coffee and points to a table that's stacked high with wrapped pastries and the fruit Kash and I bought yesterday. The sight of food makes me equally nauseous and hungry. Fergus, Zeke, and Hugo seem to be the only ones eating, though nibbling as if they can't stomach it but know they need to.

"Have you managed anything yet?" I ask Allegra. "Because you should, you know."

She watches me sip my coffee and try in vain to let the hot liquid warm me from the inside.

"I had two bites of a banana and threw it back up. I can't stop thinking about Jia, trying to wrap my head around the fact that she's gone. She won't eat anything ever again. She's still here, and there's nothing I can do to help her. We're here and she's up there. Her parents don't even know, and they won't until we get out of here. We have to get the phones, Bess."

"I agree. That should be our next move but we're going to need a plan."

"We split up and look, find them fast, and get out."

"Well, yeah, that will probably be the plan. Are you okay? Everyone is surprisingly calm."

"We don't have a choice. There will be no losing it until we're out. Understand?"

"Yes, boss."

She looks around the room, making sure no one can hear us. I follow her gaze and notice that the banner has fallen down on one side and a couple of pom-poms are lying on the floor. "She was our best friend, Bessie. The others are happy to sit around and wait, and that's because they don't care."

"Of course they care."

Allegra gives me an empty look before wandering off toward the destroyed decorations. As soon as she's out of earshot, Kash comes up to me.

"We're running with the theory this was caused by Jia's injury, right? Like she had internal trauma, and it would've taken a surgeon."

"Yeah . . ."

Kash bites her lip. "So how do we explain the phones and the cars and the person you saw? Why do we keep ignoring that?"

Because we're scared to death and want to ignore the glaringly obvious. An accident and holing up here for a couple of days are easier to deal with.

"No one is ignoring that, but the person I saw was Hugo,

remember? The storm was—*is*—severe. I couldn't see clearly, but he said he was exploring up there."

"And the phones? The cars?" she repeats, wanting an answer I only have a guess for.

"Those were done on purpose, no question. But that doesn't mean it's linked to Jia. Nor does it mean whoever is behind it is still here. I mean, would you stay here?"

"I guess not."

I think the graffiti and phone theft are the same person, but murder is on a completely different level.

The bridge was crossable before it broke with us on it. So it's possible they did leave. It seems like a lot of personal risk, though. If this person was watching, they would've seen what happened to Jia and still gone ahead with their plan.

"What are you two whispering about?" Hugo asks, making us both jump.

Zeke walks over, holding a croissant and a mug of tea. It's a weird image, all things considered, but I'm suddenly starving, my mouth filling with saliva. "Yeah, looks intense."

"Just going over some things. You know, for the millionth time," I reply.

Kash smiles weakly. "Trying to make sense of it, I guess."

Allegra reappears. "I can see at least three secret conversations happening in here. I know that you guys think Jia's death was caused by the accident." She manages to pack in as much sarcasm as humanly possible. "But I think you're wrong. I think someone killed Jia, the same someone who has prevented us from calling for help. We're not safe now."

Kash and I look at each other. Allegra does a have a habit of flitting between the best- and worst-case scenarios, but this is quick even for her. It's like she can only convince her mind that everything is fine for so long and then it unravels completely.

"Whoa, back up. What evidence do we have that she was murdered?" Fergus asks, unable to sound anything other than condescending. Not that he's wrong.

"If someone smothered her, she would have fought," Shen adds.

Kash sighs sharply. "If that happened, we would have heard her. I know you're scared and grieving and it's easier to create a source you can fight so that we have answers and can avenge—"

"We're just looking at the *facts*," Allegra snaps. "Isn't it a bit of a coincidence that this all happened at the same time?"

"That's all it is, sister." Fergus approaches her like he thinks she's a grenade about to go off, placing his feet softly on the wood floor. Her eyes are ringed with red circles from crying and wild from fear. "I know you're upset—"

"Don't treat me like I'm some fragile child, Fergus. You're all ignoring the obvious, and it's time to burst the bubble."

"She's right," Hugo says. "This was always coming. It doesn't matter what happened to Jia, not right this second. We have to find the phones because, accident or murder, we need help *now*. Not after the storm."

"And we need to find out who took the phones and busted the

cars," Allegra adds, her eyes flicking to every point of entry like a wild animal. "Because they still could be wandering around the castle."

She's sinking deeper into despair. I'm balancing on the edge, one wrong step away from following her.

"Allegra, they probably took the phones and damaged the cars on their way out. They wouldn't want to be stuck here all weekend too," Fergus says. "I need you to turn the logical side of your brain back on."

"How do you know she's not?" Odette asks. "All of this is pure speculation."

Abbas walks over to her. "Odette, please don't you lose your head too."

"I'm not losing my head! Are you kidding me?" Allegra cries, deeply offended that anyone could think she's letting panic rule her.

"I don't like the idea of someone else being here with us either," Kash says, her posture hunched, arms pressing against her stomach. She looks like she's only just holding on, physically keeping herself together. "It would be smart to cover our bases."

Fergus runs his hands through his damp hair. "Kash . . ."

Zeke wraps his arm around Kash, noticing that she's not doing so well. He's always been good at knowing who needs a hug. "No, she's right. So is Allegra. So is everyone else. There are multiple explanations and Kash is right. It's only fair to cover all our bases, right? So we go looking. For the phones and for any clue that could tell us who this was."

Zeke lets his idea settle, giving us all time to think.

"Seems like the only fair way to do it," I say after a long stretch

THE PARTY | 135

of silence. If it makes Allegra and anyone else who thinks Jia was killed by someone hiding out here feel at ease, we have to do it.

Besides, it's not like we can go back to having fun.

The party is so over.

Zeke nods. "It's fair. Before we go off again, can we make sure we have weapons? I think I would be much more comfortable with weapons."

Hugo puts his mug down and walks over to join the group. "Whoa, I don't think we need to panic that much, Zeke."

"I can't be here," Abbas mutters, sitting on one of the old chairs. It creaks but he doesn't flinch.

No one pays much attention to him. I understand the freak-out— inside I'm the same—but it's just not helpful. We need to move forward now that we have a plan.

"Sit and eat, Bessie. And anyone else who hasn't yet," Hugo says. "We're going to need you all to search. We'll figure out what we take with us if anyone feels more comfortable with a weapon."

Allegra perks up at the thought of some protection, her back straightening. She now has a purpose and feels heard. I'll take it because it's better than her falling apart. "We have knives. They're not that sharp, but they'll hurt; and, Shen, you have baseball bats, right? You brought them because we thought . . . that it wasn't going to be like this."

"That's good. We can use both of those," Hugo says to appease her.

Shen stands up, shaking his head. "How did we get here? I don't want to die."

"Oh, stop it. No one else is going to die. Unless, of course, you keep saying unhelpful, useless shit," Fergus snaps, sighing. He pinches the bridge of his nose. "Sorry. I'm sorry. This is just getting us nowhere. We're going to stick together to do a sweep of the castle. If we don't find the phones and get help, we wait in the ballroom for the storm to pass. Together. Does everyone understand?"

One by one, we all agree. It's quite possibly the easiest yes I've ever given. I don't know what's going on here, but I do know I don't trust anything for sure right now. Checking out the castle and then barricading ourselves in a room until the storm is over is our best bet.

"Bessie and Zeke think it could be Oscar from the save the castle group behind this," Fergus says. "What does he look like?"

"He did look at us strangely when we were walking away," Kash says.

"He must be the one who graffitied the cellar. It seems too juvenile for adults."

"Tell them about the fire," Kash says.

"Right. One of the members, Oscar didn't mention who, said he'd rather the castle burn to the ground than become rich people's homes."

"And you think this guy or Oscar is the one doing this?" Fergus asks, lifting a brow as if I've just told him I believe fairies have pinched our phones.

"I can hear how it sounds, but I thought it was relevant. We know someone else has been here. Those people have a grudge, and one of them could have seen us."

"Yeah, but when would he have done it?" Abbas asks. "Because

Odette and I were up until about two a.m., and we had our phones then. We were sitting in the window seat talking for ages and couldn't see the moat that clearly, but it wasn't as high as it is now."

"This person could've stolen the phones after that and left," Kash offers.

"That seems the most likely scenario. We're probably alone here. If you mess with someone, you don't stick around to potentially get caught. Not if you're smart," I tell them.

"He might be stuck here," Odette comments.

"He might be a lot of things. None of which are helpful currently." Kash points to the ceiling. "If Oscar has our phones and broke our cars, we should keep an eye out for him. He's our age, tall, kind of built like Fergus and Hugo. He has dark hair, tan skin, and brown eyes. That's who we're looking for. Okay?"

"Oh, you have to be kidding me. This is one bored teen. Are you kidding me?" Abbas says.

I leave them to argue because there's no point in going over it again. What I need right now is another hot drink because I'm still so cold. My stomach churns painfully, demanding food.

Hugo follows me to the kettle. "I'll make more coffee. You grab a pastry."

"Thanks."

"They're really losing it, huh?"

I tilt my head. "They're scared, Hugo. One of our friends is dead and they're trying to make sense of it."

Badly, perhaps, but fear and trauma don't always help you to think clearly. I can attest to that.

"Oh, I understand that. For a second, after Jia and when we'd just found the phones missing, I did wonder."

"Whether they were connected?"

"Yes . . . and for a second I thought about . . ." He scratches his jaw. "Something I overheard Allegra say last night. She was drunk and whittling on to Shen about her dad."

"I'm still listening," I say, prompting him to continue.

He laughs at my impatience. "Sorry. Bad time for a dramatic pause."

"Hugo!"

"She seemed upset. Angry, even, because she doesn't want her dad to develop and sell."

"Why would she care about that? She loves money."

"I think she wants the castle for herself."

"Allegra wants to live in the middle of nowhere in an old building?"

That's the very opposite of her personality. She's always wanted a town house in Chelsea where she can do lunch with friends every day and shop in the city.

I shake my head. "No. I don't think so."

"Look, you know her better than I do. I just thought I'd mention it, since we're considering dozens of ridiculous theories."

The thought of Allegra running off in the night to steal phones and damage cars isn't something my mind will even conjure. Besides, one of those cars is hers.

"Yeah, I appreciate that you had to say something. Have you thought it might be her since this morning?"

He shrugs one shoulder lazily. "Not really. Didn't even remember the conversation until just now. Add to that the fact that I had a few beers last night . . . Like I said, I just wanted to mention it."

Does it mean something that he only mentioned it to me? That fact seems to suggest that he won't be asking Allegra what she meant.

"What were her exact words?"

"Now, that's a good question, and one I don't have an answer for, Bess. I'm sorry. Just generally that she's pissed at him because this place could be like . . . what was it? Something out of *Bridgerton*! You watch that?"

"Obviously," I reply. "She's obsessed with the show, but I'm not sure she'd want to live it."

"Okay. Ignore me, then. Here's your coffee. I'm going to get a weapon and get ready."

I look over my shoulder as he walks away, wondering if he really did hear Allegra say those things.

It's not consistent with Allegra's personality . . . but I also don't know why Hugo would lie.

13

We go off in twos, absolutely no way to communicate with other pairs besides yelling. You know, for everybody who may or may not be in the castle to hear. At least sound carries in the castle, echoing through the long hallways so it's impossible to know the location of the yeller.

Kash and I both have blunt, rusty old butter knives that will do some damage if we really need them to. I just hope it won't come to that. I am not a fighter.

We're checking out the second floor. Which feels like a good option, since Jia is there and I'm assuming if there is a killer, they will keep away from fear of getting caught. Though I don't feel safe anywhere in this castle.

Allegra and Shen are taking the first floor.

Odette and Hugo, the top.

Abbas and Zeke, the cellar. No one's bothered much by the

graffiti. It's just another thing on the list, paling in comparison to the death of our friend. It doesn't tell us who's doing this, so there's not much point in dwelling on it.

I look out the window as we walk out of the ballroom. The storm has turned the world a crystally blue-gray color that's as pretty as it is threatening. It means the wind and rain have no intention of stopping any time soon.

"Bessie, I just want to say that if we die here, you're my best friend and—"

"Wow, Kash. Can we not go there? If we start to think like that, we'll lose hope."

"Already losing it over here."

"You're my best friend and I need you. We'll stick together and get through this. Let's just keep looking for the phones, okay?"

She nods but her dark eyes are full of worry. I'm not sure she even really heard me, and I fear that she's starting to check out.

"There aren't many places to hide things here. A few pieces of antique furniture in most rooms, but nothing that'll drag this search out. This shouldn't take us too long, Kash, and then we'll get you more coffee."

She side-eyes me incredulously. "Sure, but the castle is *huge;* there are like fifty rooms. Be honest with me and yourself. Do you think we'll find the phones?"

"Not really. Not if the person left in the early hours, but we have to at least rule it out. There's a chance, and I'm not waiting here another day if we can reach someone on the outside."

We make it to the top of the stairs and stop. Kash is right, there are a lot of rooms in this place. Maybe not quite fifty, but it still feels like an impossibly long task.

Stick with your positive attitude. Not many places to hide.

"No, you're right. We all need to be doing something proactive. Anything to be able to say we didn't just sit around chatting while our friend decomposed in the bedroom."

Her words steal my breath and my hand flies to my throat. "Kash!"

"I'm sorry, but it's the truth."

"You don't need to be so harsh. Don't say that in front of anyone else. Let's start in that room and work our way down," I say, pointing to where I want to go.

"After you," she mutters, avoiding eye contact.

I lick my lips and reach for the polished handle. The tall door creaks as if it's not been opened for a hundred years, the hinges seized with rust.

We step back as the door swings toward the wall. It's a softly painted cream bedroom with an old oak four-poster bed, stripped down to the wooden slats. There are an uncomfortable number of cherub paintings in small frames over a chest of drawers. An empty glass vase sits on top collecting dust.

"It doesn't look like anyone's been in here recently. There are no prints in the dust on the floor," I say. The floorboards look gray rather than brown, and the rug half under the bed is frayed at the edges and threadbare.

"Great, let's go."

I turn to her. "What's wrong?"

Her mouth falls open and then closes like a fish. She does this twice, as if she's stalling for time. "Do you mean other than the usual? We should just take our chances and leave."

As she speaks, the wind rattles the rotting wooden window frame, nearly drowning out her voice. The glass looks like it's not far from shattering, the castle beginning to crumble around us.

"We can't just go. Don't you want to know exactly what's happening here before we leave Jia to get help?"

"What's the point? She's dead, Bessie. We don't need to be next."

"Kash," I whisper, never hearing her sound so cold before.

She pulls her arm away as I go to reach out. "Don't. You think I want to leave her? She was my friend too. But we need to be smart about this. She wouldn't want us to be killed looking for answers!"

"We're together. We'll be fine."

"That's just what you're telling yourself! This is a mistake," she says, walking to the window and staring out over the grounds. "It's bad out there, but we can get across the moat. I'm sure."

I move to stand by her side. It's awful outside. Trees look like they're fighting to stay in the ground, clinging on for dear life as the wind tries to rip the roots right out of the dirt.

"Kash, I understand that you're scared, I am too, but I've just been out there and it's—"

I snap my teeth together as something dark drops past the window in front of us with a scream that's quickly swallowed by the storm.

Kash and I leap back, grabbing on to each other.

"What was that?" she asks, looking from the window to me and back again. "What the hell was that, Bessie?"

I let go of her and step up to the glass with my heart in my stomach.

Please, please, please. I don't want to accept what that was . . . but I think I already know.

Above us I hear footsteps running, but I can't figure out if it's one or two sets over the sound of the wind and my pulse thudding in my ears.

I peer down and gasp, the sudden rush of oxygen in my lungs making me dizzy. On the ground, face down in the rain, is *Odette*.

"Oh my god!" I say, jumping back from the window and pressing my palm to my mouth before I throw up.

"What?" Kash asks, her voice ice-cold.

"W-we need to go," I mutter, grabbing Kash and tugging her toward the door.

The footsteps above us grow louder, and I finally hear a bellow of "Odette! Odette! Help!" Hugo's voice pierces through the ceiling as if he's right on top of us.

"Outside!" I shout back in case he didn't see. How the hell could that have happened? They were supposed to be together, but it sounds like he'd maybe lost her. Kash is on my heels as we sprint to the stairs and take them dangerously fast.

Was she pushed or did she slip?

No, it doesn't make sense for her to hang out of a window in this weather. It couldn't have been an accident. She wouldn't jump.

"It's Odette. Oh god, oh god, oh god," Kash chants behind me.

"What's going on?" Allegra asks. She runs toward us in the foyer, Fergus and Shen right behind her.

"Odette fell out of the window," I reply, running past them and tugging the door open.

Fell. Pushed.

Pushed.

"What?" Allegra screeches, the sound slicing through me like a knife in butter.

Hugo shouts, but the second the door is open it's impossible to hear anything other than the growls of the wind and distant crack of thunder. The thunderstorm is returning. We can't risk going into the moat if it reaches us.

I sprint right, my sight instantly compromised, and scream as a wooden planter whips past me, rolling like tumbleweed and breaking into pieces on the waterlogged lawn, mud and dead plants flying around it.

For the second time this morning, I'm running into the rain.

"Odette!" I scream, praying there is something we can do to help her but knowing there likely isn't. She fell from the third floor.

Hugo catches up, passing me just as I'm about to reach her.

"Don't move her!" Kash yells, crouching down a second later and wiping water from her face.

Shen joins her and together they feel for a pulse and check if she's breathing.

There isn't going to be a pulse.

I stand up, giving them space. Odette's arm is lying at a strange angle, likely shattered when she tried to break her fall. I shelter my eyes and look up at the turret; the window at the top is wide open. Bile climbs up my throat.

I turn my attention back to Odette. The worst part is her head. She's stomach down; her head is twisted to the side and an odd shape from when she landed hard. Blood on the ground is pumping from underneath her, rain slowly diluting it.

Abbas shouts, stumbling forward, and Hugo catches him before he hits the stone path.

I watch on in horror, wondering how this could happen. If Odette was pushed, wouldn't she have left with her back to the window, so shouldn't she be face up?

Could she have been thrown face-first?

Kash and Shen look at each other, and Shen shakes his head.

Odette is dead.

"No! Help her!" Abbas shouts, choking on his words.

Hugo's eyes widen and he clings to Abbas harder, both realizing that there's nothing we can do for their friend. She's gone.

"Do something! Come on, Shen. Kash. Do something! You have to try!" Abbas pushes away from Hugo, shoving him with such force that Hugo stumbles backward into the brick wall.

I crouch down with Abbas as he reaches for Odette, taking her good hand in his and shouting her name. "Wake up, Odette. I know you can. Come on, open your eyes!"

"Abbas? Abbas, she's gone," I say softly, sobbing on my words. "We need to get inside."

He shakes his head, water pouring from his hair. "I can't . . . I'm not leaving her. I'm not leaving her out here."

"We're taking her," I tell him, the thought of leaving her exposed to the elements making me sick. "But we need to go now."

"I've got her, Abbas!" Fergus shouts. "It's okay, mate."

I grab Abbas's arm and help him up, gritting my teeth as he makes very little effort to move. Abbas looks at me with wide, haunted eyes, leaning heavily against me.

"It's okay," I tell him, and start walking to get him going.

I look up and see nothing but tiny bullets of water as they pelt my face. No, she wouldn't have jumped. No way. Someone had to have pushed her from up there, maybe while she was looking out the window, searching for a way out. Where the hell was Hugo when that happened? We were supposed to stay in our pairs for safety.

Fergus moves Odette's arm, trying to position it better so he can roll her onto her back. I turn away as I hear the crunch of broken bone in her arm over the pouring rain. The sound churns my stomach and makes me shudder.

For some reason it seems so much worse now that she's dead.

Abbas notices too, missing a step and almost sending us both flying to the ground. I think I hear his whispers through the wind, apologizing to her over and over for what's happened.

Abbas was nowhere near her. What does he have to be sorry about?

Shouldn't Hugo be the one apologizing?

I glance up, looking for him. Everyone else fusses around Odette, trying to keep her arms by her sides while Fergus carries her.

He's still leaning against the wall, wide-eyed, staring distantly at Odette.

Fergus passes us, carrying her. Odette's head is now rolled into his chest as if she's having a nap. I get up and follow them, reaching for Hugo on my way past, since he doesn't appear to see anything or anyone.

"Come on," I tell him, tugging on his hand when he just won't budge. Now I have two people I need to lead back inside. "Hugo."

He looks utterly exhausted, chin down, shoulders slumped, hair stuck to his head. It's as if Odette's fall shattered his entire being. I can't imagine the guilt that's weighing him down right now.

After another second, he jolts and moves my way, following me toward the castle entrance. He's unhelpful, stumbling slowly, so that I have to tug him along to get out of the storm.

Abbas at least pulls himself together enough to properly take his own weight and make my job easier. Zeke takes pity on us and wraps an arm around Abbas's shoulders, helping me get him inside.

"Where are you putting her?" I ask, and close the door behind us, blocking the storm. With Hugo and me at the back, everyone else is already halfway along the hall, moving quickly but robotically, nearly frozen with shock.

"Open the door, Kash," Fergus says, nodding to the room on his left.

The servants' kitchen. It's a good plan—the room is colder than the rest of the castle, stone floor and walls, a window that doesn't quite fit the frame properly.

Allegra brushes Odette's wet hair out of her face on the side of her head that isn't . . . damaged. "I'm sorry, we have no choice but to leave you in here."

"I'm not going anywhere," Abbas says. "I'm staying with her until we can get help."

"Are you certain you want to do that?" Kash asks. "I don't think it's a good idea."

"We'll figure out a way to go soon. Someone will come. The wind will die down and we'll leave," Abbas says. "Until then, I'm not leaving my best friend alone."

"Any amount of time that you're locked in a room with your friend like this isn't good," I say softly, understanding why he wants to but knowing how traumatic it's going to be. I jolt, blinking away a flash of claustrophobia and a sharp image of smashed glass and fresh blood.

"I'm staying."

Jolted by . . . what? Was it a memory, or did my mind conjure what I think happened to Odette? But the window didn't look broken.

Hugo runs his hands through his curls. "We'll find a way out for her. We have to." He sucks in a breath that sounds like it took all his energy to take. "We'll do it for you, Odette." Then he silently walks from the room, hands still in his hair.

I leave the others to figure out the next plan and follow Hugo, needing to understand what happened up there because it doesn't add up.

He doesn't go far; I find him leaning his forehead against the faded wallpaper. He looks so small against the high wall, the castle swamping his crumpled frame.

"Are you okay?" I ask, wondering if the guilt that's eating him up is because he wasn't there when she was pushed . . . or because he was.

14

"Hugo, are you okay?" I repeat, unsure if he can even hear me. "Come on, talk to me. I'm worried about you."

He shakes his head, hair rubbing noisily against the peeling wallpaper. "It shouldn't have been her. It should've been me."

I lean against the wall beside him, conceding to the fact that he's not moving yet, both of us dripping water onto the floor. "No, it shouldn't have. Why would you say that?"

"Because it's true. She didn't deserve to die. I left her, Bessie. I can't believe I did that. We split up. It was quiet, and there were only a few rooms up there. We thought we were safe and now she's dead."

So that's why he wasn't with her. They split up.

I try to push away the bolt of anger that surges through my chest. *Why* would they risk that? "That wasn't your fault," I say instead, trying to shove my fury away. "Hugo, you didn't know what was going to happen."

He steps away from the wall and turns to scowl at me, as if he wants me to agree and shout at him. "Didn't you hear me? I let her go into that room alone, Bessie, and now she's dead."

"I know that." I saw her fall past the window. "Tell me what happened."

He scrubs his hands along his cheeks and groans. "She said it'd be quicker to take a room each. God, there was no noise up there, Bess. Nothing. All we could hear were the footsteps below us. She said we should each take two rooms and get back to you guys. She was worried that something was going to happen to Abbas and the rest of you. I shouldn't have listened. I knew it wasn't safe. I damn well *knew* it, but I went along with it anyway. I let her walk into that room, all to save us thirty seconds of searching."

"It wasn't your fault," I repeat more firmly, but my heart isn't quite into it. The carelessness of her death makes me want to scream. I've felt it building since I discovered Jia and we realized our phones were missing.

Somehow I'm managing to keep the sheer panic and anguish contained.

"It doesn't matter that it was her idea. I still went along with it, and Odette paid the price."

"Stop. She's not a child, and you're not responsible for her. I understand the guilt. Jia died while lying beside me. I didn't even sleep particularly well, but I slept straight through that. If I hadn't, maybe she would still be here."

"It's not the same thing."

It's also not a competition. No one's grief or guilt is bigger than the rest of ours.

I close my eyes and pinch my nose, startled when a flash of blood on my palms burns my retinas. The image is so realistic that I have to look down and check.

There is no blood on my hands.

"Come on, guys, we're going back to the ballroom," Zeke says, slapping Hugo on the shoulder.

"Abbas?" I ask, pushing the vision out of my mind.

"Staying put for now. We need to convince him to come with us, though. He can't stay in there with her."

"I'll get him back," Hugo says.

"Ballroom first," I tell him. "Abbas isn't going anywhere just yet, but if you go to him with a plan, he might. Just give him a minute, yeah?"

Hugo looks back to the door where Abbas and Odette are, his face contorted with pain. "He loves her."

"I know."

"He's never going to forgive me."

"Hugo, come on. We can deal with this later."

Fergus lets us into the ballroom and Hugo heads straight for his bag.

"No one goes anywhere alone again," Hugo says, dropping to his knees beside his things and shaking his head. He rifles through his bag, head bowed. "We can't lose anyone else."

"Is he okay?" Kash whispers, pulling me to the corner of the room where our bags were dumped.

"No." I take another set of dry clothes out of my bag and wrap a towel around myself so I can change in relative privacy. The boys are on the other side, occupied. I'm also finding it hard to care about anything other than Jia, Odette, and escaping this place.

"What happened up there? He was meant to be with her."

I glance over my shoulder to make sure he can't hear. "They split up. Thought they were alone. It was her idea, apparently."

"*Apparently*. You don't believe him?"

"I believe him, Kash. He's drowning in guilt." The towel almost drops as I peel my wet top off. "I just can't work out why they'd split, even to save time."

When I'm dressed, I hang my wet clothes beside everyone else's and join them on the floor. The cold is bone-deep, and even though I'm dry I don't think I'll ever warm up. Maybe that's the shock.

Kash's question is still bothering me.

It's not that I think Hugo is in on this, but what if someone in our group is?

The second the thought enters my mind I feel horrendous for doubting my friends. I need some sugar and carbs; my body is running on fumes and it's affecting my ability to think straight.

"I'm going to make hot drinks to warm us up," Allegra says, reading my mind. "Fergus and Zeke can take a mug to Abbas with his bag."

"We're splitting up again?" Kash asks, pulling on a sweatshirt.

"No, the boys are walking halfway along the hallway and coming straight back," she replies, boiling the kettle.

Making tea and coffee seems like such a mundane thing to do

in a situation like this, but we need the caffeine. The kettle wobbles and then clicks, stopping before it's boiled. I open my mouth, but my unspoken question is answered when the light above us flicks off.

With the rain beginning to fizzle out and clouds parting, we're not in darkness, but we need the electricity before night.

Please, no. How much more can we take?

"What the hell is that?" Shen asks. "That's not good, right?"

"What if the killer's broken the generator along with the cars," Kash says, hysteria dripping off every word. "He's not going to stop. We should leave now."

Fergus moves into the middle, ready to hold court. "Take a breath. The weather warning is still in place, Kash. Danger to life, remember. Anyone think they're stronger than a tree? No, I didn't think so. You've seen it out there. People die or get injured when they go outside."

Kash doesn't look at all convinced. "You really think we're safer in here than out there? People are dead. Now the power has gone."

"The generator has probably just run out of fuel. There's more, so let's all stay calm." Fergus sounds sure of himself, at least. I hold on to that with every ounce of strength I have left.

"Okay, so we refuel the generator and then hide out here," Zeke says. "We do have the fuel, right?"

"I'm not a moron, Zeke. I brought it with us. It's in the cellar."

"I didn't see any when I was down there," I tell him.

"There are three cellars, Bessie."

Since when? That makes absolutely no sense, because on the plans Kash has there is only one cellar. Why would the other two be hidden? It's as if the castle was built to get away with murder.

Kash is frowning from her makeshift bed, wrapped in a blanket as she tries to warm up. I can tell she's doing the math too. One cellar on the plan. An extra two in reality. Why?

There has to be accurate documentation somewhere.

"All right, we'll drop Abbas's bag and go from there."

"The kettle is hot enough to make a drink. Take him this. He's going to be freezing, and there's no fire in the kitchen."

"There's a small fireplace. We can give him some wood," Zeke says, picking up Abbas's bag.

"It hasn't been cleaned out in years. If he puts a match to that the whole place could go up in flames. We'll take his bedding. It'll have to be enough," Fergus says. "Maybe we can convince him to come back with us anyway. Shen, you should stay here with the girls."

Shen turns to us three when Zeke, Hugo, and Fergus leave. "Do you think it's safe sending them out there with Hugo? He was alone with Odette."

"He was in a different room," I say.

"Yeah, yeah, I've heard the story, Bessie. Do we believe it?"

"Shen, he wouldn't kill his best friend," I tell him.

"I've been thinking about it too. In fact, it's all I've thought about since we saw Odette. He was alone with her. It was just the two of them up there and he could easily lie about splitting up," Kash says, like she has it all figured out.

"All I'm saying is I want proof before believing one of our friends is killing us. Is that too much to ask for?"

Kash lifts her palms. "It's not. Look, he was pretty cut up about Odette, I'll give you that."

"Yeah, it's probably guilt because he pushed her," Allegra mutters, her hand tightening around the mug. "We can't trust him."

Shen sits beside her, grabbing a coffee that is probably not hot enough. "Chill out, Allegra. We don't know anything for sure, and speculating isn't going to get us anywhere."

"Okay, Mr. Serious, that's not actually helpful right now, because the killer is covering their tracks. Besides, we know for a fact that Hugo was alone with Odette, then they split up." Allegra doesn't sound like herself. She's cold again.

"That means he's careless, not a murderer."

"Could mean he's a liar."

I turn to Kash. "See what you started."

She doesn't have time to respond, because the door flies open and Hugo runs back inside.

The four of us jump to our feet, and my first thought is that he's coming for us. But he stops in the middle of the room, eyes wide, and mumbles, "Abbas is gone."

Shen is the one who moves closer first. "What?"

"We walked into the kitchen to give him the drink and his bag, *and he is gone.*"

"He didn't leave a note or anything? Nothing to show where he's going?" Shen asks.

Hugo's face is a picture of sarcasm. "No, he didn't leave a note! Fergus and Zeke are going on to the generator, told me to tell you what's happened. They don't think we should go looking, but that's my best friend out there."

"Why don't they think we should look for him?" Shen says.

"Unsafe. As if we didn't already get the memo. I bet they'd go looking if it was one of you."

"Where do you think he would go?" I ask, walking past Shen but stopping a few feet in front of Hugo.

"I don't know. He was pissed off enough to go after the killer." He laughs, but it holds no humor. "He was convinced straight off that there was a killer. Maybe if I'd listened to him and gone after this asshole instead of looking for phones, Odette would be alive."

"We don't know that, mate," Shen replies. "But you can't seriously want to go find this guy. Not now."

"Abbas does. I think if I sit in here and pretend that everything will be fine when the wind stops, my other friend is going to die."

"No way, Hugo. Not happening. We're waiting for Zeke and Fergus to get back, and then we are *not* leaving this room until tomorrow," I say. "We stick to the plan. It's the best chance we have."

He lifts a brow and squares his shoulders, but I don't care how big or sure he tries to make himself appear. I know I'm right.

"When we leave this room, we die. You know that, so what is the one thing that makes sense, Hugo?"

He huffs, shaking his head and staring at me like I'm a stranger. "Look me in the eye and tell me you'd lock yourself in here if Kash was out there."

It's a demand, not a request. I could lie and tell him I would do the smart thing, but we all know it'd be rubbish.

"Hugo—"

"Abbas is expendable to you because he's not your friend."

"He *is* my friend."

"Enough!" Shen snaps. "Hugo, you understand why Bessie wants us in here and safe. Bessie, you understand why Hugo needs to find Abbas. You both get it, so *stop* arguing."

"How long does it take to get to the secret cellar boiler room?" Kash asks. "Shouldn't they have the generator back on by now?"

Allegra folds her arms rather theatrically. "Why do you think it's a secret?"

"It's not on the plans. Not all of the rooms are, it seems."

"All three cellars are on the plans, Kash," she responds, frowning as if she thinks we'd have something to gain by lying about that. "I've seen them a thousand times. Current and proposed."

"Allegra, you know I check out every place I go. I'm telling you there is only one cellar on the plans."

Or only one on the plans we saw. It doesn't make sense that there would be a false set. Wasn't Allegra the one who gave them to Kash? Did she really not notice that she'd printed the wrong ones?

It's on the tip of my tongue to ask when I'm cut off.

"Whatever," Allegra says, waving her hand to dismiss the whole thing. "We don't have time for that now because the others should be back already. Fergus knows what he's doing."

"Fergus knows how to work a generator?" Shen asks, barking a laugh that feels forced. "I can't imagine that."

"Our dad got him to do it when we were here once."

Nope, I still can't picture it.

"So, you're saying it's suspicious that they're not back yet?" Kash asks, wringing her hands. "Because it sure sounds like that. Only, the lights still aren't on, so what's delayed them?"

"I bet you want to go searching now," Hugo says, with no small amount of sarcasm.

"We all care what happens to Abbas. You know that!" I tell him, tired of his accusatory tone.

Hugo goes to take a step closer to me when the lamp flicks back on. He looks at me and smirks. "No need to go searching now. You can stay safe in here."

Anger simmers under my skin. "You have no idea how much I want to punch you."

"But you won't because you're a good girl."

"Excuse me?"

"Come on, Bessie. You don't really expect us to believe you're that sweet and innocent, do you?"

Keep calm. One of his best friends is dead and the other is missing.

"Hugo, did you hit your head? Because you're not making sense."

"Convenient that you don't remember."

Hold on . . . I don't think we're talking about this weekend anymore.

There is so much that he wants to say—I can see it all bubbling inside him, begging to be freed. I wish he would let it all out. "Why don't you enlighten me, Hugo? Since you seem to know me better than I know myself."

Kash puts her hand on my shoulder. "Stop, Bessie. He's worried about Abbas. It's not worth the argument."

Hugo lifts a brow again, a small action telling her that she's dead wrong. I need to sit down and have an honest conversation with him when we get home, because the Raif thing is far from over.

"I hate to break up the party, guys, but can we focus on the fact that they're not back from the cellar? It's at the end of the hall, right?" Shen says from the doorway.

"Maybe they ran into Abbas. He could've changed his mind about the killer and gone to find them," Kash says, her hopeful words almost making me roll my eyes. We don't have much luck when we go our separate ways.

An unease claws at my gut, telling me that something is wrong again. The urge to run screaming Fergus's name along the corridors until I find him is overwhelming.

"What do we do?" Shen asks, hesitating by the door, split between helping the others and barricading us in this room.

"I don't know but—" I don't have time to finish recommending that we give them a couple more minutes because there's suddenly a guttural scream for help bouncing off every wall in the castle.

Shen and Hugo fly out of the room without hesitation. Allegra steps back, hands flying to her mouth. "Oh my god. Who was that?"

"I can't stay," I tell them, the pull to find Fergus far outweighing my desire to hide away and survive.

"Bessie, no!" Kash shouts as I run after the guys.

Hugo is right. I won't hide while my friends are in trouble.

15

I don't think.

One day, that will be carved onto my headstone.

I run, not looking where Shen and Hugo are going, not trying to follow any one of them for safety in numbers, just running in the direction I believe the noise came from. Even knowing how sound travels in this place.

With the castle like a labyrinth, I don't know *exactly* where the scream came from, this is just my best guess.

I try to listen as I run, but Shen's and Hugo's footsteps are coming from different directions, I'm pretty certain. Someone else's too, maybe. Is it one more set? Two? Three? I can't be sure, but it would make sense for it to be two. Zeke, Abbas, and Fergus wouldn't ignore a cry for help.

The scream came from above, that much I know, so I run to the main staircase and it's there I realize I'm *completely* alone. The others could be using the servants' stairs or be way ahead of me.

"Where are you?" I shout, not worrying about trying to keep quiet since we're all stomping around the castle anyway. My stomach clenches as I rush up the stairs, my feet thundering on the threadbare carpet. The fear of being alone is something I'm trying my hardest not to dwell on. I sweep it away, ignoring the trembling of my hands as I push open the first door I come across.

It's a room I've been in on my tour, floral wallpaper, small oak single bed with a dusty mattress, a set of drawers, and a side table leaning against the bed, one of its legs lying on the wood floor.

But something is different, because the drawers have moved.

What the . . .

Why would anyone move them? The three drawers sit on legs, making it impossible to be used to hide behind.

Unless there's something behind the main part of the drawers.

The entrance to a secret room perhaps . . . one you'd have to climb into?

I look over my shoulder, heart racing to the point I feel faint, but no one is behind me; my friends sound far away, distant echoes of footsteps and calls for others to speak up.

My head is telling me to run. I should do just that.

But we've established that I'm no longer smart, so despite the heaviness in my stomach, I creep toward the drawers and look where the dust has been disturbed on the ground, scratches etched into the floorboards. That's it! Under the drawers adjacent to the wall is a floorboard that does not fit properly. It's slightly wonky and shorter than the others, with an obvious gap around it.

Not something you'd see if you were standing, but up close it's clear.

Okay, there is no secret entrance to another room. Nope, this is a terribly hidden hole in the floor. No wonder they put drawers over it. Might as well just hide your secrets inside your pillow.

Usually I wouldn't snoop, but this has been used recently and it could be by the killer, because at this point we're fairly certain there is a killer. Odette wouldn't jump. But what could be stuffed in here? There is no murder weapon.

I reach under and pull up the board, my pulse thumping rather too quickly for my liking. "Seriously awful hiding spot, wow," I mutter under my breath, and take out a newspaper that's been rolled to fit the small space. My shoulders slump when I see there is nothing else inside.

All right, that's kind of boring.

Something catches my eye as I go to shove it back. A headline in the paper that reads THREE TEENS SURVIVE DANGEROUS DRIVING ACCIDENT.

What . . .

That was *us*.

My scalp prickles as I unravel the paper to read the full article, but something outside the room makes me freeze. I can't just sit in here.

There's no time to read and see if anything is relevant yet— my friends are still running around trying to find whoever was screaming—so I stuff it into the pocket of my hoodie and run from the room, wondering how many more hiding spots and secret rooms are in the building.

"Where are you guys?" I shout, no longer knowing who to search for specifically or who to trust, my mind still reeling from the find.

Is this weekend about us?

"Bessie?" I hear after a second. "Bess, is that you?"

It takes a heartbeat, but I recognize the voice. Hugo.

Do I want to go to him when it sounds like he's alone? If something happened to the person he was with a second time, no one else would believe he was innocent.

I hesitate long enough and then decide to trust him. He's angry, not homicidal. "Hugo, where are you?"

He doesn't reply because he spots me from across the hall, the stairwell between us. The relief at no longer being alone is palpable.

"I can't find Abbas. I hear footsteps, but I can't find him!" he says, gripping the banister with white knuckles. "I can't find him. Where the hell is he?"

"I don't know," I say, taking a few steps forward. Something is stopping me from approaching him, a little voice in the back of my head reminding me that it's not out of the realm of possibility for it to be one of us.

Stop it. He's not the one doing this.

"We'll find him," I say.

Hugo looks wrecked, like he could be knocked down with a single breath. "I can't lose him too."

"You won't."

"Then why can't I find him, and why won't he reply?"

His question is answered with another scream, this one muffled with gurgling that makes me want to run away and pretend I never heard anything. I gasp. Who was that?

Hugo's eyes widen and he turns in the direction of the noise.

I gain on him as he goes to move. "Wait, wait, wait," I say, running past portraits of people watching us from the walls. It feels like we're putting on a show for them. "Hugo, we could be heading straight for the killer!"

"I have to," he replies.

"Not alone."

He flings his arm out so I can't pass. "Stay behind me."

"Hugo—"

"I will not have your death on my conscience too! Stay behind me." He keeps his arm to his side, preventing me from catching up to him.

"Okay," I whisper, staying half a step behind as he turns, and we jog along the hallway. Footsteps fill the castle as everyone tries to find the source of the scream.

We don't get far, because we slam straight into Fergus and Shen.

"Oh my god," I say, my shoulders finally losing some of their tension, but the relief to see them safe is short-lived as I notice the twin expressions of horror. There's a distant look in Fergus's eyes that I haven't seen since after the accident.

Hugo takes a ragged breath and shakes his head. "Don't . . ."

"Where are Abbas and Zeke?" I ask.

Fergus gulps and glances back at the room they've just left.

"Do not go in there," Shen says, catching me as I go to walk past them. "Don't."

Fergus puts his palm on the door handle and shakes his head. "Shen's right. You don't want to go in here."

"W-who's in there, Shen?" I ask, not entirely sure I want to know the answer, because it's obviously not good news.

He opens and closes his mouth like a fish, his eyes looking around as if he's physically trying to search for the words.

"I'm so sorry, mate," Fergus says to Hugo. "It's Abbas."

"No!" Hugo doubles over, struggling to take another breath.

Instinctively I reach out and hold him. "Oh god, Hugo. I'm sorry," I say, tears stinging behind my eyelids.

"I need to see." He stands taller and tries to push past Fergus, who blocks him. I stumble backward at his sudden movement. "I need to see! Get out of my way!"

"Trust me, you don't want to," Fergus says.

"Move!" Hugo roars, and Fergus has no choice but to let him through.

I take a step, not wanting to go in there but knowing that I have to. I need to see, and I can't let Hugo do this alone.

Fergus shakes his head, telling me not to, but he doesn't try to stop me. Abbas is my friend and I want to know what we're dealing with. My mind will only conjure something worse if I don't see.

I step inside the room, the metallic stench of blood making me retch. What the hell? My heart slams against my rib cage as I turn my head. "Oh god," I mutter, covering my mouth with my fist as bile hits the back of my throat.

I was wrong. This is worse than anything I could have dreamed.

My head spins, instantly making me so dizzy that I have to lean against the wall to stop myself from hitting the floor.

Hugo coughs but he doesn't move, his eyes fixed on the scene in the bathtub.

I look away and then turn back, praying that the image will have changed.

When it doesn't, I nearly vomit.

It's now looking likely that Jia was suffocated, Odette was pushed. This time the killer got their hands dirty, because there is blood *everywhere*. Splatters and streaks stain the tile. Red against white up the walls and on the painted wood floor.

I turn slowly to look at Abbas's face. Bright red blood streaks down his ears and mouth. His eyes are wide, stuck in a permanent state of terror.

Hugo stumbles into the wall next to me, gagging, his shoulder smearing some of the splatters. "What . . . what am I looking at, Bessie?"

I understand his confusion completely, because although I know what I'm seeing, it doesn't make sense. There is so much blood and so much violence in this room. I blink heavily, as if I can wipe the image from my mind.

"Guys, please come out of there," Shen says, his voice low and gravelly. "You need to leave that room."

I take two steps across the floor, carefully placing my feet so that I don't step in any more blood, and reach out for Hugo.

He has no reaction when I touch his arm; it's like he doesn't even know I'm here. "Hugo, they're right. We can't stay in here," I mutter, trying to keep to shallow breaths.

The thick metallic smell clogs my throat.

"Look at him, Bessie. Stab wounds."

"I can see," I reply softly, counting five and not wanting to look closer. The killer must be covered in blood. My chest burns, red-hot anger searing through every cell in my body. This murder is so brutal. "We should move fast, sweep the castle," I say, knowing revenge will get Hugo moving.

"What?" Fergus asks as I stumble toward the door, steadying myself on the wall. "Absolutely not, Bessie."

"Look at Abbas! The killer will need somewhere to wash up and change. That takes time. We can catch him and end this."

Hugo jolts suddenly, waking up at the sound of my plan just as I thought. He's angry and devastated enough to act on those feelings alone. It makes him dangerous, so I'm aware that I need to keep an eye on him.

"I want to take this asshole down myself."

"Hold on," I say. "The noise I heard was from the other end of the hall, not the bathroom. At least, I think. I was headed that way before I ran into Hugo and then you two."

"You think the killer went to hide out there?" Hugo asks.

I shrug. "It's possible."

The rooms along the front of the castle aren't visible from

here—it's a safer place to hide. The rest of us were making a lot of noise running upstairs, so it makes sense that he would still be on this level. He wouldn't have known which staircase was safe.

Hugo darts past us, running back in the direction we just came from.

I gasp and call out, "Hugo!"

Fergus and Shen move with me; we run the short distance to the front of the building, feet like a stampede on the noisy floor.

"Check the rooms!" Hugo barks, pushing the farthest door open. "Don't go all the way inside alone."

Oh, I was not planning to. It's only when I'm shoving the door and bracing myself that I realize I've come to the girls' room. No, I never wanted to step foot in here again.

I blink. Once. Twice.

No.

"Guys," I mutter, unable to take my eyes off the *empty* spot on Jia's makeshift bed.

She's . . . gone.

My eyes widen and I hear the air leave my lungs. Someone has moved her. "Oh my god. Guys!"

"What is it?" Hugo asks impatiently, crossing the hallway.

I clear my throat and grab hold of his arm. "Jia's gone."

"What?" Shen knocks into us as he rushes over. "No! What . . . oh my god. This doesn't make sense. What the hell is going on? Who would take her?"

"So are we still thinking she died from the accident outside? Because, in case you can't read between the lines, I don't," Fergus says, leaning a forearm against the doorframe and staring at the empty room with wide eyes.

"I think we're all on board," Hugo replies. Jia was undoubtedly the first victim.

I squeeze Hugo's arm harder, unsure which one of us needs the reassurance more. "We need to figure this out because I'm seriously freaking over here," I say. "We should leave. Right now. I know it's dangerous, but we should just go."

"Where did *she* go?" Shen asks, turning back to us.

"She didn't go anywhere, she's dead. Someone took her and we have to go!" I can feel the hysteria building inside me and I'm not sure how much longer I can keep it together.

"But why?"

"Mental torture," I say. First we're trapped, and now not only are we running around the castle fighting for our lives but our dead friend is missing.

Raising the stakes so that not only do we have to worry about who's next but also where our friends are. I want to stop playing this asshole's game and just go.

But my mind has other ideas, forcing me to face things I can't even begin to cope with. Like what is happening to them?

It's almost too much already. I feel the quickening of my shallow breath.

"Wait, hold up." Hugo tugs my arm so I face him. "Bessie, breathe a second. Come on. I'm freaking out too, but we need to think."

It's Fergus's hand on my shoulder that slows my pulse. "You've got this, Bess. We still need you. Breathe with me."

"What reason does this person have to move Jia?" Shen asks, almost to himself. His face is ghostly white, nothing like his usual complexion.

"Who the hell cares?" Fergus snaps, moving away from the wall as I roll the tension from my shoulders. "I say we find them and make them pay. Take control of this situation."

I'm all for taking control. It's a word that Fergus has used a few times when I've had a panic attack. He knows I want to be the one in control. I don't feel like I am at the moment, and that's terrifying.

Hugo nods, gritting his teeth. "I'm in."

He's in a scary place. His two best friends are dead, and I'm thinking he doesn't believe there's a reason to be cautious anymore.

Shen lifts his palms. "Just hold on a second. I'm with you both, I really am. But we've proved twice now that doing that gets someone killed. Three people are dead. *Three*. How many more before we think smarter?"

"Do share this smarter plan with the rest of us," Hugo says, his sarcasm shining through his fear. His hands are balls of anger, and his face is as red as the blood that coats the bathroom. "Because my best friends are dead. Jia is gone. You saw Abbas. He was *slaughtered*!"

I look away, as if lowering my eyes will stop the visual of the scene. I'll see that for the rest of my life.

I blink heavily as the image of blood flicks through my mind. Quick snippets like a slideshow. Glass. Blood. Glass and blood.

What on earth is going on?

"This guy came for Jia. Now he's just been up here . . . you know," he says, pointing toward the bathroom where Abbas lies because he doesn't want to say the words. "So he's off cleaning up, and while he's doing that we go down and slam the ballroom door so he thinks we're back in there. But we hide in the servants' kitchen and wait for him to come get Odette."

I inhale deeply. What could he want with them? If he even is going to come for Odette.

She's in the servants' kitchen, completely alone and vulnerable. Since we're all up here it would make sense to get her next. I don't think Kash and Allegra left the ballroom. They're probably doing the smart thing and hiding in there.

Hugo clenches his jaw but nods because, let's face it, the plan isn't bad. There's just one thing. . . .

"What do we do when or if he comes for Odette?" I ask.

Fergus wraps an arm around my shoulder, effectively pulling me away from Hugo, and it's only when his hand rubs along my arm that I realize I'm shaking. "I'd like to know that too. It's the most important part of the plan."

I sink into his side, soaking in his faux-calm energy. In moments like this I have no idea why we broke up. His fingertips skate over my arm. I remember the circular patterns from when he used to do this in the hospital last year.

"When he comes in, we jump out and grab him. Tie him up until we can get help tomorrow," Shen replies as if it's obvious.

"Are you on board?" I ask Hugo, leaning harder into Fergus. The brutality of Abbas's death rocks me to the core. In my head I see blood again . . . but the image is wrong. There's shattered glass mixed up in it. I shake my head to kick out the picture.

Why do I keep seeing glass?

He nods once. "Let's do it. For them."

I'm not sure what exactly he's ready to do for them, but I hope he'll stick to the plan. I'm holding on by a thread and don't think I can handle more blood and death. The killer needs to be stopped.

Hugo and Shen go first. There isn't enough time to pull Fergus to the side to talk about this, so I just have to hope he gets what I'm not saying. I lift my brows and he frowns. I dart my eyes to Hugo and back.

Fergus hurries me along, nodding to show that he's got what I'm trying to say. At least we both think we understand each other. Keep an eye on Hugo. There's a big chance he might do something reckless.

No one could blame him ... but an act of revenge might get him and us murdered.

We make noise on the stairs and on the way to the ballroom.

Hugo flings the door open. I go to approach him, but he holds his finger to his lips, silencing a wide-eyed Allegra and Kash.

"Zeke!" I say, my heart sinking to my toes, because how the hell could I forget him? He's not here, so anything could have happened to him. "Where is he?"

Hugo looks across at me, shaking his head. "Stick to the plan," he whispers, pleading with me not to change anything. "We haven't heard anything else, and it hasn't been long since ... Abbas."

After a second I nod my agreement, because Zeke is safer too if we catch this guy. The killer was distracted with Abbas, so chances are Zeke is okay. He will hear us and hopefully believe we've gone back to the ballroom. He'll come back.

Fergus closes the door, leaving Allegra and Kash worried and confused on the other side. "Quietly," he whispers, leading us along the hallway.

The servants' kitchen wasn't closed properly, so we make it inside nearly silently. I shudder, the cold not leaving my body yet.

"You okay?" Fergus whispers, holding my arms and bending so we're at eye level.

"I don't think so."

"Shh, we have to hide," Hugo says, slipping into a tall, empty cupboard on the wall adjacent to the door. Shen goes with him, but there's no space for anyone else.

Fergus scowls at him for a second and then opens a floor cabinet. "It's going to be okay. You can fit in here. Do *not* come out first, Bessie. Wait for us. Promise me."

"Yeah, I promise." I actually have no desire to be the first jack out of the box.

"Come on," he says. There are no shelves left inside, but from the sawdust along the edges I think there used to be and it broke.

I fold myself into it and Fergus closes the door. It smells like mold in here, the way it does if you've forgotten about a loaf of bread and find it weeks later. My heart instantly races with the lack of light and tight quarters. I place one palm on the floor of the cabinet and the other on my chest, as if that will slow my pulse.

With the loss of sight, I'm able to focus better on what I can hear.

Which, right now, is absolutely nothing.

We haven't discussed how long we will hide for, so I'm not sure when I can leave. There's no guarantee that he'll come for Odette, but this is a good plan if he does.

Maybe he'll go for Abbas first. But that doesn't quite make sense, because he wouldn't need to clean up if he was going to move him shortly after.

If he even is cleaning up.

Stop second-guessing the bloody plan.

I close my eyes and focus on what I need to do right now. It's so easy to get caught up in what might come next. The scent of sawdust and mold climbs farther up my nostrils. How long before Odette begins to smell?

Don't think about that.

I wish I'd stayed back with Allegra and Kash instead of believing I was strong enough for this.

It doesn't take long for my butt to start going numb and my neck to ache at my impersonation of a contortionist in this small cupboard.

Any number of minutes could have passed. It feels like thirty but probably more like ten when I hear footsteps.

One set. Getting louder.

I hold my breath when the door opens. The sound is so quiet against the pounding in my ears that I probably wouldn't notice if I wasn't really listening.

The footsteps echo until it feels like they're right beside me. I look to the door but see nothing. The cabinet is cloaked in darkness, the doors fitting so well they let in no light at all.

But I can sense the presence beside me, and my lungs stop working. I gently press my palms into the bottom of the cupboard so I can spring out if they open the door. Hopefully the element of surprise will give me enough time to get away.

Except a door bangs open from somewhere in the room.

Oh god.

A second later another.

I gasp. The boys are out of hiding. I fling my door open, maybe only three seconds after the first one.

I look up from my hiding spot to see Fergus hanging off the back of someone dressed in dark, baggy clothing. From the other side of the room, Shen and Hugo run.

"Knife!" Fergus shouts as I climb out of the cabinet open-mouthed.

Fergus goes to leap back, but the killer is faster and shoves him so hard that he takes Hugo out, sending them both flying like dominoes; they land hard against the stainless-steel island.

"Fergus!" I scream.

Where is the knife?

The killer sprints from the room, face hidden due to the oversize clothes, the hood hanging down his face. I only got to see him for a fraction of a second.

I do, very clearly, finally see the knife, though.

"Get off!" Hugo roars.

I run to the doorway with Shen and we make it just in time to see him sprint toward the back of the castle, that knife tight in his fist.

I think he's white—his hand looked pale even in the dim lighting. Oscar is tan, very similar to Hugo, but I'm not counting on this since I only got a glimpse. It's definitely not Zeke, whose skin tone is a lot darker.

Thank god it's not Zeke.

Neither of us is able to make our legs move to chase this guy down.

Hugo shoves Fergus, who rolls to the side and groans loudly.

"My arm!" he shouts as Hugo gets to his feet.

I rush to Fergus's side, panicked that he's injured. "Are you okay?"

"Yeah," he replies through gritted teeth, clearly in pain.

I touch his arms and chest, making sure that the pain is from the fall and not a knife wound.

"He's gone, Hugo," Shen says, blocking his way. "Don't. He'll be ready for us now. We've missed our chance. Stop! We'll get him, but not like this."

"No!" Hugo pushes Shen's chest but he doesn't budge. "No, no, no."

I get to my feet because Shen needs backup. I step in front of him and raise my palms. "Hugo, look at me. Shen is right, we can't chase him. He has a *knife*, and he knows we're after him. Think about it, his plan didn't go well either. It's too risky now."

"I'll go alone. Which way?" he demands, touching the back of his head and wincing. When he moves his hand again, his fingers are covered in blood.

"I'm not telling you."

"We go back to the ballroom," Fergus says, getting to his feet and shaking his hands to calm his nerves. I don't think he saw the knife until he was already on his back.

"Did you see who it was?" Shen asks.

"No, I was too busy trying to not get stabbed!" Fergus looks at Shen in disgust, as if he thinks he's being blamed for the plan going wrong. Did Fergus act too quickly? We didn't have a code word for when we were supposed to leave our hiding places.

This wasn't his fault, but the rest of us hang back, giving him some space to lick his wounds. We don't blame him, but he's clearly blaming himself. That could have been our best chance to end this. We failed, and the price for that is potentially very high.

Fergus is already halfway across the room when we get back. Allegra throws her arms in the air as she sees us approach. "Well? What on earth was that?"

She and Kash are sitting on one of the beds, holding planks of wood that are meant for the fire.

Shen flops onto the floor, bending his knees to rest his arms on them. "We had a plan. Didn't work out."

Allegra raises her brows so high they almost touch her hairline.

So much has happened in the last ten minutes, and they don't know any of it.

Shen groans. "Abbas is dead," he says.

I turn to Hugo as Shen talks, because I don't need to hear it. I was there. I'll never forget. Fergus does the same. He sits on the windowsill and stares out into the drizzle, making it clear that he doesn't want to talk to anyone.

Hugo sits down with his head bowed. I join him, not really sure what to say but knowing I need to try. He's just found his best friend dead in the most horrific way imaginable.

"Hugo," I say, and I'm met with complete silence.

"There's blood on my shoe," he mutters after the longest time.

"Oh," I reply, looking down. On the white midsole of his sneakers is a smudge of red. His best friend's blood.

I don't want to check mine, because I probably stepped in it too. There was just so much on every surface. It must've been a quick and frenzied attack. I push the thought away, needing to keep a level head.

"I'm so sorry, Hugo. Abbas didn't deserve that, and I promise you I will do everything I can to get justice for him. For Jia and Odette too."

"Do you think this is going to go any way other than how this asshole wants? We tried and failed," he mutters, defeated.

"We didn't have long to think of something. It could have worked, and it still can. We know what we're dealing with now."

He raises his head, turning slowly to look at me. "You want to pull the same trick? Don't you think he'll be ready and waiting for that?"

I shrug. "I honestly have no idea what he's waiting for or what he assumes we'll do next. I still think hiding out and grabbing him is what we need to do. We just have to—"

"Stop. He has a knife, like you said, and he'll be prepared for this shit again. It's over. We've lost."

"Don't say that. If we lose, we die. I won't give up and just let him pick us off one by one, and neither should you."

"Oh yeah, mate, that's a great plan," Fergus says, standing up.

Hugo waves him away. "Go back to your window, Fergus. You're no help."

"At least I tried! Where were you?"

Hugo stands up, fists clenched by his side. "I was right behind you!" he growls.

"You weren't fast enough and he got away!"

Shen jumps to his feet as Fergus and Hugo take a step closer to each other. "Let's calm down a minute."

Oh great.

Neither listens to him. "You're the one who let go," Hugo says.

"Because I saw the knife in his hand!" Fergus shouts. "What was I supposed to do?"

"Grab his arm!"

"All right, next time you can go first and see how you get on."

"No one told you to go first. You just did it."

Fergus steps forward and shoves Hugo. "Someone had to!"

Hugo throws himself at Fergus and gets in a solid punch to his jaw, the crack making me wince.

"Stop it!" I shout.

Shen pushes between them as Fergus retracts his arm to throw the next punch.

"Hey, no! Enough!" Shen places a palm on each of their chests, holding them apart. "This isn't helping."

"Why did you go first, Fergus? Why didn't he stab you? How were you on his back?"

There's a heavy accusation in there that Fergus does not care for. His eyes narrow. "He turned to run when he saw me jump out of the cupboard."

"Convenient," Hugo replies.

"Say that again."

"I said *convenient*. The guy had a knife, and he turns to run away from you."

"It wasn't just me there. You and Shen were behind me. Bessie too."

"I'm just saying, it doesn't add up. Could it be because you know exactly what's going on here?"

"Oh, shut up!"

Shen drops his arms, turning to stand beside Fergus. "Come on, mate," he says to Hugo. "We're not the odd ones out here."

"What does that mean?" I ask, trying to keep up with the accusations flying around.

"He's not in our year, Bessie. Why's he here?"

"I was invited, prick."

I step forward to block Hugo when he takes a step closer. "Don't."

"What the hell is going on?" Allegra asks. "Have you all lost it? Because the guy with a knife obviously wasn't either of you."

Hugo looks at her like he thinks she's simple. "We know that, Allegra. Jesus. I'm saying, right now, that I think Fergus knows who this guy is."

"Bullshit," Fergus growls.

"Stop it!" I shout, throwing my arms up. "This is exactly what the killer wants, so can we stop playing straight into his hands, please? You two don't have to kiss and make up but you sure do need to shut the hell up!"

Hugo blinks twice. "I don't think I've ever seen you this angry."

"Sit down and get comfortable, because unless we come up with an airtight plan, we're all staying here."

"Bessie's right," Shen says, backing me up. "Everyone *calm down*. We need to take a minute . . . after what we've just seen."

Hugo's shoulders slump at Shen's words. Fergus takes a step back. Both drop the fight, because they're just reacting to what we saw upstairs. Neither of them wants to turn on the other.

Hugo sits back down, taking the same defeated, head-down position.

Now we're not only trapped. We're fractured.

16

An hour passes. Then two. We sit in relative silence in the ballroom. I started getting hungry a while ago, but I honestly don't think I can stomach anything after seeing what the killer did to Abbas.

The smell of cheese wafts around the room and makes me want to vomit.

Shen is making sandwiches and Allegra's making mugs of tea and coffee, both preferring to do something practical in a situation that is completely out of control. I wish I could do the same. All I've managed to do is sit and try to convince myself that we can get out of this. It seems so hopeless.

Kash and Fergus sit close to where the food is being prepared, neither looking particularly like they want to eat, though.

Hugo also hasn't moved. He hasn't actually moved *at all*, didn't even come to the bathroom next door when we all took turns peeing and guarding. Hasn't spoken in a while either.

We haven't been back to check if Odette and Abbas are still where they last were. It went so horribly last time, and Fergus could have been stabbed. We were incredibly lucky the killer didn't want to take on four at the same time.

We can use that to our advantage by sticking together and being more prepared next time. Because I'm certain now there will be a next time.

I get up to stretch my legs, just to give myself something to do.

"Bess, here," Shen says, offering me a sandwich. "You need to try and eat, okay?"

I take the plate but my stomach churns, rejecting the food before I've even had a bite. "Thanks. Shen, Zeke . . ."

"Don't think about that right now. We need to believe he's okay. We haven't heard otherwise. He's probably hiding."

What if he's not? It's been hours and we've heard nothing. Which is a good sign and adds weight to the hiding theory, I suppose.

We've just left him out there.

He was in favor of hiding out until we could get away. Maybe he saw Abbas and decided running around wasn't safe. There are plenty of rooms he could be in.

He will be fine.

"I just feel awful leaving him."

Because let's face it, there's a chance he could be dead. What if the two screams we heard weren't both Abbas?

No. I have to believe that Zeke is okay and hiding.

"I feel the same, but you know what will happen if we go running around out there again. Eat up. It's the best we can do right now."

I sit next to Kash, who is chewing slowly as if she's trying incredibly hard to keep her food down. "You okay?" I ask.

She shakes her head, eyes fixed on Hugo. "I can't imagine what it would be like to find you or one of the others like Abbas."

She's lucky that she didn't see him, but Shen told her everything, what it looked like in there, so she can imagine. I bet she wishes she'd never asked.

"I know. I've tried talking to him, but I don't think he's hearing me."

"I can't believe I thought he might be involved in this."

"The person I saw had light skin, I'm almost certain of it," I tell her.

"You saw him?"

"His hand. But it was kind of dark, and then there was the all-consuming terror. It was a second's glance, but I think so."

"Okay. But we're thinking there could be more than one person doing this, right?"

"There could be ten for all we know."

That's a horrifying thought.

I get her point. We can't rule anyone out. Not yet.

I take a bite of my sandwich, my mind racing so fast I don't even taste the food. It's only because I'm so distracted that I manage to eat half of it.

"Bess, you want to give this to Hugo?" Shen asks, passing me a plate. "I don't think he wants to speak to me or Fergus right now."

How surprising. After that fight, I'm thinking it's best if they both keep their distance from Hugo until things settle.

"Yeah, I'll see if he'll eat."

I chuck the rest of my sandwich and grab a bottle of water.

If Hugo hears me approach, he doesn't show it.

I sit down, hand him the plate, and put the water beside him. "Hugo, you need to eat something," I say. "Please."

He takes it but puts the paper plate between his feet. His shoulders are hunched, head down; he's not wanting to talk or eat.

"Please try to have some of it."

"Can't," he mutters.

"I'm sorry about Odette and Abbas. And I'm sorry that you saw Abbas like that."

The image, the *blood,* isn't something I will ever be able to forget. Every time I blink, I see him. He must've been so scared.

If we were quicker and had found him on the first scream, maybe we could've saved his life.

We can't make that mistake again. Not ever. If Zeke shouts out, I'm gone.

I want to tell Hugo that I understand he's devastated about his friends, and he should take all the time he needs to mourn, but we still need him.

"I've been friends with Abbas since pre-prep." He shakes his head, eyes wide as if he's replaying their deaths over and over in his mind. "We joined each other on family holidays, spent most of the summer together, had plans to travel after uni. We were going to take a year and explore the world, starting with Japan. He said he was going to show me around Pakistan, despite the fact that he was born in Oxford and has only been to his parents' home country once before. He was like a brother to me, and now he's gone."

"I know," I whisper. The loss of Abbas, Jia, and Odette isn't something I can put into words. It's too big. Too much.

"He's never done anything bad to anyone. I don't understand why this happened. Why him, and why like that? The brutality . . ."

"I don't think it has anything to do with him. This isn't personal."

He lifts his head. "Oh, it's totally personal."

"Now, yes. I—I get that. What I mean is, this group doesn't know any of us. They just don't want the apartments to happen."

He turns his nose up like I'm missing something major. "Is that motive to kill?"

"I don't know, but people have killed for less," I say, needing it to be true. "And I don't think it's the whole group. Oscar said a couple were extreme in their belief that the development shouldn't happen. It doesn't need to make sense to us, only to the killer."

"What does murdering our friends solve?"

I shrug. "Maybe that will put people off living here. Maybe it'll get it torn down, like what happens with murder houses. They want to stop it being developed, right? The Beauforts have the money to cut through any of the planner's red tape."

"You said they wanted to burn it. Why wouldn't they just do that? Why kill too? It doesn't make sense."

"No, it doesn't make sense. I wish I could answer that for you, Hugo, but I don't get it either. I guess if really horrible things happened, it would ensure the building was torn down. Fire damage could be fixed, and they'd be left with the same problem." I shrug again because this is all wild speculation and I'm just trying to help.

"Three people are dead, and although the storm is better it's still too dangerous. The water is creeping closer and closer to the castle, decreasing the likelihood of any successful chance at leaving tomorrow."

Successful chance. Meaning we all manage to get out of here alive. Either the killer gets us or the weather does.

"We're going to get through this. Please don't give up," I say.

"Right, because we can get through anything."

"We can. You just have to have a little faith."

Hugo huffs. "Odette had faith. Look where that got her. She's going to be stuffed in a box and shipped to her parents in France."

"Hey," I say, placing my hand over his clenched fist. "She wouldn't want you to give up, and we need you. I need you because this is falling apart fast."

He sighs, and it sounds like he's finding it almost impossible to breathe. "I'm not sure how much I can give you. First Raif and now them."

Even just the mention of his name is enough to catapult me back to that night. My palms turn clammy. I squeeze my eyes shut, the blood image flashing through my mind again.

Glass. Blood.

Are these flashes from that night? I can't be certain that I actually saw shattered glass and blood or if my mind is just trying to piece that night together. I was knocked out cold and woke up in the hospital. I guess it's possible that I was conscious for a little while, but I have no recollection.

"Raif isn't dead."

"No, but he's not the same."

You can't drive erratically, crash a car with your friends inside, and expect to come out of it the same. I know the guilt eats away at him; it's why he refused to come back to school.

We've forgiven him, but he hasn't forgiven himself.

"No one blames Raif, Hugo. It was an *accident*," I tell him again.

One that had me in the ICU for three days and a hospital ward for another week. It took a while, but I'm fine. Fergus is also fine. Superficial cuts and bruises.

Raif was knocked out too but came around in the ambulance, apparently.

"He's still a mess."

"I've tried calling and texting him."

"He feels too guilty to talk to you."

"But we're fine and we want to talk to him."

Hugo lifts his head. "But you all could've died. *You* almost did. It haunts him, Bess, and I don't know what to do to help."

"Let me try. All I need is for you to let me in the house."

The ghost of a smile touches his lips. "When we get out of here, I might take you up on that."

I nudge his arm. "You said *when*."

His face brightens a fraction more, but the sadness is still in his eyes. "Yeah, well, maybe I'm moving on to the angry stage of grief.

The one where I want to get the hell away from this castle and bring down whoever killed my friends."

"I'll take that. I want them behind bars too."

He looks around the room, taking everyone else in. Allegra and Shen are now cuddled up on a makeshift bed chatting quietly, crying quietly. Kash has lain down and is pretending to be asleep, and Fergus is back staring out of the window.

"Do you honestly think we'll all make it?" he asks.

"I have to, or what's the point in trying?"

"You're the glass-half-full girl. I like it."

"Alternative is—"

"The glass is dead," he says, cutting me off.

All right, he's making ill-timed jokes, so maybe he's even past the despair stage of the weekend. This thing isn't over until we can get across that moat without drowning or having trees and debris squashing us, so it's a welcome change.

"Where are you two going?" Fergus asks as Allegra and Shen get up.

"The castle is . . ." Allegra shakes her head. I think she was about to say safe. "I need to do something. We need to find my best friend. She wouldn't hide and leave me."

"Whoa. Three people are dead and we could be next. We need to find a way past that moat when we can. That has to be our priority." Hugo sounds so sure of himself that I almost agree. But how can we leave Jia?

"We have to find Jia," Allegra repeats. "She was my best friend

THE PARTY | 191

and I'm not leaving her wherever she is. This sick bastard might be cutting her up."

Her words make my stomach churn. "Let's not jump to conclusions!" I squeal, shaking my head as my brain betrays me, showing me Allegra's theory.

"It's body disposal one-oh-one, Bessie!" she says, her breathing heavier and on the cusp of hyperventilation. I don't think I've ever seen her so pale.

"Allegra, are you okay?"

"I feel so . . . um."

Hugo moves so fast, he startles me. He catches Allegra before she hits the floor. Oh my god.

"Allegra!" Shen says, running toward us. "What's happening to her?"

"Is she okay?" I ask as Hugo holds her in his arms. She looks exhausted, as if she's taking a nap the way she does in every foreign-language class. Allegra is one of those awful people who expects everyone else to know English rather than trying to learn a little of another country's tongue.

"She'll be fine."

I place my palm on her forehead. "This is too much for her."

"Knowing there's a killer in the castle?" he asks, walking ahead of me.

Shen walks along beside them, toward the pile of blankets, keeping an eye on her, holding her wrist to take her pulse.

"Yeah, that. You don't think whoever took Jia really did that to dispose of her, do you?"

"What other reason would he have, Bessie?"

"Allegra is right, we need to find her," Kash says.

When her body is returned to her parents, it needs to be unharmed.

"Get the door, Shen," he says.

In his arms Allegra starts to come around, groaning and fluttering her eyelids.

"I'm going to lay you right here," Hugo says. There's a softness in his voice that I haven't heard since yesterday.

"She fainted," Kash says, smoothing out the sleeping bag on Allegra's camping mattress.

"Pulse is stable," Shen says. "She's fine. Probably needs to eat. She's made food but has refused to eat it."

Hugo runs his hands along his cheeks. "Guys, I need to check Odette."

I guess Allegra's words have gotten to him too. He doesn't want anything horrendous to happen to Odette's body either.

I turn to him and take a breath. I'm finding it increasingly hard to remain calm. I just want to scream.

"I—I have to know," he mutters.

"Of course . . . but look what happened last time."

"Where's Zeke, Bessie? Don't you want to find him too?"

"Obviously!"

"Zeke will be hiding," Fergus says.

"How do you know? Unless you're in—"

"Do not finish that sentence!" Fergus snaps.

"Whatever. I can't stay here. I have to know." He spins on his heel and runs from the room, shoving the door so hard it slams and bounces off the wall, almost closing again.

"Hugo, wait! You can't go alone," I yell, following him. "We don't know what we're running into. Stop!"

"Bessie, no!" Kash shouts, but I'm already out the door.

"Stay together," I call over my shoulder. "Hugo, wait up!"

He doesn't listen, sprinting along the hallway and around the corner. I keep up, following just behind him. The creaky floorboards in the foyer scream beneath my feet. Hugo gasps, grabs the banister, and swings around at the bottom, heading to the front door.

My arms wheel as I stop myself and change direction with him. What the hell is he doing?

The front door is heavy, but the way Hugo rips it open makes it look like it's made of cardboard. I narrowly miss running into it. Outside is just as bloody awful as before. I'm beginning to think I'm going to spend the entire time here soaked through. Will the storm ever be over?

The rain is heavier again, coming down like pellets. Hugo doesn't let up, the weather no match for his desire to reach his friends. Whatever this person is doing with bodies can't be good. I'm not willing to let them get Odette or Abbas either.

He runs almost straight into the wall of the outhouse but manages to correct his footing before he does. Where the hell is he going?

"Hugo!"

Mud squelches beneath my feet as we leave the path and cut across toward the brick building.

"What are you doing?"

He turns just as he's about to go inside, finally hearing that I'm behind him. "Careful!" he shouts, his voice barely audible above the howling wind.

We walk through the stone archway and into the building, which is somehow colder than outside. It's pitch-black inside.

"Why are we in here?" I speak each word between heavy breaths.

"I thought I saw something in the window, and it made me realize that this asshole could be hiding outside."

All right, that makes sense and could be why we can't find him, but we're infinitely worse off in the open.

"I can't see anything," I say.

He doesn't respond, but his labored breathing gives away how frightened he is also.

"I can only feel the wall," Hugo says. He sounds close by, but I can't see him at all.

The hairs on the back of my neck stand up. I don't like this.

"Neither can I," I reply, feeling my way along the floor using the walls.

I hear a thud and gasp, spinning around in the darkness. "Hugo?"

"No."

My heart stops.

That's not Hugo.

Holding out my hands in front of me for protection, I whisper, "Hugo, where are you?"

The only reply I get is a howl of wind. As I go to take a step, I'm shoved backward. My body slams so hard against the brick wall that everything goes black instantly.

17

I blink heavily, and it takes me a minute to realize that I'm on the floor. Pain radiates through my back as if I've been stabbed. For a moment I forget where I am and what I'm supposed to be doing. Panic that I may actually have been stabbed is all I can think about.

But it doesn't take long to realize that I'm okay, and then everything comes flooding back. The death, the isolation, the person who's just attacked us. I was shoved and hit my back on the wall.

I gasp, another flash of blood in my mind. I don't know if it's Abbas or something else, but it doesn't last long. Bloodied hands and the echo of a scream.

Was that from this weekend? I haven't had blood on my hands.

"Hugo?" I call, looking up but seeing nothing.

I don't get far because someone grabs me. I scream, thrashing my hands and trying to claw at whoever has me pinned face down on the stone. "Help! Hugo!"

I thought the killer had fled. *He's here.*

I try to roll over, but his grip is too tight for me to move.

"What do you want?" I shout, sobbing. "We're just here for a party. Please let us go. We have nothing to do with the development! Please!"

He leans down, his bony elbows digging into my shoulder blades. I scream out again, louder, when I feel his face near mine.

"Shouldn't have done it," he says, and slams his elbow into my head.

The voice. Do I recognize it? I'm unsure. It's hard to place it when I can hear my thudding pulse and heavy, terrified breaths clearer than anything else.

Another scream rips from my throat as pain radiates across my skull. I flail underneath him, images of the accident flashing through the throbbing pain. I can feel it, the beeping from the machines in the ICU, the panic of waking up in that bed.

The headaches that seemed to last forever.

"Get off, get off!" I yell over and over, kicking my legs and wriggling my body. "I'm not doing anything."

Where is Hugo, and why isn't he helping me?

He hits me again, the blow just as hard as the first one, and I think this might be it.

I'm going to die.

My face falls heavy against the ice-cold stone, my eyes losing focus as the world turns blurry. Black dots dance in front of me, growing bigger and multiplying until darkness is all I see.

* * *

"Bessie? Bessie?"

I groan against the pain that feels like daggers poking my brain. Groggily I pry my eyes open.

"Can you hear me?"

It takes longer than I'd like to place the voice, because it's slightly different than usual, laced with pain, but it's Hugo. *Thank god, it's Hugo.*

"Bessie, can you open your eyes?"

I thought they were open.

"I—I don't know. Where am I?" I mutter, my voice barely a whisper, my body so heavy it wouldn't surprise me to discover I'm covered in boulders.

"We're in the brick shed. I woke up a second ago. I have a killer headache. Are you okay?"

"He shoved me, pinned me down. We have twin headaches."

I open my eyes more successfully this time. It's still dark but I can just make out Hugo in front of me.

"It's okay," Hugo says. "Let me help you get up. We need to go inside. I'm so sorry, Bessie. I never should have come out here."

"It's not your fault I followed," I reply, leaning on him while getting to my feet.

My head swims as if I've just gotten off the teacups at the fair. Nausea rolling through me in waves.

"I didn't hear footsteps, just a thud," I tell him.

"That thud would've been my head on the wall. I didn't hear anything before that either. Easy. You feeling okay?" he asks.

"Yeah, I'm fine," I lie. "Did you hear the voice?"

"I heard nothing, I'm sorry."

"I think . . . I think it was deep and almost sounded like a recording, but I couldn't hear well."

"Do you mean like he was changing his voice?"

"Possibly. He would want to disguise himself. Oh, and I am certain it was a guy."

Hugo nods. "All right, let's get back inside with the others."

"Why didn't he kill us?"

"I don't know, Bess. Something to figure out when we're inside and safe."

I want to remind him that we're not safe inside, but it feels pointless.

Hugo leads me out of the shed. The rain has subsided to more of a drizzle now, a light spray that constantly hits my face. It's slowing, at least. I'm grateful for the light, but it gives me a chance to see the cut on the side of Hugo's head.

"Oh my god, you're bleeding."

"I can feel it. I'm fine," he replies, keeping his gaze forward and marching us back to the castle as if I am his naughty child.

We walk into the castle, and the lack of sound anywhere instantly has the hairs on the back of my neck standing up again.

Hugo must feel it too, because he looks in every direction and whispers, "Just get to the ballroom. Watch your step."

My head pounds with every movement I make. "I feel like someone's taken a sledgehammer to my skull."

"That will be the concussion."

"I remember it from last year."

I'm not sure this is the same, though. It's not as bad.

"Right," he says. "Here we are, next door."

"Hugo, my head wasn't smashed that bad."

He laughs. "You remember how to walk and where to go. Got it."

"Do you think the others are okay?"

"I hope so, Bess. Right now, and until we find them, we're all we've got. Sorry, that sounded more dramatic than I intended."

Despite the searing pain, I laugh. "I think you've earned the right to be dramatic."

Hugo helps me shuffle into the deserted ballroom. That's not a good sign. Where the hell could everyone else be? It's deathly quiet. I look around, trying to figure out what's changed.

The castle is different. So quiet it could be empty.

"Can you hear silence too?"

"Um . . . ," he murmurs, staring at me like he's unsure if the whacks to my head have done more damage than just knocking me out and giving me a wicked headache.

"Only wind," I say.

"Sorry?"

I roll my eyes. "Listen. The rain has finally stopped, but the last forecast we saw said rain until tomorrow, so it could start back up at any minute."

"You're right. Here, you change and grab some pills for your head. I'll check the window. Maybe the others have gone to look outside. If the water level's receding, we can get out of here."

If they went out, we would've seen them, surely.

Does he mean that we should just go? Me and him alone? I can't leave here without Kash.

"What do you see?" I ask, grabbing my water and pills once I'm dry again.

I swallow two while waiting on the bloody weather report from Hugo.

"The place is still flooded. Moat like a lake, blah blah, the usual. The wind is still bad, but no more rain. The clouds are parting, so hopefully it won't return." He turns back. "We're still stuck, but we'll probably be able to see the stars tonight."

"Tell me how that's a good thing."

He presses his damp T-shirt to the small cut on the side of his head. Okay, he's now shirtless. "I wish I could think of a positive spin, but it just means that the sky will look nice while we're dying."

"Oh. Cool."

He laughs, cricking his neck as he walks over to me. He grabs his bag and pulls fresh clothes out of it. "I say we wait ten minutes for those pills to start working and then go look for the others. Do you think you can manage that . . . with the concussion?"

I smirk. "Sure. Walking off a mild concussion is a thing, right?"

"Can you see okay? No blurriness or double vision?"

"Well, there are four of you. Is that bad?"

His face falls for a second before he realizes I'm joking.

"Sorry, just trying to bring a little light humor to our continuing life-or-death situation." I stretch my back out, wincing against the ache. The pain meds better take care of that too.

He pulls a dry sweater over his head. "Yes. Excellent. How good are you in woodshop?"

"Not terrible. Are you okay? This is kind of a strange time to discuss academic strengths."

"We have an abundance of wood and a lake."

I look up at him and burst out laughing, clawing at my head but unable to shake the image of us whittling wood to make a boat.

"You can stop laughing now."

"I can't. Hugo . . ."

"Do you have a better idea?"

That stops me. I rub my temples as the pain spreads lower. "Well, no. But a boat?"

"I'm not saying we build a ship, Bessie. A raft. Something that will float. Hell, Rose survived on a plank of wood. All we need to do is get across the moat."

"Who's Jack in this scenario?"

"Can we leave the *Titanic* references alone and be serious for a minute?"

"Fine. How is building something safer than swimming? The wind is still strong, you said that yourself."

"There's a chance we'll stay on the raft and not enter the freezing cold water. The danger is the wind causing things to fall on us, but if we're on a raft there's a reduced chance of drowning or dying from hypothermia."

"Loving your use of the word *reduced*. No promises. No sugar-coating."

He smiles. "I think people should say it how it is."

"Oh my god, Bessie!"

I gasp and spin around, instantly regretting the sudden movement as the knife in my head digs deeper.

"Kash," I whisper, the relief overwhelming me. She's okay.

She sprints toward me, with Allegra, *Zeke*, and Shen behind her. Zeke's okay.

I open my arms as she rushes over to hug me. "You're okay," I say.

"We didn't find anything. It's so weird, it's like this guy is disappearing. We can't find him or any evidence that he's even here. Zeke was hiding in a pantry."

"I didn't know what to do," he mutters, neck turning red.

"You did the right thing. Absolutely," I tell him.

Zeke nods. "This guy has to be hiding out somewhere. It's not like Jia and Odette rose from the dead and walked off," he says. "I tried to listen, to see if I could find him. He's either light on his feet or not using the main hallways."

"Hold up. Odette is gone?" Hugo asks with what sounds like his last-ever breath.

"Sorry, mate. We'll find them, though."

Allegra puts her hands on her hips. "Fergus went after you two. Where is my brother?"

"We haven't seen him. We were attacked in that creepy little brick shed."

Zeke drops to his knees in front of me. "You were attacked. Damn, Bessie, are you okay?"

"Concussed, probably. Lightly. I'm good, though. Hugo was hurt worse."

"I really wasn't."

"You're staying with me for the foreseeable future. You got that?" Zeke says.

"Right, Zeke can take on the big bad guy single-handedly," Hugo says, his voice rough. Someone doesn't like the accusation that he couldn't protect me. As if that's his job. "We didn't hear anyone coming. There was no warning and nothing we could do."

One, I can take care of myself when I'm not being shoved in the dark. Two, I'm not Hugo's responsibility.

"Hey! Where's my brother?" Allegra screeches, throwing her hands in the air. "I'm glad Bessie and Hugo aren't dead, but can we focus on the next disaster, which is *my missing brother*! You must be worried, Bess."

"Of course I am! But I had the head injury to keep me momentarily distracted. We'll find him." Plus, I didn't know he was missing until two seconds ago. Fergus has to be okay. I can't even allow myself to consider that he might not be. It's *not* an option.

"Why did he go off? He was right behind you both."

Hugo walks up to her. "Impossible. We would have seen him if he was."

"See, that seems a bit suspicious. You go off, and one of the people you were with is concussed and the other missing," Shen says, sidestepping closer to Allegra and squaring his shoulders.

In a fight, my money would absolutely be on Hugo.

Hugo's pretty eyes change in a heartbeat. He looks like he wants to strangle Shen, and if Shen doesn't take back the blatant accusation, I think he might. "What are you saying? Because we didn't even know Fergus was following us."

"That it's awfully convenient you're alone when these things happen. Almost as if it's you."

Hugo doesn't waste a second. He shoves Shen's chest, and Shen stumbles backward. Zeke leaps up and runs between them.

"Fergus was the one creeping after us right before we were attacked, yet you blame me!" Hugo shouts.

"Hey, this is not helping!" I say. "Shen, I know you're scared and worried, but this is only making things worse. It's not Fergus or Hugo so just stop. We can't keep fighting each other."

Zeke backs me up. "All right. Let's all keep our heads."

"Oh, please. Think about it, Zeke. Everyone else failed to get here through the storm but him."

"And don't I regret that now. My friends are dead, asshole!" Hugo snaps, glaring.

Okay, screw this. I stand up, not only a little bit dizzy but full-on ready to vomit. "Hugo saved me," I say.

Allegra moves around the boys and aligns herself with me and Kash. "You said you were out of it," she says to Hugo. "How do you know it wasn't him who attacked you and then played hero when you came around?"

Hugo scoffs, looking at Allegra and Shen like they're complete strangers.

I shake my head gently, even the smallest movement drilling fresh pain into my skull. "No . . ."

"You're all talking nonsense," Hugo says. "I'm not doing this. Bessie knows it's not me. I was out of it too. He attacked me first because he knew I'd get him if he touched her."

"This is all too personal," Allegra says. "Whoever is doing this has to be connected to us."

"Your brother has a connection to us," Hugo says.

"Shut up!" Allegra screams.

"What possible motive could I have for killing our friends? Come on . . . see, you have nothing. I'll help you find your brother, but after that I'm getting out of here. You do what you want. I don't care anymore," Hugo says, walking to the side of the room and grabbing a bottle of water.

I watch him and then turn to my friends with more questions in my head than ever.

Could it be one of us?

Fergus.

Hugo.

Or is it Oscar's crew?

I hate that I don't know who to trust.

18

After the arguing dies down, we all head straight out to find Fergus. Together.

But as we get to the door, Allegra folds her arms, and my heart sinks, knowing we're about to go for round two. Or is it three? I can't keep up.

"What, Allegra?" I ask, already tired of whatever she's about to say. I'm so over the drama we're adding to this weekend. It's ridiculous and unhelpful.

"I'm not going anywhere with Hugo."

"Are you serious?" Hugo asks, an eye roll almost audible in his voice.

"Yes, I'm serious," she confirms. "Until I find my brother and he tells me you had nothing to do with his disappearance, I don't want to be anywhere near you."

"Allegra, he was attacked too," I remind her.

"He has a minuscule cut on his head. You were out, and you only have him to tell you how long that was for. Do that math, Bessie."

"I'm still here, Allegra. Fergus is the one who's missing. Perhaps *you* should do that math."

"We split up," Zeke says. "I know we shouldn't, so everyone shut up about sticking together. It's not working, is it? Hugo goes his own way."

"We can't just leave him," Kash says, her eyes wide, horrified that Zeke has suggested that.

I look up at Hugo, whose expression is filled with hurt. "Yeah, it's not happening."

"Fine. We'll split into groups of three," Allegra tells us, as if she couldn't care less that she's sending me and Kash off with someone she believes is a murderer.

Wow. It's nice to know how much she values our friendship.

"All right," Kash replies, narrowing her eyes. "See you guys later."

Are we really doing this?

"Be safe." My voice is a lot sharper and more insincere than I was going for. But I'm angry and upset.

Zeke's eyes narrow. First at me and then at Hugo. "Shout when you need us, Bessie."

When, not *if*.

Whatever.

I take a breath as we watch the three of them head for the staircase without a glance back in our direction.

That happened so fast, I can't quite wrap my head around it. Is this how it's going to be now?

"Are you two okay?" Hugo asks.

"Never better," I reply, my snippy tone not meant for him.

"We'll be all right," Kash adds.

"Thanks for standing up for me. I would understand if you went with them. You'd be safer in a bigger group."

"No, they made this happen. Can we all agree not to go into any dark rooms again? Not loving those."

Hugo grins at me. "Where's your sense of adventure?"

I stare at him. "Lead the way, Hugo."

We walk the first floor of the castle, looking in every room and quietly calling Fergus's name. As a group of three we're pretty solid and have a good view in front and behind. Each of us takes a direction to keep an eye on as we move.

"Upstairs, I guess," Hugo says, approaching the servants' staircase in the kitchen that Odette used to be resting in.

Hugo eyes the countertop, blood the only evidence that she was ever there.

I tug his hand to get him to look away. There's so much blood in this castle.

"The others went upstairs. Do you think it's a good idea to follow?" Kash asks.

"I don't trust that they'll share information with us anymore," I tell them. "We should search for ourselves."

Hugo nods. "Agreed. I'll go up first. Watch and listen for anything."

He climbs the narrow staircase. I say a little prayer in my head and follow while Kash takes the back of the line.

THE PARTY | 209

At the top of the stairs, in the storage room, Hugo turns to us and asks, "Do you hear something downstairs?"

"Yeah, their footsteps, I think. That means they haven't found anything up here," I say.

"Still not going back." Kash walks past us.

Well, okay then.

She moves along the hallway casually as if we're just going for a stroll. "Kash, more looking over your shoulder, please!"

Hugo laughs. "She's reached the same conclusion I have. I just want this over."

What's that conclusion? That our fate is already sealed, so we don't need to be cautious? I can't let those thoughts enter my head.

"In here." Kash reaches for the door, at least having the sense to step back when she flings it open. My heart stalls for a beat.

Hugo walks inside first. "Doesn't look like anyone's here," he says, moving around the large white metal bed frame.

This room is painted baby blue, and going by the bed size and the pictures of fluffy white puppies on the walls, I think it was a child's bedroom. The furniture is gone, except for a large white cabinet that I can imagine used to store toys and board games.

"Wait, look at this," I say, crouching down to examine the scratches etched into the splintering wood floor.

Kash and Hugo approach; Hugo pushes his finger into the welts and disrupts sawdust.

"Some of these are newer than others."

"Right, like someone's been moving this cabinet recently."

"We're actually thinking there's a secret room behind there?"

Kash asks. "Because that would be totally fitting and *terrifying*. Also, if you suggest we go in there—"

"We have to go in there," I say. "Fergus could be . . . or it could be nothing."

Hugo laughs. "Who are you trying to kid, Bessie? It's obviously this guy's lair."

"Fine, but it could also be where Jia and Odette are."

No one has gone back into the bathroom to check on Abbas. I don't ever want to see that scene again, and that makes me feel incredibly guilty. We don't know if he's still there or has been taken.

"You know what's a better idea? Dressing in warm clothing and waiting outside by the bridge until the wind has died down, and yes, I know there is no bridge now, but you get what I mean. I think we're safer out there than in here. Fewer places for the killer to hide." Kash takes a breath, but she's not done. "Because I don't feel safe here."

"Well, we're not safe."

I whack Hugo's arm. "Not helping! Kash, you can wait here if you don't want to go in that room. There's a closet you can hide in until we've checked it out."

She tilts her head. "I'm not getting back in the closet."

"Hey, at least you still have your sense of humor," I tell her, smiling.

Despite her attempt at a stern expression, she giggles. "I'm going into the murder room with you. You're my best friend, my ride-or-die, remember?"

"I don't think that's the murder room," I reply.

Hugo stands and holds the side of the cabinet. "No, it's probably just where he hides the bodies."

Kash and I stand back. "He's terrible at motivational speaking," she whispers.

"True, but he's strong and has already saved me once."

"Did he fight the guy off?"

"No, but the pattern seems to be kill, let the body be discovered, then steal it. The person who attacked me could have assumed they'd killed us both."

"Are we going to stand around and chat, or shall we go in there?" Hugo asks.

Kash and I look up.

The cabinet is now open, on a hinge like a door. The only thing I can see is darkness. I groan, not wanting to do this at all. If it's the place where he's taken the bodies, do we really want to discover that? We don't know what he's done to them.

"Oh, I'm so not looking forward to this," I mutter, my pulse skittish.

We have no flashlight either, so we're going in without any vision whatsoever.

"We get the medal for bad decisions—I just want to point that out," Hugo says, moving into the dark.

He holds his hand out and I take it; I do the same for Kash. It's left me rather defenseless, so I hope they whack someone if they run at us. I don't want to let go of either of them.

"I don't know if I should hope Fergus is down here or not," Kash whispers.

Same. If he's there he's dead. If he's not we might be very soon.

"Steep steps," Hugo warns us.

I look down and can only just see the first one, the light from the window refusing to go any farther. Maybe we should do the same.

We descend the creepiest staircase in the world, losing all vision. If there was someone down there using the room as a base and a morgue, they'd need a light. My breathing shallows the farther down I go.

What did I say about not going back into dark rooms?

In front of me, Hugo's breathing also changes, evidence of his fear. He's going first, and we have no clue what we're about to walk into. I squeeze his hand to remind him that he's not alone.

Behind me, Kash whimpers, her hand trembling in mine but still holding me so tight my knuckles burn. It's a welcome distraction, to be fair.

"Whoa. Okay, I'm at the bottom," Hugo says.

I take the step after him, stomping the last one when I've reached the end. We're underground, and that's about all I can tell. The room is cloaked in darkness, I can't make anything out at all.

"What do we do now?" I whisper.

"We'll have to feel our way around," he replies.

Kash gasps. "No way! I'm not stumbling across them with my hands in the dark."

"Shh," I hush. "I don't think they're here. There's no smell. Other than mildew."

"Bessie's right, Kash. They're not in here. But that doesn't mean evidence of whoever's doing this isn't here."

It's a nice theory, but it's not like we're going to find a notebook with Oscar's name on it that details every kill. I wiggle my nose, the damp, moldy smell nearly making me sneeze.

"This really isn't the time, but does it make a difference if we do know?" I ask.

"It'd be good to clear my name, Bessie."

"Fair point. So . . . let's search."

Hugo drops my hand, but Kash doesn't. I'm not exactly in a hurry to get split up again so I shuffle forward with her, my free arm extended in front of me. I slowly wave it up and down and to the side, feeling for anything that could possibly help us.

We must move around the small, square room a hundred times searching. I run my hands along the rough exposed-brick wall again, and Hugo mutters something under his breath. The next thing I hear is his footsteps cross the little room, and then another muttered word.

"What happened?" I ask.

"I kicked something."

Kash gasps. "Tell me it's not one of our friends."

"No." I hear him move again. "Wait, I think it's a backpack. Let's get back upstairs. Watch your step; this was in the middle of the room."

Clever hiding it there since we've been sticking to the walls to navigate.

I've never been happier to leave a room before. We run up the stairs and back into the last of the daylight.

Hugo is holding a black bag. He sits down in the cute little kid's room and unzips it.

We're doing this right here, I guess.

Kash and I sit too, the three of us making a circle so we have eyes in every direction.

Hugo tips the bag upside down with absolutely no care for what could be inside.

"Old photos of the castle. That's what we risked our life for," Kash says as a pile of rectangle-shaped images drop to the floorboards.

"There might be more things in the bag," I tell her. "Be patient."

Hugo is rifling through it still, trying to find something useful. A couple of empty wrappers drift down. My frustration grows with every passing second that we don't find anything that could help us.

"Helpful," Kash murmurs.

So far we have photos and granola bar wrappers. The nice ones that Allegra eats because apparently all the others are full of artificial rubbish.

"What else is in the creep's bag of tricks?" Kash asks, staring up at the swirls in the ceiling.

"Jackpot," Hugo says, lifting out a clear ziplock bag that holds our phones. "Check them, see if any still have battery."

Kash sits up and grabs her phone after Hugo tips them out. I take mine and it's dead. It's been over twenty-four hours, and they

THE PARTY | 215

probably weren't fully charged when this asshole took them. "Oh my god."

I pick up the next one and the next.

"Oh my god, Fergus has battery! One percent but it's there."

"Call the cops," Kash says, as if I'm considering taking selfies on Snapchat first.

"On it." And I really am about to, but I spot a notification. My pulse thumps faster.

Kash and Hugo continue checking phones, and he reaches back into the bag.

I click on the chat, enter his password when prompted, grateful that he hasn't changed it, and glance at the last comment.

IT'S ON

My breath catches in my throat. It's at that moment the phone dies.

"No!" I tap the screen and press the side buttons, but it's absolutely useless. "No, no, no!"

"Oh, come on, Bess. It's dead?" Hugo asks.

"Yeah . . ." I look up, realizing what I've done. If the call had made it through to the operator, maybe someone would've come looking, but I had to read the message instead. "I—I was just about to dial."

Kash frowns, turning my way. "Dial? Wasn't it locked? You just hold down the side button."

"I know Fergus's code. Didn't think. I'm so sorry, guys."

"It's not your fault. It was a long shot. Didn't think anything would've been left on any of them."

"I don't suppose there are any chargers lying around anywhere," Kash says.

Hugo throws the stack of photos beside him. "I was hoping they'd be in the bag, but I suppose that would be too easy."

"It's okay."

I don't know what to think about that text message. There is more context needed, because without any punctuation it could be a statement or a question. It's a stretch, but it could be someone asking Fergus if the party is still on because of the storm. I hope.

It could be someone asking if the murder spree is on.

No way.

"I have a charger in Zeke's car," Kash says after a few moments of silence. "I know that's not helpful."

"Right, because if we go get that there's no way I'm swimming back to the Beauforts' castle of horrors." Also, we'd need to get the charger back here completely dry.

"Here," Hugo adds, reaching beside him with his head tilted. "I know we said these are old photos, but I'm not so sure. Take a look at this one."

He passes me the picture and leans over my shoulder.

"Oh my god, is that Fergus's car in the background?"

The photo is taken from the window in the turret, overlooking the grounds. In the corner is the side of Fergus's car. The license plate isn't visible, but it'd be a rather big coincidence if it was someone else's. Besides, his parents do own the castle.

"That's what I'm thinking," he replies. "Why would the killer have surveillance-style photos of Fergus's car hidden in his bag?"

"Exactly. When do you think it was taken?" I ask, staring at the photo.

"Must've been winter, given the lack of leaves on the trees."

"This past winter?"

"Fergus got the car last spring so it would have to be."

"Guess the season is a fun game and everything, but what does this tell us?" Kash asks. "Someone took photos of the castle and stuffed them in a bag with snacks."

"We don't know the why or who yet. But they must be relevant, or why hide them with our phones?"

Hugo scratches his jaw. "I've got nothing."

"Let me see the photos again," I say. "We must be missing something. Double-check the bag."

I lay the photos out and try to put them in some sort of order based on the trees. So apparently I am playing a game of guess the season.

"Anything?" Hugo asks.

"Not yet."

"Me neither. I'll look again. Why just keep photos, phones, and wrappers?"

"Check for broken seams in case anything is hidden inside."

Hugo stops, his eyes sliding across to me. "Excuse me?"

"It's a thing. Clearly you've never watched border control shows."

"What are we even going to do if we figure out who this is?" Kash asks.

"Well, I thought about staying away from them," Hugo retorts.

I roll my eyes at him. Though it would be nice to know precisely who to avoid, I'm just going to run from anyone who isn't in our group. "We can tell the police."

"We have to survive until then," Kash says, "and it doesn't look like the flood is receding. The stupid river's nearby. Why hasn't more been done to—"

"I have something here," Hugo says, digging his hand into the bag. "You were right, Bessie, there's a rip at the bottom that goes inside the bag."

Kash and I wait silently as he retracts his hand so slowly, I want to rip the bag out of his grasp and do it myself.

He holds up a folded piece of lined paper.

"Any chance that's the full details of whoever's evil plan?" Kash asks.

"Kind of," he whispers, his eyes darting between us. "It's a kill list. It looks like he's going in order . . . and, Bess, you're next."

19

I slam my hands down on the floorboards, my heart skipping a beat at hearing I'm supposed to be the next victim.

"Give me that," I demand, though I'm reaching out and snatching it before I realize I'm even moving.

My eyes widen as I stare at my name, written in beautiful cursive. Directly above my name is *Abbas,* then *Odette,* then *Jia.*

"Oh my god," I whisper, my voice hard as steel.

In my peripheral vision I see Hugo's hands curl into fists on his lap, his knuckles turning white. "This can't be about the development," he says. "So who here would want to kill us? Abbas and Odette had done *nothing.*"

I clear my dry throat. "No, but we need to figure out what someone else might think we've all done."

Kash, looking over my shoulder, says, "We're all on this list . . . all except Hugo."

"What?" Hugo snatches the note back, the thin paper almost tearing between my fingers. "I must be."

Kash glances my way, and her eyes tell me everything that she's thinking. I'm on the same page.

Hugo holds a palm up. "Hey, don't. This isn't me, and you both know that. Look, if I was doing this, I wouldn't leave my name off the list, would I? Think about it."

"I am thinking about it!" I say, noticing the desperate tone in his voice. "This is all I'm currently thinking about."

"I did *not* kill my friends. Or yours."

"All right."

"What?" Kash snaps. "All right? Are you serious, Bessie? He might be the killer. What if the other group is right? They said it was Hugo."

"I'm sitting right here," he says.

I wave his comment away. "Shut up a second. Kash, he's right. If you're writing a kill list and want to make someone look guilty, you leave that person off."

"It was hidden in the bag behind the seam! He never expected it to be found."

"Then why wouldn't I just say I didn't find anything?" he adds. "I was the one looking, so I could've said it was clear."

Kash opens her mouth and closes it again. It's an excellent point. Of course, he could be pulling a double bluff, but I don't think so. His reactions to Odette's and Abbas's deaths were genuine.

It's hard to accept that anyone you care about and have spent so much time with could want to hurt—*to kill*—you.

"Fine. Who would want to set him up, then?" she finally asks.

"It would have to be someone who doesn't like us but hates Hugo."

He snorts. "Everyone on the soccer team at school."

"I think this is bigger than the guys talking behind your back because you've worked them too hard, captain," Kash responds dryly.

"They talk behind my back?"

"Stop it, you two!"

We need to figure out who would want to frame Hugo. Hold on . . . oh my god. I might have the answer to this in my hoodie. The newspaper! I can't believe I forgot about finding that. It feels like that happened weeks ago.

I'm about to tell them about it when Hugo holds his hands up. "You believe me, right? The others think I'm a killer and . . ." He rakes his hands through his hair and takes a long breath. "I'm not the one doing this. I need you both to believe that."

"I believe you," I say, earning another look from Kash. She's not convinced and . . . I mean, *am I?*

Do I really believe Hugo over Fergus, Shen, Zeke, and Allegra? Fergus and Zeke have also been missing at different points during the weekend.

"Yeah, I believe you too," she adds with absolutely no conviction. "We should tell the others about the phones and photos. Not the list."

Hugo picks up a photo and studies it. "This is bothering me. Fergus was here when it was taken. Has anyone else been here before?"

"Allegra, obviously," I reply. "But everyone else said it was their first time."

"Could they be lying?"

I shrug. "I don't know why they would."

Kash slaps my arm with the back of her hand. "Shen knows his way around."

"So do you," Hugo says.

"I studied the floor plan," Kash replies. Shen never said that he did, all the times we've spoken about the trip at school. He even made a comment about my research when he saw me with the folder.

"Why did you study the floor plan?" Hugo asks.

Her gaze is razor-sharp as it slides from me to Hugo. "It's what I do. I've never gone anywhere without researching it ahead of time. I knew literally everything about St. Mary's before I arrived on my first day."

"But the plan you got is wrong—rooms are missing, including the one we just found this bag in. Didn't you say Allegra gave them to you?" I ask, feeling a knot forming in my stomach. I still haven't told them about the newspaper. If Hugo wasn't here, I would have by now.

"It was left on my bed. A printout of the floor plan and a map of the local area." Her eyes widen. "I assumed Allegra left it for me . . . but it could have been anyone."

Boys and girls are supposed to stick to their own dorms, no mixing whatsoever, but no one pays any attention to that rule. Allegra knows more about Kash's quirks and would be the one to think of giving her that information.

"Are you suspicious of Shen, Hugo?"

"He could've been the one who took these photos. So could

Allegra or Fergus. I think if anyone else was here before, it'd be Shen."

"I'm with you there, but there's one thing I will never believe. He couldn't kill Jia," I say, picking up another photo. "They've been friends since they were small, moved to the UK together. Ugh, it doesn't make sense for any of them to have done it. There's no motive. Why would anyone take these, and why keep them?"

"You think Fergus's car is a red herring?" Kash asks. "And the list?"

"Maybe. If someone was planning this, it would make sense to set someone else up to take the fall. Allegra has been planning the party long enough that the killer could have started their own plotting then."

"It's possible," Hugo says.

"The only person we know for sure was here when these were taken is Fergus. We have to work off of that. It's either him, which makes no sense, since his family owns this castle, or someone who's targeting him and you," I say, looking at Hugo.

"No offense, girls, but we're shit detectives."

He's not wrong. There's just not enough here to figure it out. We have to try, though; our lives quite literally depend on finding out for sure who we can and can't trust.

I have another piece of the puzzle in my damp hoodie in the ballroom and a gnawing feeling I can't put my finger on, something that's stopping me from speaking up.

What I know is that Fergus and Allegra wouldn't want the castle torn down or for its worth to decrease. Everything their parents own will eventually be theirs.

Shen wouldn't kill his oldest friend, and why would he care about the castle? If anything, he'd want it to rake in the money so he and Allegra could live happily ever after.

Hugo wouldn't kill his best friends.

Zeke . . . nope, no reason at all for him to do this. He's so laid-back and never really bothered by anything. Unless it's his soccer team losing.

The list is too personal for outsiders like the antidevelopment group.

One thing is for sure. I need to reevaluate everything I think I know about my friends, because as much as I don't think any of them have a motive, one of them obviously does.

"All right, look, we need to keep moving. Let's see if we can find Fergus and then pick a room to camp out in. We can go over everything again when we're safe," Hugo says, scooping the photos up and putting everything back in the bag.

When we're safe? When will that be?

"We should stay near the ballroom," I tell him. It'll be easier for me to sneak out and get the newspaper if we're close. I'll be able to hear if the others are in there, and I can pretend to go to the bathroom or, if I need to, wait until everyone is asleep.

"We'll stay next door," Hugo says, throwing the bag over his shoulder. "Come on."

He's not mentioned what happens if one of the others sees us with the bag, but at this point I don't think it matters. One of them would react to it anyway. Then we'd know, I suppose.

"It's silent," I whisper as we walk along the hallway to the stairs.

Hugo looks over his shoulder. "The others are probably moving around as quietly as they can too."

"They would tell us if they found something, right?"

He shrugs. "Maybe."

That maybe sounds a lot like no, but surely if they discovered the killer they would speak up.

We see nothing but an empty castle that is losing its beauty by the second, feeling dull and cold.

Now there is just death wherever I turn.

Hugo opens the door to the empty room next to the ballroom. It's relatively small, probably used by men to drink and smoke after dinner. The walls are a dark red at the top, with mahogany wood paneling on the bottom. There's a stone fireplace, but I don't know if it's safe to light a fire. There is no furniture left in here, and only a dark red velvet curtain on one side of the tall window.

"We'll need to grab our things, but we can stay in here," he says, dropping the bag.

"I'll get our stuff," I tell him a little too eagerly. I might as well mention my ulterior motive.

"I need the bathroom first. Stay with Kash and we'll all go after."

I nod, turning away so I can wince. What do I do now?

Grab the hoodie with my stuff and then sneak it to the bathroom, I guess. Kash might insist on coming with me, but I'm fine with that. I trust her.

"Back in a minute."

I turn to see Hugo walking out of the room, closing the door behind him.

"I can't believe we let him go alone." Kash is whispering, despite the fact that we're completely alone in here.

"He's gone to the toilet, Kash. I'm not joining him."

"If he takes longer than two minutes and another person turns up dead . . ."

"You still think it's him?" I ask.

"I don't know what to think, Bess. I don't trust him. He was asking me about the accident the night of the party. He's done that before, not long after it happened. But he asked again," she says. "We should go somewhere else, just me and you."

"He spoke to me about the accident a couple of times too," I admit. "Said that Raif was only at the party for a little while before he took me and Fergus home. Or attempted to. I found a newspaper article hidden in the castle—it was about the accident. But it's with my stuff in the ballroom."

Kash's jaw drops. "Whoa."

"What do you remember about that night?"

"I was too preoccupied to notice when Raif arrived, but I said bye to you when you guys were leaving. It was a normal night until the accident."

"How drunk was Fergus?" I ask.

She shrugs. "He was tipsy, but when isn't he at a party? Seemed fine, eyes glossy, walking in a straight line."

Hugo said Fergus was *hammered*.

"But why would Raif take us home if Fergus wasn't that bad? Why wouldn't he just nap at the party like he has a million times before. There are holes in that night. I don't remember it, but things don't make sense. Hugo knows more than he's saying."

Another flash of blood flicks in my mind too quickly for me to be able to figure out where it's from. But I think it's safe to assume it was the accident. Was I awake in the car for a little while?

"I'd ask you to message Raif, but that's not going to help."

"Something doesn't feel right," I say, the gnawing unease telling me to pursue this until I uncover the truth.

Could that night be connected to this weekend?

"Does anything feel right at the moment?" she asks.

"No, but I mean the night of the accident. I need to figure out the missing piece, Kash."

"You think more went down than just the accident?"

"Has to be. I just can't figure out what. Hugo's digging for a reason. Raif's reaction doesn't fit, considering we all forgave him."

"I always thought it was weird that you all lost your memory of that night. I know it happens but . . . *all* three of you."

"Hugo hinted at something similar earlier, about me and Fergus not remembering the accident."

Her brows shoot up like a cartoon character's. "Just you and Fergus? Do you think Raif remembers?"

I swallow a ball of nerves, wondering what I don't know about something I was involved in. "Maybe. I'm not sure what difference that would make."

"So why not just say that?"

I nod. "That's the problem I'm having too."

228 | NATASHA PRESTON

"You don't think something else could've happened before the wreck, do you?"

"You two okay?" Hugo asks, coming back into the room.

Kash and I startle and look up at the same time.

He laughs, not realizing exactly why we jumped. His arms are full of our bags and blankets. I hope my hoodie is among that stuff. "Sorry. I didn't mean to scare you."

"It's fine," Kash says, sounding so on edge that she's going to give us away. I don't want him to know we were discussing his brother.

What do you know, Hugo?

"Did you see any of the others?" I ask.

"They're all back in the ballroom . . . talking about me. Stopped while I picked up our things."

Thank god they're okay.

My back straightens as I take my backpack and sleeping bag. "What?"

"Apparently because I came to this party instead of the other one, that means I'm guilty." He sits down and takes a can of Pringles out of his bag.

"Did you really come just because you didn't like the guest list of the other one?" Kash asks.

He pops a Pringle in his mouth and chews, watching Kash with careful eyes. I sense there will also be a careful answer coming.

"Yes," he replies when he swallows. "Why is everyone acting like it's so out of character for this to happen? I've been to tons of Allegra's parties. You've also attended parties of people in different years. It's really not that big of a deal."

"You used to come to a lot of them with Raif."

I freeze at Kash's words.

More than anything I want to know what happened that night . . . but on the flip side, I'm terrified to find out if something else went down. What could it be, though? Was there an argument?

We didn't agree to confront him, and I think that's where she's going. Using the bulldozer approach rather than going in softly and reading between the lines.

"He doesn't want to come anymore. You know that, Kash." He pops another Pringle.

"Does he remember?" she asks, the bulldozer now out of park.

"What?" He frowns but doesn't look as surprised by her question as I thought he would. "No, I told you that. None of them do."

"Strange, isn't it?"

"Where are you going with this, Kash? I can't handle all the accusations people are throwing around."

She shrugs. "I'm just wondering what you're hiding."

Oh, all right.

I wince, looking between Kash and Hugo.

Usually I would intervene, but I am unsure of what to say, rooted by fear that I could learn something I won't like.

That night changed everything, and Hugo has started bringing it up after nearly a year. I need to know.

"I'm not hiding anything, Kash."

"I think you are."

"I wasn't there that night . . . but you were."

"What's that supposed to mean?"

I don't remember saying goodbye to Kash that night. It's a black hole.

He puts the lid on the Pringles. I take the opportunity to check my hoodie. It's in a plastic bag with my other wet clothes.

I reach my hand into the pocket and my breath catches.

It's gone.

"It means stop doubting me when you were the one at the party."

"I wasn't in the car, Hugo!"

I zone out, only half hearing their argument. It feels like a disagreement that will go around in circles and get nowhere anyway. The newspaper was in the pocket of my hoodie. It was shoved in there tight and couldn't accidentally fall out. Someone took it.

I glance up, trying to keep the panic from my face.

Who knew this was here? I was alone when I found it and told no one. By the time I took the hoodie off I'd forgotten about it due to being attacked outside.

Could Hugo have seen it when he helped me inside?

Anyone else could have, since I just discarded the hoodie on the floor. I've read plenty about that night, and each article is the same report of the accident, so I don't know how this is relevant to what's happening now.

"Just tell us!" Kash shouts. "You're not fooling anyone."

I jump at the sudden volume. What the hell did I miss?

Kash is standing, eyes narrowed and hands on hips. "Come on, Hugo. You're playing games."

"I'm not the one playing anything."

"Then who is?"

"You're paranoid, Kash. Calm the hell down!"

"Not until you tell us what you know, because right now it looks like *you're* involved in this."

I stand, dropping my damp hoodie. "Shh! The others can probably hear you."

"Stay out of this, Bessie. You clearly want to sit back and let this go," Kash snaps.

What. The. Hell. When did I become her enemy in this?

"Kash," I mutter.

Her face reddens. That perfect composure she usually has is gone. "No, I'm so fed up. Let's just get it all out, because the secrets are quite literally killing us!"

"You're the one currently tearing us apart," Hugo says, turning his nose up at her.

"Fuck you, Hugo."

"That all you have? Seriously?"

Oh my god. I look up to the ceiling, having no idea how this escalated so quickly. The stress is making us doubt each other, turning us against each other.

"I need the bathroom," Kash says, balling her hands. "No one follow me."

"Whoa, bad idea. I'll come," I say quickly, moving closer to her.

"No! I don't want you to, Bessie. Grow a spine and then you can come."

"Kash."

"Seriously, give me a minute."

Hugo blocks my way with his arm as I try to follow her. "Don't. Just let her go."

"She can't go alone." I push his arm, but he steps in front of me as Kash leaves the room. "It's not safe!"

"Door's open and we'll listen out for her. It's two doors down. Let her have a minute."

I take a breath and shake my head, tears prickling my eyes. "Do you think she meant what she said?"

"No. I think she's scared, and not having answers is playing with her mind."

"You would tell me if there was something you knew about the night of the accident, wouldn't you?" I ask.

His shoulders slump. "Of course I would. I'm trying to figure it out too."

20

"It's been too long," I say, chewing on my bottom lip and standing in the same spot I've been in since Kash left.

"Three minutes," Hugo says, watching me from the other side of the doorframe.

The bathroom door is just out of view, but if she came out of it, we'd have seen her walk into the hallway. I'm sure of it.

"Do you think the others are still in the ballroom?" I ask.

Hugo frowns and glances at the wall as if he's forgotten. "I haven't heard them in a while."

"I don't like this. Kash is alone," I say, unable to sit back any longer. Something awful could have happened to her. I dash out of the room, running along the hallway.

"Bessie, no!"

I sprint, almost not stopping myself in time and smacking into the door. "Kash, are you there?"

Hugo turns up a second later and knocks. "Kashvi?"

Why isn't she answering us?

I try the handle and it opens straightaway to an empty room. My stomach falls away. She's gone. Where? "How did we not see?"

"Bessie," Hugo says, his voice icy. "The window."

"Oh my god."

The window is open.

"Wait." Hugo grabs my arm as I go to run. "Stop. I don't think she went out there."

"Why? It's open for a reason."

"Just hold up."

I want to shake him as he moves deeper into the room. "Look, something is off here. The sill is covered in dust."

He's right. If Kash went out there, she would have disturbed the dust. There's no way she could have gone out otherwise.

"All right, but how did she get out, Hugo?"

"She didn't want us to see."

"But we would have."

"Would we?" he says. "If she only opened the door enough to slip out and kept her back to the wall, she could have got away unnoticed."

"Damn it! Why would she do that? I don't understand."

If she was taken, she would've made noise. Why make it appear as if she fled through the window? Why not make it more realistic by disturbing the dust?

She must've been panicked and in a hurry.

"She thinks I'm a killer," Hugo says.

That would be reason for her to sneak away . . . but she also left *me*.

"I feel sick," I mutter.

"I'm checking the ballroom."

"Well, she didn't go there. We would've seen that!"

Hugo doesn't listen; he walks away from me.

I clench my clammy hands, wondering what to do because I don't have long to decide. Kash isn't in here, she's somewhere else in the castle. So risky—she must be scared and totally convinced that it's Hugo.

Kash is beyond smart, but when she's in a fight-or-flight mode she doesn't think *at all*.

Hugo reaches the ballroom door and I turn on my heel, running away from him. I get to the end of the hall and around the corner before I hear him shout my name.

Keep going.

I don't stop. I run up the stairs, unsure whether I should stay with Hugo. My head, still tender from the attack, begins to throb again. All I know is that I need to be with Kash.

My chest tightens. I press my hand to my heart and try to breathe through the panic. The total loss of control is beginning to pull me under.

I sprint around the corner, without a clue where I'm going—my mind filled with fear and the desire to keep moving—when arms curl around my body and a hand presses over my mouth.

I try to scream, but the palm is too tight. "Shh, Bess. It's only me. It's Zeke. I'm going to let go, but please don't scream. Okay?"

Whimpering, I nod in his grasp and he drops his hands.

I spin around and hold my hands up, tears rolling down my cheeks. "What the hell are you doing?"

"Why are you alone? That's a *bad* move."

"Answer me!" I cry.

"All right. I was looking for Fergus and saw you. I hate that you and Kash are alone with Hugo." He folds his arms and arches a brow in a way that almost makes me laugh. That might be what he was going for. "Now do I get an answer?"

"Fergus still isn't back?"

Hugo made it sound like they were all together again.

"No. What happened with you?"

"Um." I shake my head, my mind reeling. "Kash and Hugo had an argument. She said she was going to the bathroom but took off, made it look like she'd gone out the window. I'm not sure what's going on, but I need to find her."

"What did they argue about?" he questions.

"The situation," I reply. It's not a total lie, but I don't know what to tell him. My trust in nearly everyone has gone. "You were in the ballroom?"

He nods. "We were, but we came out to check if Fergus was back. You should join us."

"Can we *all* come?"

"They're not going to let Hugo in."

"Then this is pointless," I say, running my hands over my face. God, I'm exhausted, and my mind is filled with bloody images, smashed glass, and more questions than answers. "I need to find Kash and Fergus."

"I'm coming with you."

He jogs to catch up as I move past him. I want to tell him to leave me, but it's not his fault that he doesn't know who to trust either.

"Allegra has a theory," Zeke says.

"Of course she does."

"It's about Raif."

"Raif is fine, Hugo said it himself," I reply, wanting to confide in him but not knowing if that's a good idea.

"If he was fine, he wouldn't have moved to another school and cut all of us out of his life. I wasn't even in the car and he's blocked me. You don't do that if you're fine."

"He's overwhelmed with guilt," I tell him as we take a left, heading toward the kitchen. There are more places she could hide there, and I think she would be smart about her dramatic exit.

"Hugo tell you that?"

"Why would he lie?"

Zeke opens the kitchen door and we both freeze.

The air leaves my lungs. Lying on the floor in a pool of blood is Hugo.

"What the . . . !" Zeke shouts and turns around, his head in his hands.

On the floor, Hugo's fingers twitch as if he's trying to force his body to move.

I startle and run toward him, dropping to my knees by his chest. "Hugo! He's not dead, Zeke. Help me!"

Zeke runs back and feels around, patting his body and looking for the source of the bleeding.

"Here!" I say, finding a wound spilling blood from his side. "I'm putting pressure on it, but we need something more permanent."

When did he get up here? It's only been about five minutes max. I shouldn't have left. He was coming to look for me.

This is my fault. I doubted him and now he's injured.

Zeke shrugs off his jacket and pulls his T-shirt over his head. The cotton rips easily between his fists. "I'll lift him while you tie this around his waist. *Tight*, okay?"

I nod and hold the shirt ready. Zeke lifts Hugo's chest, only managing to get him a couple of inches off the ground, but it's enough. Hugo groans, baring his teeth as I tie the shirt around him, double-knotting it.

"We might need something better," I say.

"Yeah, there must be a first aid kit somewhere if builders were here. I'll help you get him back and then I'll go look. They were in the servants' kitchen."

"Zeke, we still haven't found Kash, and the others should know that Hugo is innocent."

He frowns. "If she was here, wouldn't she have heard something? Hugo must've made a noise when he went down, even if he didn't see his attacker."

"The only thing that matters right now is helping Hugo and finding Kash and Fergus. Where are Shen and Allegra?"

"Went to check the top floor."

"When was the last time you saw them?"

Zeke sighs. "I'm not arguing with you. Hugo, mate, can you hear me?"

I press my palm to his chest, feeling the steady rise and fall. Zeke touches his chest and nods.

Pulse and breathing are both strong.

Thank god.

Hugo groans and murmurs, "St-stabbed."

"We can see that, mate. Do you think you can stand?"

He nods at Zeke and tries to sit up, gritting his teeth through the pain. "I don't think it's deep, but wow it hurts."

"I have some painkillers in my bag. Ibuprofen is good for stab wounds, I'm sure," I joke, making him chuckle and then wince. His face is almost gray. "Sorry. Did you see who did this?"

"Bastard jumped me from behind. I didn't have the chance to look. I'm okay, I think it was more of a shock. I can walk."

"You're probably still in shock, Hugo. We'll help you."

Zeke and I get him to his feet, and he's able to hold a surprising amount of his own weight. It must hurt like hell.

"Zeke, you need to tell the others."

"Yeah." Hugo grunts as we start walking.

Hugo was attacked in the hallway. That means that the killer is getting braver. Maybe a little more desperate. The storm is passing, so that must mean he's getting closer to losing his list of targets.

I was supposed to be next, so is the list a red herring? Nothing is quite what it seems and it's giving me a headache.

We shuffle slowly along the hallway.

"In here," Zeke says, nodding toward the ballroom.

"We can't."

"Hugo's hurt, and we have more supplies. They're going to know they were wrong about him." Zeke side-eyes Hugo. "I was wrong too."

"Thanks."

Zeke kicks the door open.

Shen and Allegra both gasp as we guide Hugo along, though he's doing most of the work now. That has to be a good sign. I think I would scream the entire world down if I was stabbed.

"What happened?" Allegra asks, leaping to her feet.

I'm so happy to see them, but there's still no Fergus and that's making me feel sick.

Shen, noticing blood seeping through the T-shirt, runs to the pile of bags. I hope he has a first aid kit in there.

"Where's Fergus?" I ask, my voice desperate.

"I don't know. Where's Kash?"

"Missing. I ran into Zeke on my way to find her. We found Hugo first."

I turn to Hugo, who splutters. "You're going to be okay," I say. But the words have only just left my mouth when his head lolls to the side.

21

"Hugo!" I shout, hoping I can get him to respond. "Hugo!"

"Put pressure on it, Shen. I'll get the first aid kit out of your bag," Allegra says.

"Does anyone have a charger? We found the phones but they're all drained," I tell them, kneeling in front of Hugo. I keep my head down, but my eyes are watching the others, gauging their reactions.

Allegra's mouth drops open and she momentarily freezes with the first aid kit tight in her hand. Shen and Zeke turn to me so sharply I'm surprised they don't have whiplash.

"Where's Kash?" Shen asks. "I need her."

"I don't know. I was looking for her, but we found Hugo," I explain.

"I'm here!"

I look up to see Kash running into the room. I want to leap up and hug her, but I can't leave Hugo's side.

"Kash," I say, the relief nearly making me cry.

"I'm sorry," she says, taking the first aid kit and looking at Hugo. "What happened?"

"He was stabbed," I tell her. "What happened to you?"

"I couldn't stay. I'm sorry, Bess. It all got to be too much, and I panicked. I was hiding out when I heard you and Zeke. Part of me wanted to hide there and protect myself but I couldn't," she says, turning her attention from me to the job she needs to do.

"I have a charger in my car," Zeke says as we step back to allow Shen and Kash to help Hugo.

"Hugo, can you hear me?" Shen asks, pressing on the wound. There doesn't seem to be a lot of blood, even when we first found him, so I hope that means it wasn't deep.

He frowns and opens his eyes. "Hurts."

"Lie still, mate, you have a stab wound."

"I can feel it," he says through gritted teeth, his eyes finding mine. I don't know if he heard me telling them about the phones. It's not really the most important thing right now.

"It's okay," I tell him, referring to what we found as well as his welfare. I'm not about to give them the list. We all know we're in trouble here. Kash isn't ready for the fallout of that one either.

"Okay, this isn't too bad," Shen says, peering at the wound as he releases pressure. "How is the pain?"

"Like a six."

"You might get away without needing stitches. There are some suture strips in the bag. The bleeding has stopped."

"Already?" I ask when Hugo throws his forearm over his eyes.

"You're rather dramatic for someone who has just been told a little bit of tape will make it better."

He doesn't move his arm, but he does grin. "You're full of sympathy, Bess, thanks."

I take his free hand in mine because although I joke, I was petrified that he was going to die.

Shen grabs the strips, holding gauze ready to wrap the wound.

I peek as he works, his hands moving with efficiency. He'll be a fantastic doctor. They both will.

Shen and Kash lay three strips on the wound. It looks just like a neat red line. Hugo was so lucky, because it looks like the knife caught him with the side of the blade rather than going in straight.

"How deep is it?" Zeke asks.

Shen flicks his eyes up for a second. "Not deep. He's fine."

"It won't need stitching if it's already stopped bleeding, surely."

"Wouldn't think so, but we're not actually doctors, Zeke," Kash says.

"Give them space," Allegra says, pulling Zeke back. "We need to patch him up, find a charger, get my brother, and get help."

"Where did you find the phones? The chargers weren't with them?" Zeke asks.

"Found them in a room upstairs." Not a lie. "I'm not even going to dignify your charger question with a response."

"Okay, Hugo, I'm going to need you to sit up, but do it slowly. I'm going to bandage the wound too, but if you take it easy, it shouldn't open up again," Shen says.

He supports Hugo's arm to take some of the pressure off him. "Okay?" Shen asks.

"Burns." Hugo puts his hands behind him to rest. Shen wraps the bandage around his stomach, going round and round until he reaches the end.

"It's getting dark out," Zeke says. "We should stay here. Sleep in shifts."

"No way! I'm not napping in here while my brother is out there!"

"Allegra, think about it. Fergus has been gone awhile and in that time—"

"No, Zeke. I know what you're about to say and you're wrong."

Shen approaches Allegra with caution, palms raised as if he's expecting her to attack. I think she might. She's been uncharacteristically quiet recently.

"Listen to him."

She steps back, waving him away. "Oh my god, you think Fergus is the killer too?"

"No one thinks that," I interject, trying to save Shen from being at the top of her hate list. "I know Fergus would never hurt any of us. You know we can't risk our lives. If we want any chance of getting out, then we need to stay here and wait for morning."

She shakes her head, tears spilling down her cheeks. "He's my brother."

"I love him too, Allegra," I say, getting to my feet and wrapping her in a hug, the potential loss of Fergus too much to even think about. Him being the killer is even worse. "He would be telling us to stay here."

The way she holds on to me shows her fear. I don't know if that's because she thinks he's in danger or if she's starting to consider that he might be doing this.

She lets go and wipes her tears. "All right. I'll stay. But if I hear him shout, I will not sit here."

"None of us will," Shen says. "Come on, we'll grab something to eat, go to sleep, and get the hell out of here at first light."

Allegra lets Shen pull her to the bed she made.

I look around the depressing room and bite my lip. Now that we're all back together I don't know how much to share. They don't seem to have found out anything. Or they did and have decided to keep it from us.

"You okay?" Kash whispers.

Zeke and Hugo are sitting on the windowsill, looking out across the gardens. With the light fading it's harder to play lookout; all I can see is their reflections.

Neither of them has changed yet and both have blood on them.

"I was so worried about you."

"I'm sorry."

"I still don't understand."

"I just couldn't stay. All these thoughts were screaming in my head, and nothing made them stop. I thought Hugo was going to kill us. I went to the bathroom and splashed water on my face. I heard a noise and realized it could be him or anyone. I know it's stupid now, but at the time I just needed to make it look like I'd run. Which I did."

"You wanted the killer to think you'd gone outside."

She shrugs, her cheeks turning red. "It wasn't a good plan, but it was the best I could come up with in the seconds I had. I really am sorry that I left you."

"It's okay. Did you see anything while you were hiding?"

"Only the inside of a cupboard. Cowardly, I know."

"Actually, it was probably the smart thing to do."

Considering it could be anyone.

"Fergus or Hugo. Has to be one of them, right? I just can't figure it out," I say.

"Not now. We show them the phones but nothing else. I'm going to figure out who gave me the plans. You need to work on the night of the accident."

I let her walk away, because it's pointless arguing. My memory of that night isn't coming back. Raif won't take my calls. Fergus is . . . somewhere.

I'm so completely exhausted I can barely keep my eyes open.

"I'll take the first watch," Zeke says. "The rest of you should get some sleep."

"It's not late," Shen replies.

"But who knows what's going to happen next? We should get some rest while we can. Hugo certainly needs it."

"Yeah, good idea. Come on, Allegra, let's sleep. Wake me in an hour, Zeke, and I'll take over," Shen says.

Hugo winces, stepping down from the window as if he needs to prove that he's still capable. The wound might be little more than a graze, but it still hurt him. The fear of dying probably made it worse. "I'll grab our stuff. Again."

Shen leaps to his feet. "Hold up. I'll come with you before I rest."

"All right, we were just next door."

I yawn, running my hands through my hair, and wait for my bedding.

When Hugo and Shen return, they pass Kash our stuff, the bag nowhere to be seen. I assume Hugo would have stuffed it inside his things to hide it from Shen.

I lay my head on my pillow, my limbs and eyelids so heavy that I don't even care what anyone has to say about the phones. I yawn again and close my eyes.

Gasping, I sit up, wrapped in my sleeping bag.

"It's okay, Bess."

Startled, I spin around to see Hugo sitting on the windowsill.

"God," I say, running my hands over my face, trying to wake myself up. My body is heavy as lead and just wants to lie down again. "Did you sleep at all?"

"I got a couple of hours. Sun's just starting to rise, so I was about to wake everyone else."

I look over my shoulder, watching everyone else sleep for a few seconds, making sure they're not listening. I can't believe I slept so long, but I was physically and mentally done.

"You have the bag?" I whisper.

"It's hidden. Everyone has their phones back. Yours is by your pillow," Hugo says.

It's pointless without any charge. Might as well be my little cousin's plastic one.

"Have you heard anything from Fergus?"

"Not a word. Kind of pissed at him for this," he says, pointing to his side. He's changed clothes and his complexion is nearly back to usual.

"You didn't see him," I say.

"No, but come on, Bess."

No.

"Hey, guys," Zeke says, stretching out. "I'm ready to get the hell out of here."

"Not before coffee," Hugo says, getting to his feet and walking over to the little kitchen area.

Allegra and Shen wake up when Hugo begins to boil the kettle.

"Fergus?" Allegra says.

I shake my head and get to my feet. "Sorry."

Her shoulders slump. "We're going to find him."

"Of course, we will," Shen replies.

I walk to the window and watch the sun peek between the trees, making the flooded grounds glisten. It's a beautiful day to escape hell. There are some dark clouds just noticeable in the distance but it's nice here . . . for now, anyway.

Zeke steps beside me. "Another break in the rain."

Smiling, I glance up at him. "I'm taking that as a good omen. You still want to swim across that?" I ask as the sun rises over the horizon. Sunday morning. The wind is still raging, debris from trees flying across the lawn. It's hard to remember how pristine the lawn used to look.

"More than I want to spend another day in this castle," Zeke replies.

Fair point.

"Do you think Hugo will be okay?"

"Apparently the bandage is water-*resistant*, so I don't think his wound will stay dry, but we'll take him straight to the hospital."

Kash nods, nudging me. "I like that idea. Swim. Cars. Hospital. I'm never coming back to the countryside ever again."

It's not the countryside that's trying to kill us, but I understand. I'm ready to spend the rest of my life in the city too. I detest castles.

"Coffee's ready," Shen says. "Grab something to eat. We might have another long day." He's trying so hard to be upbeat and encouraging, but the fear in his voice shines through.

"How do we get across the moat in the wind?" Allegra asks.

"We go in together. Stay close. When Fergus, Zeke, and I fell in, we very quickly lost each other. I was ahead of them on the bridge but somehow behind them soon after entering the water."

Kash's eyes dart to the window. She's not the strongest swimmer, despite our weekly lessons at school, but she can make it. She has to.

The person I'm most worried about is Hugo. He shouldn't get his wound wet at all, and here we are about to take him swimming in a dirty moat.

"Hugo is going to get an infection," Kash says.

"Thanks for the confidence you have there," he replies sarcastically, picking up a coffee.

"It's just a fact. You go in dirty water with an open wound and you get an infection. Our priority when we get over the other side must be getting to a hospital."

Shen nods his agreement. "Hopefully more people will be on the road, since the storm is passing."

"If the roads aren't flooded and blocked," Allegra says.

"There will be someone out there. Emergency services, at least."

We just need one person to help us. As long as they can call the police and get Hugo to the hospital, those who won't fit in the car can stand on the side of the road and wait. We can do this.

I take a mug of coffee and a granola bar, consuming both without even tasting them, knowing I will need the calories if I'm going to run and swim. My stomach wants to reject the food, but I force it down with a grimace.

No one says much, all of us in our own worlds, trying to put all the pieces together. I do briefly wonder if we all come to the same or similar conclusion. Do we all suspect Fergus? Hugo? Me?

I suppose it doesn't really matter at this point, we're so close to getting away. I can wait for answers.

Allegra and Shen, first to finish eating, go to the bathroom along the hall. I can't see Kash wanting to go alone again. At least I hope not.

I gaze outside as I chew my last bite, the texture like cardboard. It's only when I throw the green wrapper in the bin that it hits me. This is the same bar as the ones found in the bag.

Allegra's favorites. Can that really be a coincidence?

"Anyone else need to use the bathroom?" I ask, giving Kash a look.

"I do," she replies.

"You should have someone else with you," Zeke says, looking around the nearly empty room.

"Allegra and Shen are out there. We'll group up with them. You should stay with Hugo. Come on, Kash."

I grab her hand and pull her along, a chill sliding down my spine. She nearly spills her coffee, managing to put it down on the side table before I drag her out of the room.

"What's gotten into you?" she asks as we look down the long hallway.

"It's clear." I jog past the bathroom, not hearing any voices inside, but I think Shen will have his hands over his ears and his eyes closed as Allegra pees.

"Bess, what are you doing? The bathroom is back there. Bess?"

"I'll explain, just come with me." I pull her up the staircase; she lets me, but I can tell her patience is running thin.

"Bessie!"

"Trust me!"

She goes quiet as I lead her up to the very top floor, putting as much distance between us and Allegra as humanly possible.

I open a random door at the end of the hallway, not even remembering what's inside but knowing it's not the turret where Odette was pushed.

After a second to be sure no one is inside, I pull her in and close the door behind us.

"I just ate one of those granola bars we found in the bag!" I tell her as if that will explain absolutely everything that's just exploded in my head, unraveling like the conclusion of a movie.

"Those were wrappers. What are you talking about?"

"Oh my god, not the exact ones. Allegra didn't have any in the ballroom, so I didn't think she had them with her here. But she must have because *I just ate one.*" I'm breathing so hard that my head is dizzy.

"Calm down so you can explain, Bess. I'm only loosely following this."

I take a breath to settle the unfair frustration I feel toward her for being so slow to catch up. "Kash, those particular bars weren't with all the food until this morning. I think while Allegra was setting up her things in the ballroom after our night in the girls' room, she accidentally put them with the rest of the food. Maybe she was hiding them."

"Why?"

"Because they were in that secret bag with the phones and photos."

"So you're saying Allegra is getting mixed up with her party bag and kill bag? You think she's behind all this? She might have kept them back because she didn't want to share. Bess, it's a stretch."

"Okay. I'm aware that I'm probably forcing connections, but letting something slip could be deadly. What if I'm right?"

"Allegra? Really?"

"Her and someone else."

"I'll go with it for now. Fergus?" she asks.

"I don't know. . . ." I really don't want to believe he could be part of it. "He said he wanted the castle, so I'm not sure how murdering his friends in it will achieve that. He can't have it if he's in prison, and there's no way the killer has done all of this killing and moving bodies without leaving DNA evidence behind. Fergus is far too intelligent and levelheaded for that."

She tilts her head. "Right. But Allegra is arrogant enough to think she can get away with it. Why, though?"

"We only thought she wouldn't want to live here because of the location—and how dated it is—but what if that's what she wants us to believe? She's smart enough to come up with a brilliant plan but hotheaded enough to execute it poorly."

I put my hands on my head and pace, the pieces finally slotting into place. "Think about it. Jia's murder was clean; we would've believed it was an accident if it wasn't for the phones. Odette's too. But we were fighting back and looking for clues, all of us ready to out the killer. Her plan was falling apart, she didn't expect us to fight so hard, didn't expect we'd start finding her hiding places. Abbas's murder was horrific, a total loss of control."

"All right. Could she be doing this alone? Just her losing control?" Kash speculates.

"I don't think she was ever completely alone, was she? Shen never said anything about losing her for a while."

"I think you just answered your own question."

"Allegra and Shen."

She nods slowly. "They want the castle. If they kill everyone, no one will want to live here. Her dad won't sell. She'll inherit."

I feel the blood drain from my face. "Oh my god, do you think that means they've killed Fergus?"

"No way . . . her twin."

My heart beats faster and a cool sweat breaks out over my neck and palms. "But he's the last hurdle. With him alive she will only inherit fifty percent, Kash. He could be hurt somewhere or even dead!"

I press my hands to my chest, my lungs freezing like ice. It's a feeling I know all too well. A panic attack is coming.

Kash senses it straightaway. "Whoa, whoa, calm down. Come on, breathe. In for three, out for five. He's alive until proven otherwise, okay? Bess, we'll find him. That's it. In through your nose. Out through your mouth. Good."

No, I am most certainly not okay, but I manage to suck in enough oxygen, dispersing the dancing dots in front of my eyes. Kash comes back into sharp focus, and I nod. "I'm okay."

"Good, you—" She pauses and turns to the door. "What's that?"

Footsteps out in the hallway echo into the room as if the person is already inside.

"They haven't called out," I whisper, which means we absolutely do not either.

Kash gasps, "Bessie."

"Shh," I hush, pressing my hand over her mouth.

They're coming.

Pure fear reflects in her wide eyes when I face her.

"It's the killer." Her voice is barely audible through my fingers.

"We're going to get away. We just need to be quiet and listen."

Keep yourself together.

There is no longer any time for me to freak out.

She nods and I remove my hand, satisfied that she's not going to panic and run screaming.

We're in one of the small shower rooms. Tiles have been drilled from the walls, a hole in the floor where the pipes to the sink used to be. There's still a toilet and shower but neither one is usable given their decayed state.

"We should just wait here," she whispers.

"There's nowhere to hide if he comes in. We need to get back to the ballroom with Hugo and Zeke. If Allegra and Shen aren't there, it will confirm what we know."

If nothing else, there is light and things we can use as weapons.

"I don't want to go out there, Bessie."

It's not at the top of my list either. Our options are limited, and things have changed. A lot. Allegra is *angry*.

"Bess, let's just hide against this wall so if they open the door, we'll be behind it."

"I only hear one set of footsteps. And whichever one of them comes into the room? They'll see us in an instant."

"I'm not going."

"Shh."

I press my ear to the door, the distant thud of footsteps echoing along the hallway. I think they're getting farther away . . . and closer again.

"Oh my god, is she coming back?" she mutters.

I hold my hand up, telling her to shut up because it's difficult enough to hear with the wind rattling the window frame and my pulse thumping.

"I can't hear anything," I say. "I think he or she or they are gone, so we should make a run for it."

Kash starts to shake her head, so I grab her hand. "Hey, we can't stay here. We have nothing to defend ourselves with."

"The tile. We can use broken pieces. Some are sharp and will make good weapons. Out there we can be hunted. We're safer in here. Two against one. We can charge at the same time."

So only one of us will get stabbed. Great.

She shakes her head, tears in her eyes. "Please, Bessie. I can't go out there. We'll either die or find another friend dead. I don't want to see what happened to Fergus!"

Neither do I. I'm not sure how I would recover from seeing him dead.

Was this how panicked she got when she ran from us earlier?

"All right. I get it. Okay, I want you to get the sharpest tile you can find and hide against the wall."

"Whoa, you're leaving me?"

"We can't all be split up, Kash. I'll get Hugo and Zeke and bring them back here."

She grabs my wrist when I turn to leave. "Bessie, no. It's not safe. What if Hugo's with them! I know you think we have it all figured out but there's still something majorly off with him. Not to mention the fact that he's escaped the killer twice with only minor injuries."

That stops me dead in my tracks. How would Hugo fit in with Allegra, though?

"Oh my god, this is giving me a migraine."

"We're on our own."

"No. Look, if you're right about Hugo being involved, he'll find a way to separate himself from us."

That's what's happened all along. The only issue we have is everyone has been missing at some point, some alone and some with another incriminating person. I can't say for sure that only Hugo has been away from the group when a murder has taken place.

"Bessie, you're going to die," she rasps.

"Come with me, then. We'll take the tile like you want and do this together."

She shakes her head, tears finally rolling down her cheeks. I can see her fading right in front of me. Kash is independent and strong but also compassionate and sensitive. I've never seen her so shattered before. "I *can't* go out there again. Please don't make me."

I'll admit that kind of stings. She thinks I'm going to be killed if I leave but won't come to help. But I suppose it's no different than asking her to come with me and risk her life . . . and she's *so* scared.

"Keep your back against that wall and don't make a sound," I tell her. "I *will* come back for you."

She dips her chin, shaking her head. "I'm sorry."

"You're scared. It's okay."

"Don't leave me for long, and please be careful." She grabs my wrist. "Don't trust Hugo either."

"I'll find the others and come straight back."

I reach for the door handle, my lungs like deflated balloons. That'll work in my favor; I thought I was going to start hyperventilating.

"Be careful," she murmurs again as I push the handle down and slowly pull the door.

The hallway is dark, only one window right at the very end to give any light. Which isn't doing a very good job, since those dark clouds have caught us. The first drops of rain hit the glass.

Damn it.

The dimness might be good for disguise, but the hallway is long and full of rooms that could possibly house a murderer.

I pull the door closed behind me, glancing up and down to make sure I'm alone.

My stomach clenches. I'm completely alone.

Be brave. Keep moving.

The footsteps have disappeared, but I'm not certain where they went. I move sideways so I can watch both directions someone could rush me from, slightly crouched so I'm ready to react. Watching me would probably be comical, since I resemble a bloody crab.

At the end of the hallway, I stop to listen before turning toward the stairwell. The layout of the castle is now ingrained in my memory as well as Kash's. With the exception of any other secret rooms Allegra didn't want us to know about.

I'm met with only the sound of wind shaking the castle windows and the sudden torrent of rain.

I need to get down two flights of stairs without being seen or heard. Which feels like an easy task right now, because the castle is a ghost town. It's so quiet I wouldn't be surprised if no one else is in the building anymore.

The stairs are in the middle of a large foyer, rooms around them. I creep closer to the railing and peer over, looking down at the floor below. Only the foyer on that level and a small square of the first floor are visible, but both are clear.

It's too quiet.

I take a breath and glance over my shoulder to make sure no one is behind me. Also with a little bit of hope that Kash is following after all.

The hallway is still empty, other than a spindly black spider on the wall.

She's hiding on the top floor, farthest from where I'm about to be. It'd take too long to reach her if she was attacked.

I tiptoe along the railing, keeping my eyes on the stairs and floors below. All I have with me is the butter knife still in my hoodie pocket. I should've taken a shard of tile; they're a lot sharper.

When I reach the stairs, I have a sudden change of heart. This is such a bad idea—there will be a point where if someone's down there, they will see me first.

I won't have as much time to react.

Maybe I should go back with Kash and hide out until the others find us. We should be in the moat by now, ready to run to safety.

Don't think about that, you chicken.

Not to mention the fact that we agreed not to do something so risky again, like going off alone or rushing into situations we're unsure of. A promise we broke over and over.

And here I am.

Reckless seems to be all I have left.

Perhaps desperate too.

Kash and I were only supposed to pee and get back, not split up. *It's not for long—you're going back for her.*

I creep down the stairs, holding my breath and wincing every time a board creaks, which is about every other step.

My back aches as I crouch, trying to look as far as I can while I descend.

Somewhere off in the distance I hear voices cutting through the rain. It's impossible to pick out words or even who the voices belong to, but I don't think I hear Allegra. Her voice is light and high, almost musical.

I reach the bottom step, breathing as quietly as I can to make the least amount of noise possible. The storm is covering my tracks as well as theirs, but noise still breaks through. I need it to be theirs and not mine.

What happens if we all die here? I don't know when the builders are due back. Our bodies could be rotting here for days.

My parents might not know what's happened to me for a while. The thought almost has my mind spinning. *Stop thinking like that.* Our classmates know where we are. As soon as word got out that we're missing after tomorrow, they would say something.

With that lovely thought, I peek around the corner, checking the hallway to the west wing of the castle.

That's where the voices are drifting from, I'm sure of it.

I can't think what would've brought them up there, since there are only bedrooms and bathrooms, but Kash and I ended up in a similar situation. They could be hiding.

Wouldn't you whisper if you were hiding, though?

My palms turn clammy. Shit, that's probably the killer. *Killers.* You wouldn't keep quiet if you had nothing to fear.

Allegra. Shen. Hugo.

At least two of them.

One of the voices laughs and a bolt of anger surges through my chest. Are you fucking kidding me? My friends are dying and it's a joke to them.

I replay the sound in my head, but I can't place it, and I can't even tell if it was male or female. My hand twitches. I want to storm in there right now and put this butter knife through their heads.

On instinct and anger, I move closer to the noise, balling my hands into fists.

I *have* to know.

The walls are clad in wood and peeling wallpaper, so I can't move that closely to them without alerting the entire castle of my whereabouts. I keep as close as I can, hoping to blend in.

I creep closer, the voices so loud I can almost pick out words.

There are few places to hide out here, just a random couple of end tables dotted along the hallway that probably used to hold large splays of colorful and fragrant flowers.

Footsteps join the voices and my heart leaps. I pad along the threadbare carpet and duck behind one of the tables. It's not as big as I need it to be, but I manage to squeeze myself beside it and tuck my legs against my chest just as the door flies open.

22

The door closes and I curl my nails into my palms as footsteps split, one set fading and the other getting louder.

I press my lips together, praying that I won't be seen.

Fear like nothing I've felt before freezes my muscles until I'm sure I won't be able to move even if I had to.

Don't be stupid.

My stomach rolls when his legs come into view.

I glance up but it's too late; all I can see are black cargo trousers that are baggy as hell and a long black coat, plasticky so probably a cheap waterproof material.

None of my friends own a coat like that.

Not that I've seen, anyway.

He's tall with what appears to be dark hair, but I can't get a good enough look at him from under the table. It's a bad angle and there isn't enough light to rely on what I think I see.

After a couple of seconds he disappears around a corner and I rise to my feet. The other one has gone, and since there's a staircase from the servants' kitchen to the servants' quarters up here, he could be on any level.

I hear the other one's footsteps on the stairs, but I can't figure out which way he's going. Down to my friends or up to my best friend.

If I go up, we're in the same situation again. So I make my way to the stairwell, keeping light on my feet and constantly looking over my shoulder. There's no one here, no sign of where he went. The rain above is so loud it sounds like a shower of bullets.

I use the noise to my advantage and run down the stairs, my feet light on the wood. When I reach the bottom, I dart for the ballroom.

Hugo looks up as I enter and close the door behind me. My hand trembles around the handle.

His jaw drops and he stands. "Bessie, are you okay? You were gone for ages."

"No, but don't ask, because I need to focus. Okay?"

He nods, approaching me cautiously.

Kash thinks Hugo has something to do with this. I've just seen and heard two males. No faces.

Hugo could be doing this.

No.

"Whatever you want, but I need to know something. Kash. Why isn't she with you right now?"

"She's alive. Top floor hiding in a shower room."

"What? You went to the bathroom. What were you doing up there, and why are you here alone?"

I pinch the bridge of my nose, trying to think of a reason to be up there without giving away our theory. "She wouldn't come, but I had to. We weren't safe. We're not safe on our own. We have to go to her, Hugo. Where the hell are Zeke, Shen, and Allegra?"

"They went to find you and Kash. I wasn't invited; I'd like to think that's because of this." He points to his side and winces. "But the way Zeke was keeping an eye on me before they came back would disagree."

"They still suspect you?"

He nods. "Yes. They left me behind, Bessie."

"Right . . . but if they thought it was you, they wouldn't take their eyes off of you."

Unless they just wanted to get as far away from him as possible.

"Do you want to wait for the others or go to Kash now?"

"Wait! I saw them up there."

"The others?"

"No." Probably. "The killers."

He takes a step back, raising his palms. "Back up. Bess, what the hell? Who is it?"

"I didn't get a good look due to the panic and hiding under a table, but there are at least two. The one who walked past me was wearing ridiculously baggy black trousers and a long black coat."

Hugo frowns. "Ridiculously baggy trousers and a long coat. Like a disguise."

"Huh?"

"Bessie, if they're disguising themselves, it's because we might recognize them. How easy would it be to chuck on a coat and trousers and shed them again when you're done?"

"Right." Duh. I smile, letting him think that I'm only just getting it.

"Hugo, maybe we should go alone to get Kash."

Potentially a *huge* mistake, but he would surely be out of breath if he was up there and made it to the ballroom before me.

Unless of course he's athletic and in the gym four times a week.

Which he is.

"Who are you suspecting?" he asks, his tone almost gleeful, as if this is a game and we're about to make a bet. I always lose bets, so I'm not playing.

"None of them!" All of them. "We just can't leave her alone. She's terrified."

His face is a mask as he watches me. "You're lying to me. Look, I'm coming with you, so don't worry about that, but don't I deserve the truth if you're asking me to risk my life?"

He makes it sound so simple.

"This whole thing is a risk to life, Hugo."

"Right, but I could just run now."

"Go ahead."

"*Who*, Bessie?"

"It could be any one of them, Zeke included."

"He was off for quite a while yesterday and I'm not sure I believe he was just hiding away for hours. My money's on Fergus and

Allegra. They know the layout and they've been here before. Plenty of time it would take to plan."

"What would they be doing it for?" I ask, wanting to hear if he reaches the same conclusion Kash and I have.

"What they want could be to murder. You think there's no chance they'd get away with it? We both know that's not true. Every one of our parents has the money it takes to make things disappear."

"Let's just get Kash. We can figure the rest out later."

Allegra is the one who had more time in this room. She wouldn't be questioned if she was looking through my things—we share all the time. It would be easiest for her or Kash to steal the newspaper I found.

That has to be actual evidence, and not a red herring, for it to be taken.

Unless Hugo is right and all of this is the Beaufort twins taking *How to Get Away with Murder* from the screen to the stage.

A show that Allegra has binged more than once.

I've seen her in science class, almost vomiting at having to slice apart any organ. Though the organ had never done anything to piss her off or get in her way.

"I've got your back. Always, you know that."

I wish I did.

"Follow me," I tell him, opening the ballroom door and being thrown back on my ass when someone slams into me.

I scramble, kicking my feet to get purchase on the floor and move backward.

"Bess, it's okay," Fergus says.

My eyes widen. *Fergus!*

"Oh my god," I say, and before my brain has the chance to process I throw my arms around him.

He laughs and hugs me back. "Careful, Bessie, I'm pretty wrecked."

"What?" I pull back to look at him and gasp, not really noticing the first time. He has a black eye emerging; a split lip; blood on his head crusted into his hair, and all over his stomach and chest; and hunched shoulders.

"Looks worse than it is," he says, trying to smile but wincing instead.

"What happened to you?" Hugo asks, stepping back inside the room.

Allegra and Zeke are there too. It's Allegra I'm shocked by because her face is so pale she looks like she could pass out at any second; she's clinging to the necklace she's wearing that Shen bought her for her last birthday.

"I was jumped in the cellar," Fergus says. "Saw the graffiti. More than last time. We knew about some, but the whole wall . . . I was hit on the side of the head and stabbed. I fought until the world went black. Woke up with a sharp pain in my stomach that made me feel like I was dying. Managed to get my sweatshirt off, rip and tie my T-shirt around my waist, and climb the stairs. My eyesight is still a little fuzzy but I'm okay."

"You were stabbed," I whisper.

He lifts his hoodie, revealing a blood-soaked T-shirt underneath like a bandage.

"We can patch you up. There are still supplies in the first aid kit," I tell him.

"Bessie, we need to move," Fergus replies.

"But you're hurt."

He shakes his head, stroking my cheek. "I'm all right. Shen isn't. Where is Kash?"

"What happened to Shen?" I ask, my eyes flitting to Allegra.

She's a statue, gripping that necklace and staring off into the distance. Zeke is staring at her like a deer caught in headlights.

Oh no.

"Allegra," I say, approaching her slowly, my heart sinking with each step. Shen is gone. "Allegra, can you hear me?"

"Shen was attacked in front of her," Fergus says. "His throat was . . . it was slit."

"Oh my god." I gasp, and my body jolts at the horror of his words. "Allegra, I'm so sorry. Where were you?"

"Bathroom," she whispers. "I couldn't do anything. Couldn't move. This asshole jumped through the window, and I just stood there, frozen, watching Shen's neck bleed."

The window that Kash left open.

"How did you find Fergus?" I ask.

"I didn't. Eventually I walked out of the bathroom and ran into him. We ran into Zeke after that, coming downstairs."

"I went looking for you all, heard noise in the servants' kitchen but realized it was coming from upstairs. Got up there but it was empty, eventually heard voices downstairs and ran into Allegra and

Fergus . . . and Shen." He shakes his head as if to rid himself of the image.

Seeing Abbas was enough.

Fergus, still slightly hunched and holding his stomach, watches his sister with fear in his eyes. He's been through a traumatic experience and knows what Allegra has to face next.

"He's dead," Allegra mutters. "We had plans and now everything is gone."

This latest development has thrown me completely. Allegra has never looked so ready to give up. She loved Shen and they had their whole lives planned. She wouldn't destroy that herself.

Hugo glances at me, frowning as if he's going back to the drawing board too.

"I'm sorry, Allegra. Shen was one of the few truly decent people at school," Hugo says. "I understand that you don't want to do this now, but we're going for Kash. She's hiding in a shower room on the top floor."

"Why?" Zeke asks, pushing past Allegra.

"Fear," I reply. "We heard the killers. Two of them. I half saw one."

"Who is it?" Fergus asks.

"*Half* saw. I was hiding. I don't know who it is."

He runs his hand over his jaw in frustration. "How are they managing to conceal their appearance at every turn?"

"Forget that for now. Allegra and Bessie should stay here and block the door with a chair. The rest of us will get Kash," Zeke says, after taking a minute to digest my words.

"No," I say.

"Bessie, don't. Allegra is falling apart, and every time we've left this room we've been split up. It's better for you two to stay." He gestures to Allegra, trying to tell me something without using words.

I watch her folding in on herself, staring at the two gold initials hanging from the chain around her neck. A and S.

"But Hugo and Fergus are injured."

Fergus downs a couple of pills and swigs water. "I'm fine," he says, wiping his mouth with the back of his hand. "This bastard isn't going to win. Zeke's right, Allegra isn't in any fit state to go out there yet."

That means she's a total liability if the killers come for us.

So the answer is to lock me in a room with the liability.

Great.

"All right," I say, because what choice do I have?

Hugo rolls his shoulders on his way past me. "Do not take your eyes off her," he murmurs, low enough that he won't be heard by the others.

She's not the killer.

I grab a chair and shove it under the handle once Hugo closes the door.

Allegra doesn't seem aware of her surroundings.

"Hey," I say, putting my hand over hers and blocking her view of the necklace. "Allegra, can you hear me?"

"Shen's death has not altered my hearing."

The snark is a good sign. It means she's still with us. We're going to need her to be alert to run when we have Kash back.

"Then you heard what I said about seeing the killers, and you need to know that it's one . . . *two* of us."

She rears her head back, dropping her hands to her sides. "Hugo and Zeke?"

"That's one possibility."

"Well, it's not Fergus!" She looks at the door, her forehead creasing. "Tell me it's not him."

"I wish I could. I want to believe that."

"You still love him?"

I nod. "I do, but there are things he's hiding."

She whimpers and then nods, as if she's thought that all along but pushed it away. "We need to leave, Bessie. Right now. Me and you."

I laugh without a shred of humor. "And where would you like to go?"

"Across the moat, into the storm. We can disguise ourselves in the forest and not stop until we find someone to help us. That's what we were going to do anyway, right? This morning our plan was to swim and walk." She looks back at the door. "You said it's two of them. They'll all be back soon, so the smartest thing we can do is go. I know the way."

My mind spins, desperately trying to keep up and figure out what's going on inside her head. I thought it was her until two minutes ago.

Fergus is her twin. They've always had each other's back, and I honestly don't understand how she could even think about leaving him behind . . . unless, of course, she suspects he's one of the killers.

The guy who passed me upstairs could have been Fergus. He

was kind of the right build, I just can't be certain. Fergus is tall . . . but I think they were taller. I should've risked it and shuffled forward under the table to get a better look.

"You want to leave them? And *Kash*?"

She shakes her head and grips the necklace again. Tears roll down her face, the last of her two-day-old mascara streaking her cheeks. "Two of them killed Shen. We're going to be next, don't you see that? I want to get Kash out too, but we don't have time."

"We can find a way to separate us from the boys when Kash is back. They wanted us to stay behind to do the protective chivalry bit."

"Bessie, we need to go!"

"We will. Grab a bag and let's pack towels and waterproof jackets. We're going to need them to dry off and then stay dry at the other side of the moat."

"We're not going to have time to change!"

"Calm down and stop yelling at me. We've got a long walk after a freezing swim, Allegra, and the last thing we need is hypothermia. We can strip and change on the go."

"The bag won't stay dry."

I take a breath, ripping my coat from my bag. This was her idea, and she's not bloody helping. "Wrap the clothes in one of these plastic bags from the supermarket. We'll wrap the backpack in one too. It'll work."

"Okay," she replies, emptying her backpack and shoving in the towels and coats I throw at her. "Three coats."

"We're waiting for Kash."

"Bessie, come—"

"When they get back, we'll pretend to hear a noise. The boys will investigate. The three of us will get out through the window when they're gone."

"What if one of them wants to stay to protect us?"

"They literally all just left the two of us. They're not going to stay back for three."

Why is she so desperate to go now? Three of us running is safer than two. This could just be my suspicious mind, but it feels a little like she's trying to get me on my own.

But she has me alone now.

The thought sends a bolt of fear through my body that I have to ignore. "Hide that under the blanket," I tell her as she ties a plastic bag around her backpack. The thing is stretched to the max, but it'll hopefully hold out so we have something dry to run in.

"Where are they?" she asks.

"Kash is on the top floor—it'll take time for them to reach her."

I assume they're trying to move around the castle as inconspicuously as possible.

She takes a deep breath, her cheeks puffing out. "Could three of the boys be doing this?"

"I only saw two, but it's a possibility. We're getting Kash and leaving them. Which is an awful thing to do if one of them is innocent. We're leaving them to die, Allegra."

"I *hate* that too, but there's no way of telling who it is."

"You can leave Fergus?"

She whimpers, pressing her lips together. "I never would have thought so . . . but if he killed Shen I can."

"Wait . . . what if we turn it around and do the spying."

"What the actual hell, Bessie."

"No, think about it. We know where they're going. God, they're about to be alone with Kash."

"Oh. My. God. You saw two, and they wouldn't act with a third with them."

"We hope! We've just let them go get her."

"Shh, will you get it together?" she snaps.

That hits me hard, since I've been the together one this whole time. Allegra has had multiple meltdowns.

"I'm going back out there."

"Yes, that is the most ridiculous thing you could do, Bess, congratulations."

"We're sitting ducks here. It's time to stop running around scared."

All right, that's a bold claim.

"We literally just made a plan to get Kash and escape. Can you focus on that one for longer than five seconds, please?"

"Nope. They think we're hiding here, so it's the perfect opportunity. Put the chair back against the door when I'm gone," I say, not giving her a chance to argue.

I'm doing this for Jia, Odette, Abbas, and Shen.

And Kash needs me.

23

I know leaving Allegra and the ballroom is a monumentally terrible idea. I'm acutely aware that if I die now, it's all on me. The decisions I have made have led me here . . . to potentially be stabbed to death in a remote castle.

Here I am following a desire to become a spy slash amateur detective, wanting to protect my friends and bring the killer to justice. I'm done hiding, and I'm not standing by and waiting while my best friend is murdered.

Some things are worth risking your life for.

Kash is one of them.

Our plan isn't over—I'm still leaving with Allegra just as soon as I find Kash and the truth.

I take the indirect route, the servants' staircase, because it's darker and that's about all I have going for me. If you don't include the blunt knife. Which I do. Kind of.

I move quickly because they have a massive head start. Kash

could be dead already, but I have to believe her hiding spot is work-ing. I've not heard anything to suggest that she's in danger.

Moving fast and quiet should be a priority, but I don't have that luxury. All I can hope is that they can't easily see me. And that I don't die.

I try not to think about the risks I'm taking as I go.

I take the stairs on tiptoe, making just under a total racket. At the top, I press myself against the wall and peer around the corner. Empty, but I think she's up here somewhere. I didn't hear anyone on the stairs.

Three boys know she's on the top floor, and there are only four rooms up here. They've had plenty of time to check them. So where are they?

I move along the hallway, looking over my shoulder; I strain to see clearly in the dimly lit dark hallway and finally reach the shower room door.

The room is empty. *What the* . . . "Jesus, Kash, where are you?" I mutter.

For the second time today she's missing.

As I go to leave, I spot Kash's shoes on the floor by the toilet. The small, shallow built-in closet in the room has no door and would only hide a child. But on the floor in front of it is disturbed dust. One clear path, like someone's drawn a half moon in the snow.

As if there's a hidden door at the back of it, like in the room I found with Hugo and Kash.

Oh, how much I do not want to go in there. I swallow my fear and reach out. The wood depresses as I touch it like it's made of paper. I push and something clicks, the door moving toward me.

I was kind of hoping it'd be locked.

I pull it open and brace myself for a fight.

Thankfully it doesn't look like there are any stairs in here, just a damp, stale room in desperate need of airing. I take a couple of steps and collide with something solid.

My eyes slowly adjust and I see Kash sitting on the floor, doing a stellar impersonation of a statue. Thank god she's alive.

"Kash," I say, crouching down. "I was so worried. Hey, look at me. Allegra and I have a plan, so we need to go right now before the others find us. Kash, look at me." I cough as a pungent stench poisons my lungs. I'm pretty certain old, stale air is terrible for your health. It smells awful, so bad that I have to focus hard on not vomiting.

"Kash! Will you look at me. We need to get out of here. This room is . . ."

I stop talking, the smell finally registering because it's not stale oxygen.

Oh no.

Covering my mouth, I turn my head to where Kash is staring and understand why she looks traumatized.

My eyes come into sharp focus and I see, with perfect clarity, the dead bodies of Jia, Odette, Abbas, and Shen in the corner of the room.

"No," I mutter, bile rising from my stomach. I push my fist

against my lips and squeeze my eyes shut, the image of my four friends lying in a discarded heap as if they're rubbish engrained in my memory.

I look again, this time around the rest of the room. It's small, probably about ten feet by thirteen feet. Empty and, weirdly, off the shower room; I have absolutely no idea what it was used for.

Some sort of panic room would be my guess. A secret room off the library would be a bit obvious.

"There's nothing else here," I say, my hands trembling. We need to get out of here. The room is used to hold the dead. It doesn't look like this person has anything else in here. Why hide your bag in one room and bodies in the other?

She doesn't reply to me, staying in her statue state. Eyes as wide as Abbas's.

Don't look at them.

"Kash."

Her body jolts as if she's only just heard me. "I tried to hide in the cupboard, but it was too small. Clicked when I leaned against the back," she mutters, her voice a low monotone that's filled with trauma. How long has she been in here with them?

"It's okay," I lie. "Has anyone else been in here? I mean the shower room. Did you hear anyone before me?"

"I . . . maybe."

Well, she's not reliable. I wince. "They were ahead of me," I tell her, my eyes beginning to sting from the stench.

"I don't know, Bessie. I found them."

"I think they must have. They had a good few minutes on me.

If you were already in here, they could have moved on. It must mean that one of them is innocent, because if they're all guilty they would've checked this room."

"Which ones? Hugo and Zeke?" she asks, her eyes still fixed on the pile of our friends. Their arms and legs tangled. They were thrown in here like garbage, no care for the fact that they're human.

"Why do you think it's them?"

She shrugs. "Fergus's family won't make much money off the castle if it's a murder house."

"Hugo and Zeke aren't exactly best friends."

"They're friendly enough if they have the same enemy. Raif was our friend. Zeke's best friend. Hugo's brother."

"Okay, let's go," I say, having heard enough of this angle. Raif thinks we're mad at him. If any one of us was terrorizing the other, it should be us pissed at him.

I rise to my feet and listen at the flimsy door, trying to ignore the bodies. My mind does a better job of blocking the image of them all than I thought. I focus solely on Kash.

"Get up. It's quiet out there," I tell her.

"We're getting Allegra and going?"

"Yes, right now, so get up! I need you to move."

She tilts her head, breathing raggedly, as if she's finding it really hard to hold herself together. I take her hand. "I just need you to be strong for a little bit."

"O-okay. I can ... do that," she replies, getting up and brushing off her top like there's dirt all over it. There's nothing on her, but I don't think either of us will feel clean again after being in here.

I pull the door open and slip back into the shower room, placing my feet carefully so I don't crunch any tile.

Kash is right behind me and we move toward the hallway, my pulse quickening with every step. All we need to do is make it downstairs and into the ballroom. We can get out through the window then and leave this awful place forever.

It doesn't make sense that I didn't run into the boys up here. They knew the room she was in. They had to have come in here first, but where did they go next and why the hell can't I hear them? That's just another reason for Kash and me to leave with Allegra and never look back.

"It's too quiet," Kash whispers, the sound of her voice bouncing off every wall despite her hushed tone.

"Uh-huh." They won't want to call out either, not if only two of them are involved. Or they could be preoccupied killing the third.

Do not go there.

They will be creeping around like us. It gives me hope that we can make it down to Allegra unseen.

"Just keep moving," I tell her, my heart thudding so hard I want to run, to keep going until I can finally breathe again. I can't act too rashly. It'll get me killed.

There's only one way out from here, so we're in serious trouble if anyone comes along now.

Kash grabs my arm when we get near the stairs. I was going to go back down the servants' route, but I hear what she heard. Footsteps.

I spin around and run with her around the long foyer, the entrance to the stairs on the other side.

"Bessie!" Kash shouts, nearly ripping my arm out of its socket as she flies backward.

Startling, I fall hard to my knees and instantly shuffle back, raising my chin to see what the hell just happened. For a second, I see another flash. My bloodied hands, shattered glass in front of me, branches touching my chest. The image is gone seconds later and I'm catapulted back to reality.

"No, no, Kash," I say, leaping to my feet, ignoring the pain in my legs and holding up my hands to the guy who has Kash's back pinned against his chest.

"Let's just take a minute," I say, swallowing my fear. "We can talk. Sort this out."

The hallway is lighter, but with his hood pulled up high and some sort of black scarf covering his face, it's impossible to see who it is.

Kash stares at me with wide eyes and an open mouth. A blade pointed at her neck stops her from wriggling out of his grip.

"Please," I say, fear trickling through my veins.

He shakes his head but makes no attempt to hurt her.

"Tell us what you want, and you can have it. Okay? Whatever you want. Just let us go."

He shakes his head again and releases the hand around her waist. The knife doesn't move, so she doesn't either.

"All right. Can you just let her go and deal with me?"

He tilts his head and the hood moves. Not enough, but maybe I can get him to do it again so I know exactly who I'm dealing with.

"Please let Kash go. She's not part of this, is she? Or you would have killed her already. It's me you want, right? I'm part of something that made you angry."

This *has* to be about the accident.

Kash mouths "Stop," but I can't stop, because I'm trying to save her life here.

"You don't want her," I say again. "Something happened that night. Something I don't know about. We can discuss it."

I wait for a reply that comes in the form of a movement and open my mouth to shout as he flicks his hand. The knife flashes in the dimmest light as it swings out, leaving her neck but plunging into her waist.

Kash's bloodcurdling scream rings through my ears and I double over as if I was stabbed too. Her body hits the floor like a rag doll, and she presses her hands to the wound on her side.

She tilts her head up, her face scraping against the wooden floor. "Go," she rasps, and coughs blood, splattering specks of red in front of her.

"I'm sorry, Kash," I sob, my heart shattering. My best friend since I was small. I don't remember a time where she wasn't in my life.

"Go."

"I love you," I whisper, and turn on my heel. I sprint along the hallway, hand on the railing, feet thundering down the stairs. "Allegra, go!" I scream. "Go now!"

She'll be leaping out of the window in the ballroom, which is at the front left of the castle, so I'll meet her there.

I shout out at the bottom of the stairs, my arms wheeling as I try to stop too quickly. My feet stumble but I manage to keep upright. One of the killers, dressed in the exact same oversize clothing, stands by the front door, blocking my exit.

The ballroom door opens beside me; Allegra pokes her head out as if she didn't hear my words. Why the hell isn't she halfway across that lawn already?

There's no time to worry about her idiocy. I shove myself into her and slam the door shut. "Chair!"

She's already grabbing it, and together we block the doorway.

"They're out there," I say, shaking; I rake my fingers through my hair. "They're out there, and one of them just killed Kash! He killed her right in front of me. Oh my god, we need to block the door off. Find more furniture."

"Bessie, what the hell is going on?" she demands, sobbing. "You're talking too fast. Kash is . . . ?"

"Did anyone else come in here or try to?" I ask her. "Think, Allegra. Did you hear anything? This is important."

"No. Calm down. I heard nothing until shouting seconds before you came back. Will you answer my question? What's going on?"

"He stabbed Kash. Ripped her from my grasp and stabbed her. We found the other . . . their bodies. There's another hidden room on the top floor, and that's where these bastards are hiding our friends!"

I feel the withdraw from reality and have to grasp hold of the present with both hands.

Breathe. Fight.

Her mouth opens and she grabs the plastic bag. "Shen."

"Yeah, he's there, but—"

I snap my teeth together, hearing a slow knock on the door. One. Two. Three.

Allegra and I look at each other and my heart stops beating.

"We are so not answering that," she says.

"Hadn't planned to," I rasp. "Time to go."

I turn around and my stomach bottoms out. Outside, staring back at us through the window, is the other killer.

We're trapped.

24

"What do we do?" Allegra asks, shuffling closer to me.

I swallow and lick my dry lips. "Right now, I have no idea. Pray?"

"Pray!" Her eyes widen like a cartoon character's. "That's your answer?"

"I figure it'll be about as effective as screaming . . . but make us appear less afraid."

"I'm feeling pretty afraid."

"Same." I breathe in deeply through my nose in a futile attempt to curb my panic. "It's two against two now."

Or three against two, but we don't need that negativity.

"Are we thinking one of the boys is also dead?" she asks, picking up on my math.

"It's a possibility."

"We're all we have, Bessie. I'm feeling pissed off enough to take them on now."

"Same," I repeat, straightening my back. They've killed too many

286 | NATASHA PRESTON

people I love, and they're still coming for us. I am *not* going to make it easy for them.

"Look!" Allegra shouts, pointing to someone outside in the distance. I spot what she's seen and I gulp. My math was correct because the odd guy out isn't dead at all. He's running.

The killer turns as well.

Shit. We've just given him away.

"No!" I shout, earning a whack on the arm from Allegra, who has finally let go of the necklace.

The killer turns back toward the running figure, holding his knife up, and then sprints after him. It's too dark to tell who the runner is, and they all have a similar build. Who is that?

"Oh no," Allegra says, realizing what we've done.

"We can't change that. All we can do is . . ." I stop, listening to the hallway. Footsteps fade as the killer takes the chase outside.

Allegra hears too, turning around. "He's gone. Sounds like out the front door."

"Yeah, we should go out through the kitchen at the back of the castle. If he's going to help his murderer mate, they'll both be at the front."

I'm strikingly aware that I'm saying we should run and leave the other runner to his fate. But I couldn't help Kash, so what chance do I have now? The best thing Allegra and I can do is get the hell out of here.

"Go," I say, and she moves the chair while I hold the knife up, ready for anyone who might think it's a good idea to come for us.

I don't know if it's adrenaline or anger, but I'm ready. My new-found bravery is spurring me on, and I just need it to last until we're the other side of the moat.

She pulls the door open and I brace myself, but we're met with empty, silent space.

I get two steps in when Hugo sprints into the room, knocking into Allegra and sending them both flying.

"Get away from me!" she screams, crawling away before getting to her feet.

Hugo lies on the floor, his chest heaving. "Close it!" he snaps. "He's out there!"

Allegra and I look at each other and she shakes her head. Yeah, I'm not willing to lock myself in a room with a potential serial killer either.

"What happened, Hugo?"

He gets to his feet, rubbing his chest and wincing from what I assume is the pain in his side. "I don't know. I was hit when we went looking for Kash. I'm getting seriously pissed off with being attacked."

"He just let you go?"

"No, I shoved him and ran, Allegra. Had to go outside and found my way back in around the back. *Why* aren't you closing the door?"

Where's the one who knocked on the door? That could have been Hugo. He could have easily hidden in a room to change and then come back.

I narrow my eyes. "Why aren't you?"

There's nothing stopping him from closing it. Why does he want us to do it so bad? I'm not letting anyone separate me and Allegra.

Very slowly he turns his head my way.

I hold my breath, braced for the impact of his next words.

This is where he confesses.

Before he can say anything, Fergus stumbles sideways into the room and bumps into the table. His hair is a matted mess of dried blood, but he's ruffled it to try to make it neater. "She's dead," he rasps with tears in his eyes. He looks at me and I nod.

Yes, she was killed right in front of me.

Allegra and I don't move. I fight the urge to run toward him, to help him stand upright. It doesn't look like the pain meds he took are doing much.

Fergus steadies himself, leaning against the table. His eyes slowly move from Hugo to me to Allegra. "What's going on?"

"Guys!" Zeke shouts, running into the room. He spins on his heel and points to Hugo. "You stay the hell back."

"Me? You two are the ones who decided we should split up! Fergus is the one who was with Kash."

"I was not with her, I found her!" he rasps, pressing his hand to his stomach and wincing. "We need to go. I saw this guy outside."

"Fergus," Allegra whispers. She frowns, glassy-eyed and twitchy, wanting to go to him too. But, like me, she's scared and doesn't know who to trust.

Allegra, Zeke, Hugo, Fergus, and I stand in the ballroom breathing heavily and trying to piece this thing together.

I look at each of my friends and just can't seem to figure it out.

One or more of them have killed this weekend. The bodies of the people I'm closest to in the world are lying in a pile, their lives snuffed out for no reason at all.

The weight of this weekend is pulling me under, nearly suffocating me.

Hugo doesn't get a pass, because his injury isn't serious and he doesn't even need stitches.

The five of us are silent, as if the first one to speak loses. It's a heavy price to pay for coming in last.

"Where do we go from here?" Allegra asks, her cheeks stained with tears, evidence of her grief over Shen and the dilemma over Fergus. "So many of us are dead and we're still stranded. I don't trust any of you."

Fergus huffs. "That's amazing, Allegra, and thank you for the update."

"Don't patronize me, Fergus. You haven't offered anything helpful. All you do is sit around and pass judgment on what the rest of us do. Or stress over Bessie being in the same room as Hugo, though you do nothing to make sure he hasn't stabbed her through the heart."

"Hey!" Hugo snaps. "*I'm* the one who was stabbed here."

"So was I!" Fergus mutters, coughing.

He really doesn't look good, leaning and swaying to try to keep upright. How on earth is he going to get across the moat?

Allegra growls, her frustration bubbling over. "Shut up! We all need to be honest with each other. Right now."

Raising his arms, Fergus says, "Okay, Allegra. Now step forward if you're the killer. Come on. Which one of you hates the rest of us so much you want us dead?"

He turns away from his sister. "Were you all expecting a confession?"

"I'm trying, Fergus! At least I'm—"

He laughs. I'm about to tell him to stop messing around when he stands tall, rolling his shoulders as he walks into the center of the circle. His face changes, the grimace disappearing and transforming into a smirk that drips with pure evil.

No.

Allegra gasps, jumping back as Fergus pulls a knife from his pocket.

"Because, sister, you're getting one."

Oh my god.

My eyes widen and my body turns cold. Hugo and Zeke leap back to distance themselves from Fergus.

It doesn't make any sense.

Fergus. The one who nursed me back to health last year, who has continued to protect me. The one who guides me through each panic attack with calm and steely determination to make things right again.

This can't be the same person.

"What are you talking about? Stop, Fergus. This isn't funny," Allegra says, her tears falling like the rainstorm.

"Oh, for once, will you just shut up? I'm *so fucking tired* of your constant bitching and whining." He spins, stepping back so we're all clearly in his line of sight, and arches his neck, stretching out the muscles that must ache from being hunched.

"Don't even try anything," he says, pointing the knife toward us, eyes cold and detached, not once looking at me. I don't recognize him at all. "I'll be talking to my sister without any distractions. Is that understood?"

I nod, reaching out and backing the three of us up. The betrayal I feel is so physically painful I can barely stand straight. How could he do this? Shen was his best friend. He knew Kash was mine.

When Fergus turns his attention back to Allegra, Hugo whispers, "More of us than him."

Zeke shakes his head. "I think knives count as five people."

"Shh."

Allegra watches her brother with horror etched into her features. "Fergus, please . . . what have you done?"

"I've done what was needed. That's all I have ever done."

"What else was needed?" I ask, earning an elbow in the side from Zeke.

Don't prod the unstable killer. I get it and I'm so on board . . . but Fergus has hinted that it isn't the first time he's done something like this. There has also been a lot of chat about the accident.

They have to be connected. This is about that night, I'm sure. Or at least some of it is.

He smiles wickedly, taking pleasure in what he's done. I've known him for years and never saw even a hint of anything so dark inside him. He's proud of his work here . . . and he's not finished yet.

"Can't see a reason not to answer. After all, you're going to take it to your grave with you before the end of the day." He checks his watch. "We have time."

"Fergus, please," I whisper.

"I'm getting there. No need to rush, love."

I shudder at the cold emptiness of his voice. How could he just flip the switch like that? He used to meet me with warmth, even when I told him we were over.

"He's got wild eyes," Hugo mutters.

"Remember the accident." Fergus straightens his back, his posture perfect to make himself taller, and his lips curve into that sinister grin again.

"No, I don't remember anything, but you know that," I say, swallowing acid. "Fergus, just tell me the truth."

He shrugs so casually, as if this is all a game to him. "It has nothing to do with this per se, Bessie, but it was the start. The accident made me realize what humans are capable of. I've spent so much of my life being the perfect son and perfect student. All that man cares about is *money*. I've had enough."

"Dad?" Allegra asks, shock evident in her high-pitched voice. "That's not true, Fergus. He loves us."

"He shipped us off to boarding school the second he could. Never really bothered with us before that. Name one problem he hasn't solved with his fucking credit card, Allegra. Go on. Just one!" he spits, his face red, hands curled into fists.

She shakes her head, pauses, and then very slowly her eyes widen. She can't think of anything. Neither can I, because I've only met him once and it was a quick hello as he was running late for a meeting and then going away on another business trip. All the years I've known Fergus and Allegra, and I have been in their dad's presence for a grand total of ten seconds.

"There must be something, Allegra," Zeke says, shooting her a look of desperation. I'm not sure her telling Fergus their dad once baked them a cake is going to stop him from doing this.

Besides, he probably never baked a cake. Fergus isn't going to be swayed by a handful of fleeting happy moments.

"There isn't, Zeke," Fergus says, tilting his head, looking at Zeke with a raised brow. It's only for a second because he's fixed on his sister and making her realize what a useless parent their dad has been. I don't think their mum is much better, but I'm not about to bring that up.

"Stop this right now!" Allegra squeals. "You've lost your mind, Fergus, and you need help. Shen, Jia, our friends. What's going on with you? It doesn't make sense. If you want to piss Dad off there are better ways. People are dead. This isn't a game."

"Allegra, you talk too much."

"Then let me listen," she says, holding her hands up and nodding. "Tell me what's going on and I'll help you."

He laughs, a proper belly laugh that turns my stomach. Why isn't that hurting him? He has no trouble moving around now.

I gasp as I realize just how deep he's into this "game." The stabbing and blood were a ruse so we wouldn't suspect him until he was ready.

"And what could you possibly do to help me, sister?"

"We'll get you the best defense. Pay off whoever we need to. You'll do your time in a retreat. It'll be like a vacation."

Beside me, I can feel the anger rolling off Hugo in waves. He takes a step closer. "That's what you always do, isn't it? Hide the problem. Blame someone else. Whatever it takes so your life isn't inconvenienced by a small matter of consequences."

"Hugo," I whisper, reaching out for him. What on earth does he think he's doing?

He pulls his arm away before I can grab him. "No, I'm done!"

"What are you talking about, mate?" Fergus asks.

But he doesn't look confused by Hugo's words; his eyes are bright, mouth stretched wide. He looks amused. He looks like he knows *exactly* what Hugo is talking about.

"Stop pretending, *mate*."

Allegra looks at me as if she's expecting me to know. I shrug, not having a single clue what he's going on about.

Unless . . .

Wait. Pretending. Blaming others.

Raif.

The accident wasn't what it seemed.

I shake my head as a vivid image flashes past my eyelids. Blood, smashed glass, me holding my hands up. They're dripping red and then . . . something new. A voice. It's gone too quickly for me to recognize. Was it Fergus?

Stop!

Fergus rolls his eyes. "Oh that. It all ended well, so what's your problem?"

"Ended well?" Hugo roars. "My brother's life has been ruined because you switched seats with him after the accident and you think that's ending well?"

My hand flies to my throat and I gasp. No way. That can't be right. Oh my god, did I see that? The blood and glass make it clear that it was that night. I must've been awake after the crash, even if it was only long enough to hear Fergus's voice and notice the blood and glass.

Mom said I looked awful when she got to the hospital. I had cuts everywhere. Most of the scars have long faded.

Fergus throws his head back and laughs. "I'm sure that's what Raif is saying to absolve himself from any guilt."

Hugo takes another step, much to Fergus's amusement. "You remember, don't you?"

"Fergus," I say. "Tell me he's got it wrong and you haven't been lying to me this whole time."

I don't know why, at this point, it matters. But it does. Raif has been plagued by guilt for ten months.

Fergus stares at me, tilting his head. I have always been good at reading him, but he's slammed the book shut and set it on fire. I don't know what he's thinking.

"Oh my god." I take a breath and reach out for Zeke, who holds my wrist. "Raif and I were the ones with worse injuries . . . because we were on the same side of the car, weren't we? I was behind the passenger seat. He was in front of me and when the car landed on our side, our heads were knocked."

Zeke swears under his breath. "Did you really do that? Did you move him?" he asks.

Fergus's hard expression bursts and he smiles wide, baring his teeth. "Busted."

"How could you?" I ask, my head spinning. Fergus and Raif were close. They used to do nearly everything together and always had each other's back. Or so I thought. I can't believe Fergus would do that to his friend. He sat there and said nothing when Raif was drowning under the weight of his guilt.

"You did that, Fergus?" Allegra asks, and she no longer looks like she wants to check him into a retreat. He needs to be in prison. "Why would you do that? I don't understand."

His eyes flick to me before his sister. "You're asking why bother when I could have had Dad make it all disappear." It's not a question. That's what we all want to know. It's a DUI, one where no one was killed. Fergus's family could've had that squashed before we even arrived at the hospital.

"Allegra, you're completely missing the point. There may not have been any legal implications to anyone knowing I was behind the wheel, but it doesn't look good, does it? A drunk-driving conviction. The entire school knowing I was in a wreck like that, putting others' lives in danger. No."

"So you just moved him?" Hugo growls. "He was injured. That alone could have killed him!"

"What else was I supposed to do? Bessie and I had been drinking. I woke up, couldn't have been out for long. I realized we'd be found soon and made a choice. You would've done the same."

"No," I whisper again, my body bending with the weight of his confession. "No, I wouldn't."

"Oh, calm down, I didn't put you in the driver's seat, Bessie."

"How did the police not notice the head injury thing?" Allegra asks; I don't know if she's holding out hope that he's lying right now, but how closely would they have looked considering we were all unconscious when the car was found.

Well, two of us were.

One is an evil, lying bastard.

"He was heavy. All that dead weight. I was shaken up too. The car had rolled twice on that bend. The injury could've been from any point." He stands taller, puffing out his chest. "But I managed to drag him from the back seat to the front. Couldn't risk getting him out of the car to carry him around and leave marks."

I close my eyes, squeezing them tight as I try to rid my mind of that image. He did all that while I was right there. I trusted him and he betrayed me.

Fergus needs to stop talking. I can't stand hearing him anymore. I don't want his reasons or excuses. What he did is unforgivable. We need to overpower him and tie him up. At least we'd be safe until the storm passes.

Or we could lock him out and see if the storm can right his wrongs. But if we did that, wouldn't we be just as bad as him?

"Okay, so you did what you thought you had to," Allegra says, trying to appease him. I want to whack her. Fergus doesn't get the benefit of any doubt. That night changed him, turned him into the sick, twisted person before us.

What I don't understand is why us?

When he turns to her, I mouth "Grab him" to Hugo and Zeke.

Zeke rolls his shoulders, and on his nod they run forward.

Fergus shouts as they knock him to the floor, landing on his back. "Get off! Get off!" he yells, his hand tightening around the knife.

I leap to take it from him, but I'm not fast enough. Fergus stabs the knife into Zeke's thigh.

Zeke screams out, an animalistic noise I've never heard from him before—and I was there when he snapped his leg last year. He grips the wound but blood pumps between his fingers like a bright red waterfall.

The scream catapults me back and I'm in the car. A flash of glass shattering in and covering my face, arms, and legs.

I gasp, grab Zeke, and haul him backward. Blood leaks all over the floor, pumping from him. He breathes heavily through gritted teeth, forehead creased and hands curled. I press my hand to the wound, feeling the warm liquid drip down my wrist.

I see it again, a fleeting image of blood on my hands.

I was definitely awake for a moment in the car. Why can't I remember more?

"Too . . . much," he murmurs, gagging.

"You're okay," I say, trying to stay with him while my mind wants to drag me back.

Allegra crouches beside us, one arm on Zeke's shoulder, the other raised toward Fergus. "No more," she pleads. "Fergus, you have got to stop this madness. This isn't you. It's not too late. Please listen to me. I love you."

Oh, that's not true—it's entirely too late.

Zeke's eyes flutter. No matter how hard I press, the blood isn't slowing down. I sob, watching it pour between my fingers. Fergus must've cut through an artery, because there is nothing I can do to stop this. I don't know how long he's got, but if something isn't done very soon he's going to die.

"You're going to be fine," I tell him, lying through my teeth. "Zeke, look at me."

"You need to run," he whispers, and then coughs. His voice is barely audible. "Remember he's not alone. Run, Bess."

Allegra?

No.

Fergus roars, waving his knife around and aiming for Hugo, who is circling him like a predator. Hugo rolls to avoid him and tries to grab his armed wrist.

"Stop it, Fergus!" Allegra shouts as he gets to his feet and points the knife at each of us. Wild eyes, planning who to kill next.

He has completely lost it.

We might have to kill him to survive.

Allegra gets to her feet. "I understand now, Ferg. I get what you did with Raif, and now."

He laughs again, tilting his head to the side. "You know what I'm doing here?"

"No," I whisper, my eyes filling with tears as Zeke's body slumps, his head lolling to the side and hands hitting the floor. My heart shatters.

He's gone.

25

"Zeke!" I cry, shaking him to try to wake him up despite knowing that it's no use. "Zeke, please."

Allegra screams, "What have you done?"

Startled, I look up just in time to see her flee from the room as Hugo lunges at Fergus, knocking him to the ground while he's momentarily distracted. I sob, wiping my tears so I can see what's going on.

Fergus coughs, the air leaving his lungs.

"Go, Bess!" Hugo snaps, shaking Fergus until his head cracks on the floorboards.

I want to wait but Hugo hasn't killed Fergus—so I still can't be sure Hugo's not part of it. It makes no sense if he is. Raif is his brother.

Without looking back, I sprint to the heavy front door. It's wide open already, so this must be the route Allegra took. I don't have the bag with my phone, and there's no way of getting changed once I'm past the moat, but I don't care.

My cheeks burn as the brutal wind bites into my skin, my hair whipping into my eyes. The rain has gone again, for now, but I'm about to swim through a moat; there's no chance of getting out of here dry.

"Bessie!"

I whimper, hearing my name called behind me. I think it's Hugo, but I can't be sure and there is no way I'm slowing down. I press on, pushing myself to fatigue.

My feet slide on the wet ground. I scream and throw my arms out to the side to steady myself, not able to afford tripping and falling. I need to get across that moat and not stop until I find safety.

"Bess, it's me. Keep going!"

Hugo. I wipe my tears, adrenaline pumping through my veins, quads on fire as I push my legs harder than I ever have before.

"In there, Bess!" he shouts.

I look over my shoulder. "Where is he?"

"I don't know. Hide. He can see where we get into the water."

I don't need to look at him to know he means the brick outhouse. I change direction and head for it because I know he's right. Fergus is the strongest swimmer of us all, even in the wind. Our best chance is to find where he is and then swim out of his sight on the other side of the castle.

He can't see us.

Hugo and I sprint around the castle, nearly at the back now.

The grounds are so big. I can't believe I thought that was something special when we arrived. All the castle has done is trap us with a killer.

I lean against the wall and crumble. My knees bend, my shoulders slump, and I sob. "Fergus," I mutter, hiccuping.

"Shh, Bess," Hugo says, wrapping his arm around my shoulder. "It's okay."

"It's not."

"Yes, it is. We're getting through this nightmare. We just need to think about the best way to get over the moat."

"I loved him!" I say, moving away. Hugo drops his arm and nods. "I thought he was always with me after the accident because he wanted to help me, because he cared. Hugo, he just wanted to keep me close to know if I remembered."

Hugo nods. "That's what Raif believes too. I asked him again and again to tell you, but he didn't want to."

I gasp. "Why didn't *you* tell me?"

"It wasn't my place. Raif wanted to do things his way. Said he had it under control. It caused a fair few arguments, but I had to trust he knows what's best for him. It was tough after, Bessie."

"That doesn't make sense."

"I agree, but he is the one who was framed. He wasn't in a good place, he was fragile. He needed to heal, regain his full memory of that night, and figure things out. He's going to the police, he told me that himself. He just needed time first, enough that he would be believed over Fergus."

It would be Raif's word against Fergus's, and the Beaufort name holds a lot of weight.

"This is too much," I mutter, rubbing my temples as if that'll bring back my memory of that night.

"Shh," he says, pushing me through the arched doorway to an outhouse.

I look around, unable to see much, but there's a workbench and toolboxes. They look like they've been unused for years, so probably don't belong to the builders.

"Hugo, we have to go back."

He shakes his head, looking over his shoulder. "Zeke's dead, Bess. I'm so sorry, but he is. You saw ... you were right there. All we can do now is fight for us."

"But Allegra?"

"Ran and left us," he reminds me.

"She's scared."

"And we're not?"

"Hugo, please. She's not part of this."

"What? He tried to kill her too?"

"No, he didn't. He yelled at her and told her a few things she didn't want to hear, but he only came after me and Zeke. Told you you're dying this weekend."

I duck my head because I don't want to accept that he could hurt his twin. They've always had this tight bond, even when they were arguing. It's a lot to believe he will harm her, so maybe he isn't going to.

Allegra was my number one suspect before Fergus showed up with the knife. It makes total sense for this to be a twin murder spree. No one else would have each other's back through *everything*.

"Allegra too," I mutter, my mind spinning once again at how little I know my friends.

"This is really important, Bessie. Was she unaccounted for during any of the murders? I need to know if we're going to try to find her and get her out, or if we need to run from her too."

"She was the last to go to bed on Friday . . . was still playing on her phone when I eventually fell asleep. The wrong floor plans that Kash was given were left on her bed in the dorm, we think by Allegra. Her healthy granola wrappers were in that bag! She wants the castle for herself."

He reaches out and takes my hand. "She killed Jia. Her best friend."

"We don't know that for sure."

Even with all the evidence, I still don't want to believe she would do that. I've spent almost every day with her for years, confided in her, cared about her. I thought our friendship was real.

"I don't see them anywhere," Hugo says, peering around the corner of the building. "I think he's gone the other way so we should have the castle to disguise us. We're going to have to risk it now."

"I don't want to die."

He levels with me. "You're not going to die."

"Kash did, and I'm supposed to just run away and leave her?"

"If there's anyone Kash is looking out for right now it's you. Look at me, you're doing this for her. We'll get to safety and make

Fergus and Allegra pay. No amount of money in the world will get them out of this one. Can you do that?"

I nod, blinking back tears and drawing on some bravery I felt earlier. "Yes. Can you start your car without the key?"

He shrugs. "I have no idea how to hot-wire. Wouldn't even have a clue where to start. We've both run cross-country plenty of times for school. We've got this."

"We'll freeze."

"We won't."

I'm not sure where the eternal optimist side to Hugo has come from, but I appreciate it. One of us needs to be confident. Too much has happened for me to believe that we'll make it. I guess if we keep moving, we'll stay warm. Or at the very least stay above hypothermic.

"All right, it's clear. We'll head to the side, not near the broken bridge and cars. If we stay in the trees but still travel in a straight line, we'll be hidden and eventually hit the main road."

It's the best we can come up with, and I hate that there isn't a better option.

"Stay with me," I tell him.

"I've got you."

He lets me run ahead, both of us about equally strong runners. I don't look back because I know if I see Fergus or Allegra I will panic.

It's a short distance from the outbuilding to the edge of the water, because we're headed in a slightly different direction. The wind is still strong, and we have to dodge branches flying at us.

306 | NATASHA PRESTON

When I reach the moat, I don't second-guess or wait for Hugo. I run into the cold, muddy water, drops splashing up and hitting me in the face.

I hear another louder splash a second later and know Hugo has entered the water too.

"Go, Bess, go!"

I push myself harder, wading clumsily.

Then there's a third splash, one that steals my breath.

One of them is *right* behind us.

26

"Hugo?" I shout, but the harder I push the slower I seem to move. The floor of the moat is slippery, but the mud seems to want to hold on to my feet and deliver me to Fergus. I desperately try to use my hands to push the water and propel myself, but all I'm doing is wearing myself out.

When the water hits the tops of my thighs, I bend down and swim, kicking my legs and drawing my arms to the point of instant fatigue to get away. The cold almost stops me, and I have to force myself not to gasp.

The wind is against me, taking over from the mud, but I press on. All I can think about is getting away and not letting Fergus anywhere near me.

I dunk my face and swim harder, no longer able to hear anything other than splashes and my own pulse. He could be anywhere.

My head breaks the surface of the water and I see that I'm

almost at the other side. Soon I will have to stand and run, not knowing if I'm doing that alone or if Hugo has made it.

I can't hear him.

Why can't I hear him?

He would have made noise, shouted if Fergus caught up with him. What's going on?

My feet find ground so I stand, still using my arms to push myself forward. Gritting my teeth, I reach out to grab handfuls of grass and pull myself up the bank, elbow-deep in dirty water.

I splutter, spitting out the water that made it past my lips despite clamping my mouth shut.

As I'm about to run, someone grips my ankle. A scream rips from my throat as I fall flat on my face in the swampy grass.

This is where I die.

I kick my legs, trying to get him off me.

"Bessie, stop."

Fergus.

A spike of ice-cold fear trickles down my spine. "No!" I scream, rolling onto my back in an attempt to dislodge his death grip.

I look down, seeing his teeth bared and determination in his empty eyes. He's lying on the ground, arm outstretched as he holds on to me.

"Get off!" I use my free leg and aim, kicking him in the face.

He cries out, turning his head away, his grip loosening a touch. I use the opportunity to scramble backward. When I look up, I see Hugo running to me. Fergus pushes himself onto all fours.

I stand and turn, ready to run with Hugo, when I see someone in the forest line.

It's not Allegra.

Hugo's gasp is louder than the wind in the trees.

Raif steps forward with a twisted grin. He looks like he's aged about five years in the past ten months. Time hasn't been kind to him. It's clear, from the matching baggy pants and blade, that he's Fergus's partner.

They've spent months together planning this. Fergus told me Raif doesn't talk to him anymore.

This doesn't make any sense, though. Why would Raif help him?

"Raif . . . ," Hugo mutters, stunned, his eyes drifting between Fergus and Raif, wondering how he missed this. "What . . . what are you doing? I don't understand."

"I knew it!" Raif says, almost gleeful that his brother didn't see this coming. "Didn't I tell you they'd never guess?"

Fergus chuckles, rolling his eyes. "Yeah, yeah. Well done."

"Raif, he's the reason your life has changed beyond measure. What are you doing?" Hugo asks.

"Is that the real reason?" Fergus asks, making it sound like a rhetorical question. He's smug, tilting his head to the side and swinging his arms, the knife catching the light.

"Hmm," Raif says, an arrogance in his voice that turns my stomach. He's a completely different person, his personality merged with Fergus's, adopting only the worst parts. "Why, no. I don't believe it is, Fergus."

"Why don't you two stop playing games and tell us what's really going on here. You look ridiculous," I say, absolutely having enough of all the cryptic information.

"Bess," Hugo warns, moving an inch closer to me. It's two against two, but will Hugo be able to stop his brother if it comes down to it?

I don't know if he would choose me over him. Fergus certainly isn't choosing me.

"No, no. Let her talk, big bro. There is a lot I want to hear from her."

"Raif, stop this. It isn't you," I plead.

"I've changed, Bessie."

"I can see, but it doesn't need to be like this. It doesn't for either of you. Fergus, please don't do this."

"You were talking to me!" Raif spits. "Don't speak to him, don't look at him, focus on me."

Hugo holds his hand out. "Raif, that's enough. You're on the wrong side of this and you know that."

"No, you are! God, Hugo, you have no idea."

"So tell me. You say you've changed, but I still see my little brother. You're in there, Raif. Please let me help you."

Allegra said a similar thing to Fergus, and look how well that went. I don't think there's anything that can be done for Fergus or Raif.

Where the heck is Allegra, anyway? Raif must have been out here and Fergus was chasing us. If he killed his sister it would've been quickly. I just can't bring myself to accept that he would do that. Their twin bond is stronger than ... whatever is going on here, I'm sure of it.

"I wasn't quite telling the truth about the night of the accident." Fergus walks over to Raif and the two of them stand together like bouncers, a joined force to show us we're not getting past. It's so jarring to see Raif here that I almost don't want to believe it.

We'll see about that.

"What do you mean?" Hugo asks.

"I think Raif will want to take it from here."

I jolt, seeing a car flip from the inside. A flash of shattered glass and a scream that makes my head pound even from the broken memory of it.

"You see, something was bothering me from that night. I have no recollection of getting behind the wheel, yet I woke up in hospital to a fucking police officer telling me I almost killed my friends."

"Yeah, because he moved you!" Hugo snaps, pointing to killer number one.

"No." Raif slowly turns his narrowed eyes to me. "Psych. *She* did."

I rear backward as if he's struck me, another flicker of glass before Raif comes back into focus. "No. No, I didn't. What are you talking about?"

"Do you remember that night?" he asks.

I shake my head, trying to draw the memories to the surface. They're coming in one-second flashes and so far haven't been anything helpful. "No . . . but I know I wasn't driving. I still can't drive now!"

All right, lots of us have driven cars before being old enough but only on private property, where it's not illegal.

"Raif, I didn't do that, I swear."

"You said you remember Fergus moving you," Hugo tells him. "Why would you tell me that if it was Bessie?"

"It wasn't me!" I say, my heart nearly beating out of my chest. "Raif, I didn't do that. Fergus, please!"

"I'm sorry, Bess. I tried to protect you for as long as I could, but he started to remember." Fergus sure as hell doesn't look sorry for throwing me under the bus.

I sob, shaking my head. Why would they try to pin this on me? What if Hugo believes them? I haven't passed my test and I'm not a confident driver. They wouldn't have gotten in a car with me, particularly if I'd been drinking.

And I wouldn't drive like that.

"No. No, no, no. That's not what happened. Raif, what do you remember? Don't listen to what Fergus is telling you."

"Being moved," he growls. "I was groggy and being dragged in and out of the car!"

"You remember Bessie doing that?" Hugo asks.

"He can't because *I didn't.*"

Hugo cuts me a look that tells me to shut up. I can't stand back and listen to them try to blame me.

"I can see her face now."

"I'm not following, Raif. You told me it was Fergus, and you seemed pretty sure of that fact."

Fergus rolls back on the balls of his feet. "He thought it was me but kept seeing Bessie. Asked me to meet him a couple of months back. I had to tell him the truth. Glad I did now; he wanted a way to get back at me and Bess, but I had a better idea."

"That idea was mass murder?" Hugo says. "How dare you bring my brother into this!"

"Oh, don't act as if this was all my idea. Raif isn't that easy to manipulate. He wanted this too. In fact, it was his idea to turn this weekend into our little murder spree. It was too soon for my liking. I preferred a few more months to plan, but he was confident. Nice call on that, by the way."

"Thank you," Raif replies, smiling at Fergus with pride in his eyes. They make me feel physically sick.

"Will you stop. Fergus, tell the truth," I say, wiping tears from my cheeks. "I didn't do that. I wouldn't. Please don't do this to me."

Hugo takes another step closer to me as my vision turns blurry and I feel a tightening sensation in my chest.

I don't have time for a panic attack—one thing left behind from that night that I can't seem to kick. Fergus is usually the one to step forward and help me; now he's watching like my suffering is entertainment.

"Please, Fergus."

"Sorry, Bess."

"No." I shake my head, my insides crumbling at another flash of blood in my mind. "No."

Hugo stops himself from reaching out, retracting his hand before he touches me. "What happened? The truth, Fergus."

"We were at the party. Bess and I were drunk and got into

an argument. I don't even remember what it was about now. Raif turned up as Bess got in my car. He saw me jump in, trying to stop her, and hopped in the back."

I squeeze my eyes closed, forcing out the images of his words. That can't be the truth. I couldn't have done that.

"No," I whisper.

"I don't remember a lot about the drive. Raif and I were trying to get you to stop, but you were crying and wouldn't listen. Then all of a sudden we were upside down. The car rolled and I lost consciousness. I came around a couple of times, but the world was fuzzy. I saw you moving, Bess. You were out of the car, and the next thing I know I'm in the hospital and being told that you're in intensive care and Raif was driving."

"N-no."

Hugo sighs heavily. I don't know if that's because he's relieved Raif didn't cause the accident or if this is too much for him as well.

"Yes!" Raif spits. "You did that, Bessie. You moved us and I took the fall. How could you? I hate you for it. You let everyone believe it was me."

I shake my head. "I didn't do that. It doesn't make sense. I was knocked out."

"You were," Fergus says. "But it wasn't for the whole time. I'm sure you aggravated your injuries from the crash by moving dead weight while still hurt. No offense, Raif."

"None taken, mate."

"Stop!" I snap, sniffing. "Hugo, I didn't. Please believe me."

He side-eyes me, and it's the first time I notice that he's put a bit of distance between us.

"Why didn't you tell me?" Hugo asks Raif.

"Because by the time I figured it out and confronted Fergus, he already had a couple of ideas." He laughs, looking at his partner. "Very good ones."

"Those very good ideas turned to excellent ideas when you came on board."

"I appreciate that."

"Enough!" Hugo shouts. "This ends *now*. You're going to stop, Raif. Right the fuck now."

Raif takes a step forward, holding the knife up. "You will not tell me what to do. This ends when *I* say."

Fergus's face flickers with irritation before he covers it. Oh. Someone doesn't like being challenged for top killer. I knew that already, but his sick partnership with Raif has clearly never been tested.

"What happens next?" Hugo asks, standing his ground even after his brother pointed a knife at him. "Have you thought that far ahead?"

"Of course we have," Raif says, trying to make it sound like he's offended by the question, but I can see the truth in his lie. He's not actually sure. He doesn't have a plan B or C or D.

What kind of killer doesn't plan for one or more eventualities?

"You don't need to worry about what we do next," Fergus says. "Neither of you is going to be around to see it."

But Fergus has a plan, he always does. Their friendship isn't as solid as Raif thinks.

"He knows what he's doing," I say, pointing to Fergus.

Images of that night flicker in my mind, but I don't know if they're real or if my mind is conjuring what I've been told. A scream first. Then I see Raif in the back. Then Raif in the front.

Blood.

The stars.

Glass.

I shake the patchy memories away. None of it feels real and I don't want to keep having these images . . . but I know I have to remember or people could believe Fergus and Raif's story.

"Getting it yet?" Fergus asks as I press my fingers to my temples.

"No," I say, clenching my hands into fists as my stomach turns to lead. What if it happened like they said? I shake my head, trying to bat away a new image, one of pushing the driver door open. *No, no, no.* How do I know if I'm only seeing what they're telling me? I can't even trust my own mind.

"You don't need us for whatever you plan on doing next," Hugo says. "We end this right here. We figure out what we're going to tell people and we all walk out of here."

Fergus and Raif laugh, starting and stopping in unison, as if they rehearsed it.

"I killed your friends, and you think I'm going to let you leave?"

I gasp, eyes widening. "Raif."

"They were irritating, all of them. Pretending they were perfect, acting like they were good! You have no idea, *no idea,* what they were really like!" he spits, his voice booming over the noisy wind.

"He's right," Fergus says, much more calmly than Raif. I'm beginning to see their dynamic more clearly. Fergus is manipulating Raif, feeding him information that fits his agenda. "Jia knew all along."

"What?" I breathe.

"She knew that you're the one who was driving; she saw us leave, apparently. She admitted it and said she was going to tell the truth. I managed to stop her. Fickle little thing she was—she also loved money." He rolls his eyes. "Anyway, she began to get a conscience, and that's when I knew she had to go first."

"Fergus, stop," I whisper, but he doesn't hear me. How could she not tell me?

"What about Abbas and Odette?" Hugo's angry, demanding tone makes me believe that I will be able to get him to help me so we can leave together, even if he doesn't believe me.

"Odette was unfortunate. Abbas took delight in being chosen to play in teams above me. Just because he's older! He had every opportunity that I was owed!"

Abbas was chosen because he's a better player than Fergus. He's not owed anything. I keep that inside, knowing it's not going to get me anywhere if I antagonize him.

"Abbas earned all of that," Hugo says, defending his friend.

"No, he didn't! It was supposed to be me the university scouts were looking at! He took that away from me, and he didn't even want to play past high school!"

Abbas's death was so brutal because Fergus was jealous of his sporting success.

"What about Zeke and Kash?" I ask, as if it even matters. There will never be a reason to kill.

"He wanted you, and thanks to Kashvi that was getting closer and closer to happening."

"What?" I whisper.

This time he hears.

"Don't pretend that you two weren't getting closer! Kash told you to break up with me after the accident, and Zeke wasted no time—"

"No!" I shout. "That's not true at all. Kash never told me to break up with you; she only ever said she'd have my back no matter what I did."

"That's the same thing! She should've kept her nose out of my business."

My business, not *ours.* Does Fergus see everyone as a pawn in his game? We belong to him and we're his to keep or cast aside?

"It's not. She was your friend too. All she did was support me, Fergus. And Zeke and I were just friends. That's all either of us wanted."

"Liar!" he roars. "I could see it, so don't lie to me."

"Doesn't matter anymore," Raif says. "They are *all* dead."

Fergus frowns. He looks at me and Hugo standing together and then over at Raif. "What do you mean?"

"Sorry, mate, I also took out Allegra. She ran straight into me . . . into this," he explains, holding the knife up.

Fergus's face very slowly falls. So Allegra was never supposed to be harmed. Her name was on the list, but that's obviously something they fabricated to throw us off.

Unless it was Raif's list. He might not have wanted to murder his own brother.

"You did *what* to my sister?"

"She was in the way."

"No!" Fergus roars, shoving his knife-free hand through his hair. "No! I spare Hugo. You spare Allegra. That was the deal!" He paces a few steps back and forth, takes a deep breath, and sobs, "My sister!"

Hugo grabs my hand and tugs.

Fergus and Raif face each other, tension rolling off Fergus's shoulders. The way he looks at Raif is frightening. He's realizing he doesn't have the control he thought, and I don't want to be around when he thinks of a way to regain that control. They're both dangerous.

Hugo tugs on my hand again. I'm not sure what his plan is, but I can't see it being anything other than to outrun them.

Raif must have a car here, but he's not going to give us the key.

God, Fergus agreed to his precious car being damaged in order to trap us. That's why he didn't get out to go look and just let Zeke find it. He knew what was coming. I sidestep cautiously, trying to be fast without making huge, obvious movements.

They're still distracted in their death stare, Fergus's eyes wider than I ever thought possible. Neither is aware of the wind throwing debris at us or that the sun is setting at an alarmingly fast rate.

The longer we stand out here, the harsher the cold sets into my bones. It was easier to ignore before, but now the adrenaline is wearing off as they focus on each other.

Hugo moves again, taking me with him another few steps. For a second, when they revealed what happened the night of the accident—what I did—I thought he was going to leave me.

I wouldn't blame him if he did. I shake off another violent image of the blood inside the car. I don't know whose it was—we all had multiple injuries.

Why would I get behind the wheel?

I wouldn't.

If Fergus was with me, why would Raif jump in too?

There are so many questions I still have, but I don't think I'm going to get many more answers. Not unless I remember. Properly remember, not just visualize, what Fergus and Raif told me.

I look at Hugo, trying to ask him with my eyes what we're doing. Unfortunately I don't seem to be able to do the psychic bit with him, not like I could with Kash . . . or Fergus.

We move again, Hugo tightening his grip on me as if he's telling me we're about to execute the next part of his plan. We're still adjacent to them, but we've moved to the side so they're not directly blocking our way.

Fergus growls, "Why did you kill my sister?"

They're turning on each other. Good.

I step again, my breath catching in my throat as Fergus raises the knife.

"She was off-limits and you know it."

"Calm down, mate. I had to. She was going to turn us in."

"She wouldn't!"

"Yes, she would. You just don't want to accept it. I did what I had to do to protect us. We can't leave any witnesses."

What the hell is their endgame?

"Now," Hugo whispers while they argue.

I push off on my feet, catapulting myself forward the way I do in a race.

We get a few good long strides before they realize. Raif bellows, "Hey!" and they begin to hunt.

27

Hugo lets go of my hand. For a second I miss the safety of holding on to someone, but we're faster if we use our arms while running.

He stays close as we sprint between trees, twigs snapping beneath our feet. The damp mossy ground feels like sand. We're both breathing hard, but I'm too scared of the consequences of slowing down to stop.

We quickly lose light in the depths of the forest, the trees banding together to block out the sun.

I suck in a breath, trying to pace myself the way I would on a cross-country run but knowing I need to be a lot faster.

Behind us I can hear their footsteps and the distant sound of laughter, and it turns my stomach. How could I not see the evil in Fergus?

This is fun to them.

"He killed your twin!" I scream, knowing that will hit Fergus where it hurts. To get away we need to break up their team. They're fractured. I've already noticed that.

Hugo makes a weird growl. I'm goading Fergus into killing his brother, but I don't see another way. I have a better chance of getting away if I only have Fergus to deal with.

Raif wants revenge for the accident. Fergus is a bored rich kid.

Fergus shouts out, sounding as if he's been injured—but the footsteps don't falter, so the wound is from my words, not Raif's knife.

Good, I need that.

"Allegra deserved better!"

"Bessie, shut up!" Hugo snaps, either unsure of what I'm trying to achieve or doubting that it will work.

Sorry, Hugo, I can't.

"Bessie, you're dead!" Raif shouts, and laughs maniacally. He's out of breath and sounds farther away than Fergus.

I guess he didn't use the months he was planning murder to also work on his fitness.

Even over our heavy breathing and the rustling of the trees, I hear Hugo's gasp.

"Raif, stop!" he shouts, pushing himself faster.

I want to speed up and keep up with him, but my body is running on fading adrenaline alone. I have nothing more to give. Once that runs out, it's over.

"Allegra's . . . gone," I pant.

Hugo doesn't stop me again.

"She's dead."

I dodge trees, stepping as carefully as I can while knowing speed is the most important thing here. Wherever we all end up, Hugo and I just need to get there first.

Fergus is a strong runner, and he's clearly been working toward this because he's gaining on me. I thought he was just getting obsessed with his form, but all the extra gym sessions, some with me, were to do this. And I had no idea.

How could I not see that? Other than an occasional glance when Zeke threw an arm around me or something, I didn't know how he felt. And worse, I didn't see any signs that he was angry with Jia, Abbas, or Kash.

"Allegra!" I scream, needing him to hear his sister's name over and over until he snaps.

Fergus roars and then I hear a change in the footsteps.

Raif shouts and a thud ends the running behind us. Fergus has taken him down.

"Keep going," I tell Hugo.

But he doesn't listen; he stops and turns around.

Damn it!

My arms wheel as I stop myself too fast. "Hugo, we need to leave!"

Fergus is on the ground, Raif underneath him trying to dodge punches. I can't see where the knives have gone.

"I can't leave him."

"Hugo, no!" I reach out, but my fingertips only brush his arm as he moves toward the heap of killers on the damp ground.

Raif shoves Fergus's chest, turning his head and spitting blood onto the ground.

Against my better instinct, I run toward them.

Raif's knife is beside him; I'm not quick enough and he spots it too. His fist closes around the handle and he swipes, cutting Fergus's arm.

Fergus screams, leaping up and holding the wound on his forearm.

Raif doesn't waste a second; he leaps to his feet, holding the knife out in front of him. Hugo and I stop dead, far too close to him.

We're all watching each other, waiting for someone to make the next move.

"You came back for me, brother. I'm touched," Raif says, smirking.

"Don't get too comfortable," Fergus says to Raif. "I'm going to kill him in front of you and then slit your throat."

Bile hits the back of my throat at the jovial tone he used in that threat.

Raif narrows his eyes. "She was going to ruin everything," he says, repeating his excuse as if Fergus is suddenly going to come around. Raif has seriously underestimated Fergus's bond with his twin. That was his first mistake.

In the dim light I can see the pain on Fergus's face, even as he tries to disguise it.

Hugo is too focused on them to notice that I want him to run with me again. This is our chance.

Fergus laughs. "You think you have everything figured out, Raif.

You're pathetic. It was too easy to manipulate; I actually got second-hand embarrassment."

Raif frowns, clearly not knowing what Fergus is talking about. He really believed they were equals, and I don't know what he's going to do now that he's learning they're not. I don't think he's going to take it well. "Shut up."

Fergus shakes his head. "Who did most of the killing? Who moved the bodies?" He laughs again. "All I had to do was steal a few phones, drop a couple of clues, and get my hands dirty once."

Raif moves his weight from foot to foot. "You had to pretend to be one of them." His voice is weaker now as he begins to realize he's been played. "No."

"Yes, you moron. You did all of that just because I threw you a few truths and lies about the accident. I molded you into this. *I* did all of that, and it didn't even take me that long."

I turn to run, because they're so fixated on each other we have a good chance to get away.

But I don't even move one foot before I freeze again at Fergus's next words.

"Of course Bessie wasn't the one driving."

Raif and Hugo look my way. I nearly fall down with the relief his words bring. It was a double bluff. I knew it couldn't have been me. I would never.

Raif grimaces. "What?"

"You originally thought it was me, and you were right. But I saw an opportunity to turn you into exactly what I wanted you to be, because I wasn't sure I could do it alone. We had the party weekend planned, and I knew I needed to act then. It worked. You've killed for me. Killed innocent people because you believed Bessie ruined your life. What did Jia, Odette, Abbas, Kash, Zeke, and Allegra have to do with this?"

Raif's eyes widen. I don't know if it's remorse or shame, but I hope it hurts. "N-no."

"Yes," Fergus says, lifting his brows and taking immeasurable pleasure in manipulating Raif the way he has. "You've been a very good doggy, but I have no use for you anymore."

Fergus uses Raif's shock to move before Raif has the chance to defend himself. He plunges a knife into Raif's chest.

"No!" I scream, the sound bouncing off every near tree and ringing in my ears.

"Raif!" Hugo splutters, watching his brother fall to the ground, wide-eyed and open-mouthed.

Shouting again, Hugo runs toward him. Fergus straightens up, still watching Raif, when Hugo collides with him.

Oh my god.

They hit the floor, the knife falls to the ground, and Hugo wraps his hands around Fergus's neck.

"Hugo!" I shout, not moving a step.

My head still hasn't recovered from when I was attacked. Couple that with thinking I was responsible for the accident and then learning I'm not and I'm feeling like my skull is being split in half.

I press my hands to my mouth and watch Fergus try to bat

Hugo's arms away. He pats the moss around him, feeling for his weapon, but Hugo has such a scary grip on him that he can't do anything.

Fergus makes strange gagging noises that I've never heard before, not even in the movies. I'm surprised by how much this hurts, after everything he's done.

"Fergus," I whisper as his hand movements slow. Watching him die is just as hard as watching Kash. Fergus needs to pay, but not like this.

"Hugo, stop," I plead, wanting to take a step but not being able to move. Fergus finds the knife, his fingers wrapping around it.

I move then and shout, "Knife!"

Fergus digs the blade into Hugo's side, close to where the last wound is. Hugo roars in pain, gritting his teeth, but he doesn't let go, spurred on by rage and revenge. He will do anything to avenge his murderer brother.

Fergus's eyes bulge, his face turning shades paler. Then his arms flop to his sides. He's dead.

In front of me, Hugo's side bleeds, pumping crimson onto the forest ground.

I stumble forward, tears blurring my vision, and slump to my knees. Hugo finally lets go and his body drops. He clutches his side and rolls onto his back.

"Hugo," I sob, wiping my tears and placing my hand over his chest. "You're going to be okay."

He shakes his head. "I'm not, but it's okay. You need to leave. Get far away from here."

"Not without you. I can get you to the cars. Raif must have one along the road."

He groans, his eyes rolling backward. "I can't see properly."

"Hugo, don't give up. Please."

He splutters, his breathing sounding like his lungs are full of holes. "Get out of here, Bess," he whispers with his final breath.

"No," I cry, bowing my head. His chest stills, and I know he's gone too.

I wait until I feel the cold again just to know that I'm still here. The horrors of this weekend flash through my mind on a loop.

"I'm sorry," I whisper, sobbing into my palm, and then stand.

Stepping around Hugo, I pass Raif and notice his eyelids flickering. His clothes are coated in fresh blood.

As I get level with him, those lids open. "Bess," he whispers, barely audible. He tries again but nothing comes out, his lips mouthing "Help."

I shake my head. A huge part of me wants to pick him up and help him walk back with me. I won't do it because none of my friends will get the opportunity for a second chance.

So I bend down and reach into his jeans pockets, ignoring how hard he tries to grip my arms.

"Please," he rasps.

I narrow my eyes. "Go to hell, Raif. It's where you belong."

When I pull out a key from his jeans, I feel a sense of relief that I've only felt one other time in my life. The day I was moved from the ICU and knew I was going to be okay.

I stand and walk away, not looking back as I head toward the road. Raif's car will be hidden but accessible. I'll find it and I'll get out of here.

As I make my way to the edge of the forest, I'm plagued with images of the accident. My hands appear so clearly in front of my face, I wonder if I've actually raised them. They're dripping, red, and the smell of blood turns my stomach.

I look up, willing the vision to stay with me . . . and my eyes come level with the steering wheel.

What the . . .

I'm the last one standing, but do I deserve to be?

In my mind I see Fergus beside me and hear a scream that I'm now certain was my own.

Fergus's final confession might've been another mind game.

Because . . . I think I was the one driving that night.

ACKNOWLEDGMENTS

My first thanks is always to my wonderful family for continually supporting me through the entire writing process. My boys often leave little notes of encouragement by my computer, which brings a smile to my face every time.

To my amazing team at Delacorte, thank you so much for your hard work editing, proofing, designing, promoting, and cheering for this book. There is so much you all do behind the scenes to get this book out into the wild, and I appreciate every one of you.

Thank you to Ariella and Amber for continuing to be a dream to work with. You're both amazing.

I couldn't release a book without Sam, Vic, and Zoe. Until the next writers' retreat!

A huge thank-you to bloggers and vloggers for taking time out of your day to read and support this book.

And to my readers. You absolute legends!

WOULD YOU TAKE THE DARE?

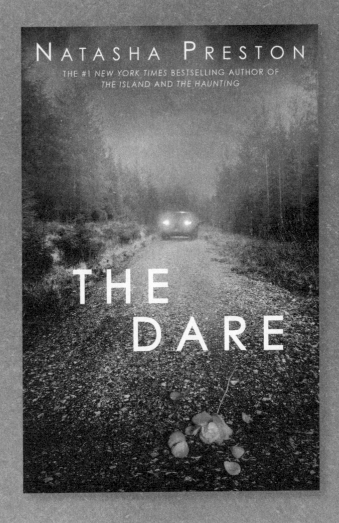

NATASHA PRESTON

THE #1 *NEW YORK TIMES* BESTSELLING AUTHOR OF
THE ISLAND AND *THE HAUNTING*

THE
DARE

1

Monday, May 22

Senior pranks are a rite of passage. Sometimes they're fun and sometimes they're killer.

They're the last dumb thing you do in high school before you get to do a whole bunch of dumb things in college.

But if you go to my school, they can stop your college dreams *dead*.

Sophomore year I couldn't wait to participate in senior pranks, but in the last two years the pranks have really escalated. The Wilder brothers—putting their last name to good use—took over. Five of them, all a year apart in age and all headed for prison if it weren't for their parents' money, came up with a way to raise the stakes.

Everett

Emmett

Rhett—*ugh*

Garrett

Truett

Their parents really went with that matching-name theme. No wonder they have issues.

I think I remember a kid ribbing Everett about it once. Only once. There's a rumor that the kid had to move to another country.

The brothers all like to exert their dominance. They assign you a prank. A dare, really. If you're brave enough—or stupid enough—to turn it down, a forfeit is forced upon you.

Arrests, expulsions, not walking at graduation, and even college rejections are what we face now. That is if we accept the dares . . . *or* if we don't. Saying no has consequences too.

I watch Rhett laugh and shove one of his followers as he makes his way into the cafeteria, cutting in the line because he doesn't have to wait like the rest of us.

My best friend, Lucia, twirls her shiny black hair around her finger. "Ignore him," she says, pushing what I think is supposed to be a burrito away from her. She's curled up with her boyfriend, Jesse, so far evading the eyes of any teachers monitoring for PDA.

Jesse throws a scowl in Rhett's direction, still holding a grudge against him for getting starting quarterback at the beginning of the year. Jesse and Atlas are better. Rhett's family is richer.

"The dares are going to start soon," I say, turning my nose up. "Rhett's probably already plotting."

With only three weeks left of school, senior pranks are right around the corner. Don't get me wrong, I'm going to go all out to prank Principal Fuller, but I don't want to get messed up in Rhett's games.

Atlas leans in, kissing my cheek. "Nothing's going to stop you and your big brain from going to UCLA."

Last year Billy Halsten had his place at Ohio State stripped because the fire he set in a trash can spread and gutted a 7-Eleven. It was his dare from the second-born Wilder brother. Not to destroy a building but to keep the fire department busy while someone else stole a CPR mannequin.

Since then, the whole thing has made me want to skip the last few weeks of school altogether. There's no way Rhett is going to listen to Fuller's warnings.

We're to keep it safe. No stupid stuff.

The Wilder brothers only do stupid stuff, and I think Rhett might be the worst one of them all.

And I already know Atlas and Jesse won't back down from a dare.

"Nothing will stop college because I'm not playing," I tell him. "We're sticking with eggs and glitter and balloons. That's enough."

Atlas pouts, and I can feel myself starting to relent. He's ridiculously good-looking—dark skin, full lips, football player's physique. He's been mine for the last three years. "Come on, babe, we'll stick to the boring pranks, I promise. But we can't miss out on this."

The ones we've planned are boring. Kind of. They'll annoy the hell out of Fuller, so it'll still be funny. He'll be cleaning glitter from his office long after we've gone.

"He's right," Luce says, jabbing a finger in my arm as Jesse bites her neck and makes her squeal. She pushes his head. "We're not skipping this just because people have been total idiots in the past."

"So you're going to listen to Rhett?" I ask, eyeing them as if they've been taken over by aliens.

Jesse scoffs, runs a hand through his white-blond hair, and glares at Rhett again. I think he hates him as much as I do. "We're not going to let him threaten us. Their family doesn't have as much power as he thinks. If there's something we don't want to do, we won't."

A burst of noise gets my attention. Ruthie cackles when Rhett pokes her in the hips. They take a seat at the table next to us, and he looks over, smirking at me. His eyes are the darkest blue I've ever seen, looking nearly black against his light skin and sandy-blond locks. He just looks rich, you know. The preppy, perfect hair and expensive clothes. He has a ring on his thumb, as if he belongs to some underground organization.

All the brothers wear them, and no one knows why, but they look ridiculous.

I've lost count of the times he's tried to break Atlas and me up, despite having Ruthie hanging off his every word.

He's a typical bored rich kid who's never had to deal with the consequences of any of his actions. It's why he and his brothers hijacked senior pranks.

And he was once my best friend.

He smiles again and I turn away.

Hate, hate, hate.

Atlas, unlike me, is still staring at him.

"Forget him," I say. "He's not worth it."

"I really wish someone would do something about him," Jesse mutters, his light eyes trying to laser into Rhett's head.

Atlas barks a laugh. "Like what?"

"Yeah, like what?" I ask, genuinely invested now.

"I don't know," Jesse says. "But I think we should figure it out."

"You want to mess with a Wilder?" Luce asks, giving him a look as if she thinks he's lost his mind. Luce is too nice and a total rule follower. She wouldn't even pack a fizzy drink on a field trip if you weren't supposed to.

I want to roll my eyes. Not because I think it's a bad idea—because someone needs to stand up to that family—but because it's a waste of our energy when we'll be going to college in a few months.

We'll be out of here, and Rhett will be at a college in state because he's not allowed to go far. His parents are *big* on control; all the brothers have gone to the same college, and all will get an apartment near their parents after so they can join the family business.

I mean, no wonder they act out. Their whole lives have already been planned, and they don't get a choice in any of it. Sounds suffocating as hell.

I still think they're all assholes, though.

"I'm just saying, I'm sure there's some way we can turn these pranks around on him," Jesse says.

"I'm game," I tell him. "We could paint little pink bunnies on his expensive car."

"Why bunnies?" Jesse asks, chuckling.

"Why not?"

"Fair. He'd hate it."

I smile. "And that's all that matters."

Atlas side-eyes me, tapping his fingers on the table. He knows that Rhett and I were close in elementary and middle school—they all do, but I've never really spoken about it.

Atlas looks like he's about to say something, but we're distracted by screams of laughter. I look up as four guys from the football team walk into the cafeteria wearing cheerleader outfits, complete with pom-poms and paint stripes on their cheeks.

The room erupts with cheers and applause.

"Why didn't you do that too!" I say, playfully hitting Atlas's arm.

Luce laughs. "Yeah, come on, I would've *paid* to see that."

The boys don't have time to answer because the honorary cheer-leaders begin to chant and jump around. Max spells out "school is shit" with his arms, and I think I actually see steam coming from Fuller's ears.

"They're good," I say, cheering and throwing a wadded-up napkin at them. Max and Charlie both leap up and attempt the splits in midair. It's a hilarious fail, and they both laugh along with everyone else.

This is the dumb stuff we're supposed to do, not burning down buildings.

Fuller is on his feet as the four boys curtsy, holding their skirts to the side. He smiles as he approaches, but it's easy to see the irritation on his face.

"All right, the fun's over," Fuller says. "Five minutes left, so hurry up."

Luce and I jump up, knowing this is our chance, leaving the boys chatting to some guys on the team.

We make our way to Fuller's office with the supplies in my bag. He always walks around the field for the last few minutes of lunchtime, after checking the cafeteria. It wouldn't surprise me if he sits out on his porch watching his neighbors.

We easily slip past the secretaries as they dash to the staff room for their iced coffee fix.

Luce giggles as I look over my shoulder, palm resting on the handle of Fuller's door.

"Go," I say, pushing the door open and slipping inside.

She closes the door behind us and tugs the zipper of my bag, almost bending me backward. "We need to hurry, I'm already sweating," Luce says. "This stuff always makes me feel like I could vomit."

"Can you not pull me over while we do it?" I say, twisting around and sliding the bag off my shoulder. "And don't stress, we're supposed to do pranks like these."

It doesn't hit the floor, thankfully, because she has hold of it, reaching in to get the water-and-glitter-filled balloons. I could only fit three in there because we've filled them as much as we dared. The latex is stretched to the max, almost making them completely translucent.

I take one out carefully, wincing as it bulges, threatening a heavy dose of karma.

"Where are we putting these?" she asks, gritting her brace-covered teeth.

"One on his chair for sure."

"You think he'll sit on it?"

"He doesn't need to, he just needs to pull the chair out and let it drop. It'll explode all over this fancy rug under his desk," I say, toeing the edge of it.

She laughs. "Okay, where else?"

"That display cabinet. We'll balance it on the edge of a shelf and close the glass door carefully."

"He'll see it."

"Doesn't matter. Use yours. It's darker, so he won't see the glitter."

I place a balloon on the chair and gently roll it back under the desk. Luce puts hers on the shelf and shuts the door, holding her hand out in case she needs to catch it. I don't bother telling her that it'll explode all over her if it drops into her hand, because, frankly, that would be hilarious.

For the last one, I balance it on top of the bulb in his tall lamp. It's right beside his desk, so if it bursts while he's sitting, he'll get wet and glittery. The balloon rests on the bulb inside the shade.

Then, because I don't want to kill anyone, I pull the plug out of the wall so he can't turn it on without noticing there's a balloon up there.

"Bit dangerous, Marley," Luce says.

I hold up the plug in my hand, and then let it drop to the floor. "I've got it covered."

She nods. "Okay, because that was almost a dumbass Rhett dare."

I point at her, then grab my bag. "Rude. Let's go, lunch is almost over."

She opens the door and we sneak out, leaving behind three glittery bombs and the promise of a bad day for Fuller.

"Think he'll find it funny?" she asks as I close the door.

"Absolutely not."

I look back over my shoulder just as Mrs. Bell and Miss Romero return to their desks, holding oversized tumblers.

We split up in the hallway. I head to math, usually absolute hell, but it's the end of the school year and we're playing an escape room game.

Our town is huge on memories, and the school does way more for the end of senior year, so we don't finish as early as other schools in the state. I could be home for summer break by now. Unfair.

Up ahead, Rhett leans against the wall, blocking the door I need to go through. As if he gets to decide where I go.

"You need to move," I say.

He lifts a brow, a cocky smirk on his lips. "Do I?"

I go to push past him, but he sidesteps so I can't get by.

"Rhett, just go away."

"I know your parents wouldn't be happy with how rude you're being."

"And I know your parents wouldn't be happy with you being a jackass."

I meet his smug smile with my own, mirroring his contempt. He's the one who ended our friendship, so I don't know why he insists on messing with me. What's the point? I'm so over his crap.

"Everything okay?" Fuller asks, walking the hallways like a security guard. As someone who loves order, he's going to hate the next three weeks.

"Fine," Rhett says, stepping back. "Just chatting with my oldest friend."

I scoff, wanting to disagree, but I also want Fuller to go to his office and Rhett to go away.

Fuller nods and continues on his way. I press my lips together to stop myself from laughing as I watch him head to his office.

"What did you do?" Rhett asks, following my gaze.

"Shhh."

I can't see from here—Fuller's office is too far away—but if things go to plan, I'll definitely hear.

"Come on, what prank did you pull?" he asks, trying to sound bored. If he didn't care about knowing, he would've left.

"Water-and-glitter bombs."

He rolls his eyes. "Are you seven?"

I don't have time to think of a witty retort because Fuller shouts out, his booming voice carrying all the way to the end of the hall.

"How many are in there?" Rhett asks, trying not to smile.

"Two more. I wish I knew which one that was."

"Go take a look."

"I'm not stupid. He'll know it was me."

There's another shout. Rhett and I jump back just as Fuller walks out of the room. I only catch a glimpse, but he's wet and sparkly. Ha.

Rhett rubs his mouth, his way of pretending that he's got an itch and he's not amused. It's a classic Rhett move and one he should know I can see through.

I open the door to math, but before I disappear into the classroom, Rhett says, "Things are about to get very interesting for you and your friends."

"Whatever," I mutter, not giving him the satisfaction of seeing how nervous that makes me. I'm still on the high of Fuller and the water balloons, so I'm not really thinking about what my nemesis has planned.

He can bring it.

What's the worst that could happen?